Miracle Glow

BELINDA BENNA

Vinci Books

vinci-books.com

Published by Vinci Books Ltd in 2026

1

A CIP catalogue record for this book is available from the British Library.

Paperback ISBN: 9781036727406

The EU GPSR authorised representative is Logos Europe, 9 rue Nicolas Poussion, 17000 La Rochelle, France contact@logoseurope.eu

By Belinda Benna

Halifax Harbor Hospital

A Glimmer of Hope

A Twist of Fate

Miracle Glow

Love and Other Dreams

The Dreams We Share

The Sky We Seek

The Colors We Desire

The Dance We Remember

The Stars We Chase

Marie & Lukas

Promise Me

Show me the Stars

By Belinda Benna

All I Need

Every Step I Take

Foreword

I researched the medical aspects of this story with care and diligence; numerous specific details have been reviewed by medical professionals.

That said, we're all human, and despite best efforts it's conceivable that some inaccuracies remain or have been unintentionally left in. If you find any, I'd be happy to hear from you so I can correct them.

I wish you many gripping, moving and heart-felt hours of reading at the Halifax Harbor Hospital!

Yours,

Belinda

Trigger Warning

Miracle Glow contains potentially triggering content. Readers are advised that some scenes may be considered disturbing.

Prologue

AUTUMN

Sometimes you meet someone who puts the broken pieces of you back together, only to lose them again. Sometimes miracles glow in our hearts, only to ultimately yield to the darkness. What remains is the realization that it was never a miracle—just a fleeting moment we desperately mistook for one.

Until this morning, I still wanted to believe that Tay and I had a future, but now there's no hope left.

I turn to him and see in his eyes that he has already known it for a long time too. A mix of despair, longing, and pain is reflected in his expression. He cups my face in his hands, and I do the same to him. We hold on to each other, even though we both know we've already lost one another.

"I'm so sorry," he repeats tonelessly. The wind carries his words away, far out to sea.

How could this have happened?

How is it possible that the only man in this world who makes me feel whole, the man who loves me despite everything that isn't perfect about me, the man who made me believe in miracles again—how is it possible that this man is slipping away from me?

His thumbs gently stroke my cheeks. "In a few years, we might get another chance."

Years? That's hundreds of weeks in which we won't be close to each other even once. Thousands of days I'll have to fall asleep and wake up without him.

"You'd be willing to wait that long?" I look deep into his eyes.

His expression turns serious. "I would wait for you until the end of time."

"So would I." My lips curl into a wistful smile. My heart doesn't know whether to break from sadness or burst from love. This moment is bittersweet, and yet it is and remains a goodbye.

"Kiss me," he pleads longingly. "Kiss me one last time."

Chapter One

AUTUMN

One and a half weeks earlier

The problem with wounds isn't the pain, but the fact that they leave scars when they heal. They're like letters, words, and lines of an ugly story that life burns deep into our skin without asking for permission. Doctors don't feel responsible for how we deal with them, how we manage to move on, how we find our way back to a happy life. They declare us "healthy," discharge us to a place they call "home," and rush off to fix the next patient.

It's time to change that, and today I'm taking the first step.

"Dr. Autumn Hall?"

The female voice startles me. I push my red hair just far enough out of my face to see the tall woman with the asymmetrical bob and teddy bear earrings. In the breast pocket of her lab coat is a pen with an oversized pink tassel.

Dr. Abby Parker—the woman I hope will soon be my boss.

I jump up from my chair. "Nice to meet you."

She waves me into her office. "Come in, come in, have a seat. Would you like something to drink? Water or coffee? We're out of milk, unfortunately, but you can have sugar if you'd like."

A bit overwhelmed by her boundless energy, I slide into the chair she offers me. "No, thank you, I'm fine."

"But it's going to take a little while, you should know that. You'll have to answer some questions—I want to find out everything about you." She whirls through the simply furnished office, past the bookshelf where a teddy bear crouches in the corner wearing a surgical mask, eyeing me with its dark button eyes. "You know what? I'll just get you a glass of water."

And just like that, she's gone. Dazed, I look around. My gaze lands on a copy of People Magazine on her desk. Tay Lawson beams from the cover.

Everything about him is perfect. The jawline, the dark eyes, the lips, the teeth. His broad shoulders, the chest muscles peeking out from the V-neck of his shirt, the muscular arms—even his fingers are perfect. Every single one of them.

I catch myself imagining how flawless every millimeter of his body must be. A painful tightness spreads in my chest. To distract myself, I read the headline.

Hollywood star takes a break while renovating his Los Angeles mansion.

I flip open the magazine, studying the pictures of his dream villa in the Hollywood Hills, as well as shots of him and his stunningly attractive wife on the red carpet. He's in a suit, she in a low-cut dress, both glowing with happiness. The next page is filled with photos of him lounging casually on a designer chair, apparently answering the questions printed alongside in the interview.

People Magazine: Your holiday starts tomorrow. You'll need it—after all, your last film was a total flop. How much did that hurt?

Tay Lawson (smiling wryly): Not in the slightest.

Once again, I look at one of the photos. He really doesn't look unhappy or wounded.

People Magazine: That's hard to believe, especially since it's obvious how much heart and soul you poured into that role.

Oh yes, I saw the movie. The pain of the male protagonist was so palpable, so real.

Tay Lawson (laughs): I'm just an excellent actor.

He certainly is. Unbelievable that it was all just acting—what a talent!

People Magazine: But the fact that you have no chance at an Oscar nomination for this role must be devastating for you. And now your biggest rival, Scott Pears, has been nominated. He's already snatched the award from you once before—you must be frustrated.

Tay Lawson (smiles): He's a great actor who deserves the Oscar.

And he's got a big heart, too.

Out of nowhere, Dr. Parker sets a glass of water in front of me. "Are you a fan?" She nods toward the open magazine. "He's pretty hot, isn't he? I certainly wouldn't kick him out of bed. And you?"

I quickly close the magazine. "I like his movies," I reply evasively to her more than inappropriate question.

She sighs, as if I've ruined her fun. "All right then, let's get started—we've got no time to waste, right?" With a flourish, she walks around the desk. No sooner has she sat down than she props her head in her hands and raises her perfectly arched brows. "So, why pediatrics? What is it about working with the little rascals that fascinates you enough to choose this specialty?"

Those are the questions I want to hear. The ones that, unlike those in People Magazine, truly matter to me.

"Sick children need special protection, and as a doctor, I can give them that." Instinctively, I think back to the time when I was a patient myself. So many years have passed, yet I still feel the same loneliness that was always with me despite the bustle. I feel the fear, taste the bitterness of unspoken questions, hear the medical terms doctors and nurses used to discuss my progress as if I weren't even there. "I want to be there for them, want to make sure that—no matter why we're treating them—they can smile." Openly and honestly. Because they're happy, not to please someone else.

Dr. Parker laughs. "Wow, that was very dramatic, Dr. Hall. You've rehearsed that well, but I must admit it sounded very convincing."

Of course it did, because it's nothing but the truth. I let her see that now with my expression. "Pediatrics is also a fascinating field," I continue, straightening my back. "Pediatric medicine is a broad discipline that encompasses many different aspects of medicine. This interdisciplinarity is a challenge I'm eager to take on."

Her expression brightens as she taps her chin with her index finger. "All right then, show me what you've got. How would you treat a child with pneumonia?"

Over the next seventy minutes, Dr. Parker grills me more intensely than any of my professors ever did at Dalhousie University, but I answer each of her questions with the utmost professionalism. I give it my all, because this job is the best possible next step toward my goal.

"And finally: Where do you see yourself in ten years?" she asks me at last.

In my own children's clinic, where not only wounds are healed, but the little ones also learn to live with the scars that will forever be a part of them.

In exactly the place I would have needed back then to avoid becoming the monster I am today.

"Wherever I can best help sick children," I reply vaguely —after all, today is about the job as a pediatric specialist.

She studies me a little longer than necessary. "And that's here at Halifax Harbor Hospital," she says suddenly. "Welcome to the team, Dr. Hall."

I got the job? Wow, that was fast.

A little firework explodes in my chest, and I reach out my hand to her. "Wonderful, I'm looking forward to working with you."

"Likewise." She signals for me to stand up from my chair. "Now, do the following: go down to HR and sign your employment contract. We'll see each other tomorrow at seven o'clock on the ward, bright and early."

I'll have to get used to her waterfall-like way of speaking, but that's no problem. I got the job—that's all that matters.

"Wait, take this with you." She now pulls the pen with the pink tassel from the breast pocket of her coat and hands it to me. "Everyone here has one, it's important. The kids like it, and you want the little ones to smile—this is perfect for that."

Yes, I do want that, but not because I have a funny pen that distracts them from their worries, but because they have none—or at least fewer. Still, I take the pen; it seems important to her.

I thank her and head to the HR office. On the way, I text the good news first to my mom, then to Sonora, who's starting her job as a surgeon at Halifax Harbor with a night shift tomorrow and is currently painting the living room of our newly founded shared apartment. Mom sends me a hug emoji back, Sonora a high five.

It takes a whole hour before I've signed the papers and received an initial orientation. When I finally get home and open the door to the apartment, I'm greeted not only by an adventurous mix of pizza and fresh paint smells but also by exuberant laughter. Are all four of my roommates already here?

"You're seriously the only person who doesn't eat takeout pizza with their fingers," I hear Nyla, who starts in the ER tomorrow, say amusedly, and I smile to myself because I know she can only mean one of us: Olive, our always-perfect glamour lady with a cleanliness obsession.

"Order is essential. You'll all thank me soon enough when I make sure this apartment doesn't descend into chaos," Olive replies right on cue.

"Hello?" I call out, making my way through the towers of moving boxes.

"Hey there," June calls back—she had her job interview in the diagnostics department today.

I walk down the hallway and find Nyla, Olive, and June in what will be our future living room, where Sonora has clearly done a stellar job painting. The dusty pink is fantastic, and once all the paint splatters are scraped off the floor, the plastic sheeting removed, and the furniture in place, this will be a great spot for the five of us to unwind after work at Halifax Harbor Hospital.

As I step into the room, I pull my employment contract out of my pocket. "Got it!" I shout, prompting cheers all around.

Nyla claps so enthusiastically that her oversized earrings

swing back and forth. Warmth floods her elfin features, and her big, doe-like eyes sparkle. June sets her slice of pizza aside to applaud as well. With her high ponytail, blue eyes, and small nose, she looks like a Barbie doll. Olive, whose Marlene Dietrich-style trousers make her look more like a glossy magazine cover model than an ICU doctor, nods at me approvingly.

Immediately, I feel my cheeks flush with joy. "Is there any Margherita?" I ask, eyeing the pizza boxes stacked on top of a pile of moving crates.

"What do you think?" June gestures for me to help myself.

As I reach for a slice, the fifth member of our group enters the living room—our surgeon Sonora, pressing both hands against her stomach. Wet strands of hair cling to her dark curls. "I think I've had enough pizza for today," she groans, joining us.

Smiling, I settle into a cross-legged position on the floor and take a bite of my pizza. Nyla studies the food selection like she's making a life-or-death decision. Olive pushes aside the clear plastic cover on the sofa and pats down the cushion before sitting.

I watch the scene thoughtfully. We're all doctors, we all studied together, and now we're all starting a new chapter at Halifax Harbor Hospital. Still, the question of whether it was the right move to leave home and move in with the girls keeps nagging at me. Even though Mom's response to the news that I got the job gave no reason for concern, I'll call her after dinner. I need to be sure she's okay, that she can manage without me.

"You know what?" June, who has since let down her ponytail, lets her gaze wander around the group.

"Waf?" I ask with my mouth full.

A warm smile creeps across June's face. "I think this is going to be amazing," she says, voicing exactly what I am hoping for.

Chapter Two

TAY

Life is a battle with brutally simple rules: whoever strikes first has the advantage, whoever hits harder wins. Letting people get close makes you vulnerable, loving someone means losing.

That's just how it is—I didn't make these rules, this is how our world works. We all have to play by them, that's how we survive. Sure, it was hard at first, but if you fight long enough, you figure out how to deal with it—and I've been fighting for as long as I can remember.

With a coffee cup in hand, I step up to the large window that frames the view of the Atlantic like a living painting. Sunlight touches the horizon, mist hovers above the sea.

Kayla is swinging in the garden, her long dark hair flying high, she laughs carefree—because she doesn't know that we're not just on holiday here. She has no idea that this is about distracting the press so we can finally have that one conversation with her that will change her life forever.

It's going to happen today. I finally have to do it, I just don't know how.

Her joyful squealing drifts in from outside, and my chest tightens more and more. To shake off the feeling, I step up to the punching bag and hit it with my right fist.

At least part of my plan is working.

The press is reporting exclusively on the renovation of our villa in Los Angeles, speculating about the new number of bathrooms and trying to get hold of the building plans.

Meanwhile, I'm here, in the vacation house on Inner Sambro Island off the coast of Nova Scotia, punching my soul out for minutes on end.

I hit harder and harder, sweat streaming down my forehead, my pulse racing.

Jab-cross-hook-cross.

Eventually, I slump against the punching bag. Outside, my daughter laughs, accompanied by the sound of waves endlessly lapping against the rocky shore. Out of the corner of my eye, I see the deep blue water, lightening toward the horizon where it merges with the endless sky.

Gasping for breath, I look outside, see all the beauty, and feel all the more that, where I am—behind the window—none of it exists.

Out there, I can fool anyone with my sunny smile. In here, I'm just me, and behind what the world sees of me, buried deep inside, lies a heart that hasn't beaten properly in years. Too many emotions are trapped there. The ones that hurt, the ones no one's allowed to see. Like the fear that everything I've ever cared about could soon shatter into a thousand pieces.

My fists find the punching bag again, and I hammer away at it until the ringing of my phone interrupts me. I strip off the boxing gloves and reach for the phone.

It's a video call from Chloe. As beautiful as ever, my wife looks stunning today with her deep red lipstick and elegant blouse. Like a dark-haired Marilyn Monroe. Behind her, the furnishings of a hotel room come into view.

"Not yet," I say instead of a greeting, since I know why she's calling.

"Why not?" Reserve is written all over her face.

"I'm waiting for the right moment." My gaze flits outside—Kayla is on the swing, her lips moving as if she's singing.

Chloe furrows her brows. "You don't have forever..."

"I know that," I interrupt her, casually grabbing a towel and dabbing the sweat from my forehead. "You wanted me to tell her, so let me do it my way. We have to be tactically smart."

"All right, you're right." She raises her hand, smiling gently. "How's my little darling? Does she miss her nanny?"

"Everything's wonderful. How's the promo tour going?" I ask with an easy smile, even though my muscles tense. "Any interesting offers?"

"The producers don't forget any more than the press does," she replies bitterly. "I warned you that role wasn't right for you. Now look where it's gotten you." A deep crease forms on her forehead. "I'm your agent—you should've listened to me."

Still, I wanted that role—desperately. To be that man in front of the camera, the one breaking under the relentless, incurable illness of his wife—that's what I needed.

"It wasn't my fault the film flopped, and you know it." Wouldn't surprise me if Scott Pears was behind it. He'd do anything for an Oscar nomination, and now he's pulled it off again.

"Everyone's talking shit about you, calling you a hollow pretty boy with no acting talent." Her tone is icy; she's ashamed, I can see it in her face. She's just as ashamed of me as my father used to be.

That's pathetic, he growls in my head, as if he still had any power over me. He doesn't. Just like Chloe doesn't.

"And we both know that's bullshit. Soon they'll find another sensation to exploit," I reply calmly, because that's exactly how it'll go. "That's Hollywood for you." Nothing but smoke and mirrors, wonderfully shallow, delightfully fake. "No reason to worry."

Now her expression freezes. "Excuse me? No reason to worry? That flop of a movie could end your career."

That flop of a movie could end your career, the words echo ominously inside me. I rub my temples to drive away the buzzing spreading through my head. Of course, I could ask her to sue the press for defamation or whatever, she's a lawyer after all. But then she'd know how much this is getting to me, and that's the last thing I want.

"Now you're seriously overreacting," I say. "By the time Kayla and I are back in Los Angeles, this will all have blown over."

She gasps, but before she can reply, something catches her attention. Frowning, she lowers her eyelids. "Wait, something's coming in."

I check to see if my daughter is okay. She's climbing the ladder to the slide and waves at me when she spots me. I stick out my tongue, and she giggles.

"Shit." Chloe's face darkens like a thundercloud, and she instantly has my full attention. "They're terminating the contract for your next film."

I smile—dominant, in control, confident—even as my chest tightens. "New offers will come." That's how it always is. That's how it has to be.

"What's wrong with you?" She touches her forehead, as

if I'm giving her a headache. "I get that you usually don't let anything rattle you, but why doesn't even this affect you?"

Because it has to be this way, in every second of my life when I'm not playing a role. Because this is what I do to survive. The times when I was emotional and vulnerable, the times when my heart was still capable of opening up to others, of showing warmth and love and passion for something—those times are long gone.

"Ah, here comes our genius." With these words, my younger brother Mike greets me as I come home from school. "Did you have a breakthrough? Can you finally do your times tables? What's two times two?"

I shrug off my jacket, hang it on the bull horns we've repurposed as a coat hook, and do my best not to touch the thing. "And you?"

"Unlike you, I actually did something useful and shot a few wolves."

Images of dead wolves flash before my mind's eye. I feel sick.

He pounds his chest proudly. "Three of them!"

"Congratulations." Sadness weighs down my voice. I'll never understand how he can enjoy killing animals. Yes, we're in Montana. Yes, we live on a ranch. Yes, here a man has only one task: to be a real man. Still, I can't get used to the things a man is supposed to do, or to how he's supposed to be.

I know I have to get tougher.

Stronger.

Mom steps out of the kitchen, a dish towel in her hand, her bangs stuck to her forehead. "Dinner's ready."

"That useless idiot didn't earn anything." My brother laughs. "While the rest of us were busting our asses, he was daydreaming again. And he still can't do math."

Mom tilts her head and looks at me expectantly. "The useless idiot is helping out at the rodeo later." Oh God, no, not the rodeo. I give

Mom a pleading look, but she just stares at me blankly. "Your dad's already there, you two will have a great time together."

"I have to study for school," I say.

"As if that would help." My brother walks past me and jabs his elbow into my side. "Don't be such a pussy."

It's true. I can't be such a pussy, because the truth is, I'll never make it out of Montana. Not with my grades. I can only live the same life as my father: a cowboy's life.

For that, I have to be tough. As tough as my father and my brother. I have to hit first before I get hit, be brave instead of scared.

I swing to hit my brother back, but miss.

"My God, what a wimp you are." He rolls his eyes at the ceiling, lets out a sigh, and struts ahead into the dining room.

Two hours later I'm sitting in the stands of the rodeo arena, feeling Mom's casserole crawl back up my throat as one horse after another bucks its way across the arena.

Next to me, Mike jumps up from the bench, cheering. "Give it to the horse!"

"Watch closely," my father admonishes me, pressing his heavy hand onto my shoulder. "Otherwise, you'll never become a real man."

I can't. The animals are deliberately being hurt, tortured for the spectators' amusement. It's horrible.

"Don't be so sensitive, boy." I feel his fingers digging into my shoulder. "There's nothing wrong with it."

I lift my gaze, looking past the horse as best I can while my brother cheers excitedly. Still, out of the corner of my eye, I see the animal's eyes widen in pain and its nostrils flare. Compassion floods me, my nausea grows worse, the crowd applauds, the rider stays on, cheers erupt.

My God, when will it finally be over?

With every passing second that this dreadful spectacle continues, I can bear it less and less.

I know I mustn't throw up again. And under no circumstances can I cry. Not this time and never again.

Still, it happens. Without my doing, tears run down my cheeks. I press my hand over my mouth to at least stifle the sobs and pull the cowboy hat lower over my face.

My little brother rolls his eyes in exasperation. "Daaad, the crybaby's bawling again."

"Pull yourself together, boy." Father's expression is full of shame as he hastily wipes my cheeks with his calloused hands.

My lips are trembling and I hate them for it.

"Pussy," Mike whispers to me.

As if on cue, fresh tears well up in the corners of my eyes.

"Stop it right now," Father hisses, glancing around. "You're a disgrace to our family."

I guess I am—and not just today.

"Enough!" Father grabs my upper arm and squeezes. "This is pathetic."

I clench my fists, imagining myself building a wall inside me. Meters thick and so high it reaches the sky. Then I shove all those useless feelings behind that barrier. Because I can't think of a better way to become the man I have to be.

My tears stop.

"Good boy," my father murmurs and gives me a firm pat on the back.

Back then, my emotions controlled me, and they left countless scars on my heart. Scars that taught me to protect myself first and foremost—even from my wife, who now looks at me with incomprehension on my phone screen.

"This is about your career, don't you understand that?" Chloe asks, trying hard to stay composed.

"I'm just keeping a cool head, and you should do the same." I raise my eyebrows pointedly, and she finally gives in and lowers her gaze.

I look out the window; my daughter is still swinging, unchanged.

"This all actually means something to me, unlike you," I hear my wife whisper.

She's wrong about that. It means far too much to me, and that's exactly why my tone turns ice-cold now. "I have to go."

"Of course." Chloe curls her lips into a smile. "My next appointment is already waiting."

Thank God. I wish her a successful day and end the call. A split second later, the corners of my mouth drop. The same fears and worries that have been haunting me for weeks threaten to overwhelm me.

The canceled contract was the last thing I needed. What if it really is over?

What if I stop getting good roles, if I no longer…

A sharp scream interrupts the downward spiral of my racing thoughts.

Was that Kayla?

I immediately look outside.

Just in time to see her fall from the climbing frame.

At first, I don't understand what's happening—then, slowly, nausea rises in me.

Damn it, this can't be real.

My phone slips from my fingers.

A dull thud reaches my ears.

She lies on the safety mat like a rag doll, her face pressed to the ground. Her glasses twisted completely, lying beside her dark hair.

For the briefest fraction of a second, the world stops turning.

Then I rush outside.

Chapter Three

AUTUMN

I stare at the fire, transfixed, stepping back to escape the flames, yet they keep coming closer.

Closer and closer.

And even closer.

Instinctively, I grab the door handle and yank at it.

It doesn't budge an inch.

I pull harder, brace myself against the door.

Nothing moves.

Now the flames reach for me, growing larger, more intense with every second.

Hotter.

A scream escapes my mouth, I jerk my eyes open.

Where am I?

There's a white ceiling with a bare lightbulb. A window without curtains, twilight falling on moving boxes, my books sticking out from them. It smells like paint.

The shared apartment—I'm in my new home. I push my sweat-soaked hair from my face, throw back the blanket, and slip into my bathrobe. The apartment is quiet, but still, I lock the door behind me after entering the bathroom.

Without looking in the mirror, I shrug off the bathrobe, then the oversized T-shirt, still damp from my nightmares. As I lather up in the shower, I feel every single ridge on my skin, all the uneven patches—but where my fingers glide over the surface, I feel no touch at all.

As if those parts didn't belong to me. As if that weren't me.

Still, like every day, I'm somehow intact and somehow not when I step out of the shower five minutes later. I get dressed, undo the knot in my hair, and tug at my bangs to cover the scar at my temple. Finally, I pull my hair over both shoulders and look at my reflection.

No monster in sight, no one's going to be scared of me—my first day of work can begin.

Two hours later, I've completed a ward round during which my boss talked nonstop without taking a breath.

"To start off, I've got an easy case for you, a bit of a warm-up, so to speak. That should suit you just fine, right?" She pulls a patient file from the shelf at the nurses' station. "Patient P100424-079, seven years old, displaced tibia fracture. Preoperative assessments, monitoring tissue pressure, and pain management until the swelling subsides enough for surgery."

Sandra, a woman in her mid-fifties with closely cropped black hair, whom Dr. Parker introduced earlier as the head nurse, glances over at us from her desk with curiosity. "You're sending her to that mysterious guy with no insurance?"

Dr. Parker grins. "That's been sorted—he's paying privately and has already made an advance payment. The paperwork will follow."

"Ooh." Sandra's eyes light up. "Intriguing."

Dr. Parker leans against the nurses' station counter as if it were a bar. "Fifty says he's a stock market millionaire," she whispers to Sandra.

Sandra raises her painted-on eyebrows. "I'm in. My bet's on professional hockey player. I mean, with that body…"

"Which room?" I interrupt the two of them—after all, we're here to help the child.

Dr. Parker gives me a disappointed look. "Don't you want to place a bet?"

"No, thanks."

"Come on, don't be so prudish. I bet you're actually full of surprises, aren't you?" she asks curiously.

I throw Sandra a pleading look, who luckily takes pity on me and nods toward the left side of the hallway. "Teddy bear room."

Relieved to get away from the two of them, I take off. I only barely register how Dr. Parker and Sandra dive back into gossip and chatter.

"Well then, let's see what the redhead's got," I still hear my boss say before I round the corner behind the sprawling green plant—and walk right into someone.

A man.

With strong chest muscles.

Who smells irresistibly of coffee.

And radiates warmth—no, it's more than that. It's heat. Damp heat.

"What the hell? Can't you watch where you're going?" a deep voice asks aggressively.

Before I can grasp what's happening, cold surrounds me. My field of vision widens—there's a well-toned forearm, a hand holding a crumpled plastic cup. A white T-shirt with a coffee stain the size of an IV bag.

Oh dear.

"Sorry, I didn't mean to…" Embarrassed, I look up and see tousled black hair and a full beard that, along with a pair of old-fashioned glasses, covers most of his face. Dark eyes stare at me impassively.

"Of course not," he grumbles with an American accent.

"I'll get you a replacement shirt and, of course, a new coffee," I suggest.

Although he lifts the corners of his mouth, he still seems reserved. "That would be good."

With an apologetic smile, I signal for him to follow me to the supply room. On the way there, I notice that my own shirt has coffee on it too. Looks like I'll have to walk around like this today—the hospital shirts have necklines that are way too low, and I don't want to scare either the kids or their parents.

The man walks silently beside me. I watch him out of the corner of my eye. There's something familiar about him, but I can't quite place it.

We enter the supply room. "Are you visiting a relative?" I ask politely.

"Where are the shirts?" He looks around, spots the right shelf, and shrugs off his jacket on the way over. Then he pulls his T-shirt off without removing his cap. Now he turns to face me, and I can't help but stare at his abs.

Are those real?

He must be an athlete. Maybe I've seen him on the news before.

"Enjoying the show?" There's a mix of amusement and provocation in his voice.

Heat rushed to my face immediately. "Sorry," I mumbled, turned around, and waited until he was done.

His upper body kept flashing before my mind's eye. His skin, so flawless compared to mine. So beautiful. So whole.

He was already brushing past me. "I'll get the coffee myself."

Before I could reply, he was out the door. I stood there, puzzled. Anyone else would probably have admitted partial blame for the little coffee mishap, apologized as well, or at least thanked me for the fresh shirt.

But him? Nothing.

Whatever. He's gone, and I'll most likely never see him again, so I shouldn't dwell on it. Besides, my patient is waiting.

Out of habit, I checked my hair and adjusted the high collar of my shirt before leaving the supply room. On the way, I studied the medical file, then entered the hospital room with the oversized teddy bear on the door.

Wow, the teddy bear room lives up to its name. I don't think I've ever seen so many in one place. On the walls, on the curtains, on the windowsill, on the bed frame, on the sheets. Teddy bears are painted or stuck everywhere.

"Hi, Kayla, I'm Autumn," I greet my patient, who looks at me alertly from among all the teddy bears.

"Are you a lady doctor?" Her eyes shine bright blue behind the oversized glasses. Her hair falls across her forehead from a deep side part, which looks very cute.

"Exactly. Where are your parents?" I don't like that the little one is completely alone.

"Don't know." She shrugs sadly.

"That's not a problem, I'm here now. May I take a look at your leg?" I ask the little one gently.

She nods. "I fell off the climbing frame, it was super high." To show how high, she stretches her arm as far up as she can. "My daddy rushed out of the house as soon as he noticed, but he didn't have a bandage to put on it."

So her dad wasn't there when she fell either—she seems to be alone a lot.

"Don't worry, here at Halifax Harbor Hospital we have bandages for every wound." Absentmindedly, I look at the broken shinbone that was set in the ER yesterday. It's badly swollen. "Does it still hurt?"

She shrugs.

I quickly check the type and dosage of the pain medication she's received so far in her medical chart. It's quite possible the effect is already wearing off. "You can tell me, it's totally okay."

"She said she's not in pain," a male voice suddenly interjects behind me.

Even before I turn around, I already suspect it. And when I see him, along with the aloofness in his dark eyes, I wonder why I didn't realize it earlier, when Kayla told me her dad wasn't there when she fell off the climbing frame.

Damn. The coffee incident earlier was with Kayla's dad.

Now he enters the hospital room, a fresh cup of coffee in hand. "You're Kayla's doctor?"

Despite the corners of his mouth being raised, a wave of hostility radiates from him. I meet it with a warm smile. "Yes, I'm Autumn, hello."

"David." He sips from his cup, his wedding ring glinting under the neon lights.

Earlier, I thought for a moment he looked familiar, but now I'm sure I was mistaken.

He raises his eyebrows and fixes me with an intense stare. "Is there a problem?"

I quickly shake my head. "I was just about to start the examination."

"Then don't let me stop you." With a forced smile, he pulls his baseball cap lower over his face and touches his beard.

There's definitely something wrong with him.

He should be worried. His daughter is injured, but he doesn't seem to care. Why is this David acting so strangely? He actually seems carefree now, with that disturbingly exaggerated smile on his lips. I search his face for answers, but find none.

Confused, I turn to Kayla. "First, we'll check if your leg is getting good blood flow." Out of the corner of my eye, I notice her dad looking around the room, as if the teddy bears interested him more than his daughter. "It might tickle a little."

"That'll be fun." Kayla looks at her father, who gives her a forced grin like flipping a switch.

God, what is wrong with him? His daughter needs him and he's giving her the cold shoulder with a fake smile.

All the more carefully, I get to work. During the examination, I keep telling her how great she's doing, that it's okay to be scared, and that I'm here for her, no matter what she needs. Meanwhile, the little girl's father buries his hands in his pockets and strolls casually over to the window, where he spends the whole time either staring out or fiddling with his phone.

Ten minutes later, I finish the examination and loop my stethoscope around my neck. "You did a wonderful job, Kayla."

She pushes her chest forward. “Because I’m already a big girl.”

“You definitely are,” I confirm, jotting down the vital signs in the medical record. “Let me know if the pain comes back, okay?”

David snorts in annoyance. As I’ve done so often in the past few minutes, I glance at him again, still unable to figure him out.

“Yesss, I will.” The oversized glasses nearly slip off Kayla’s nose as she nods.

I hold out my pinky finger to her. “Pinky promise?”

She hooks her little finger with mine. “Yes, ma’am, Doctor!”

“Call me Autumn.”

David turns to face us. The incoming light caresses his muscular silhouette, and his gaze is dominated by inaccessibility.

“What’s next?” he asks.

That you be there for your daughter, that’s what’s next, I think. “We’ll wait a few days for the swelling to go down and run the pre-op tests in the meantime. Then the fracture will be surgically fixed with screws and plates,” I explain instead, kindly, because the conversation about how he’s acting like a complete idiot toward his daughter is not one we should have in front of Kayla.

He grins at me again, this time as if I’d just told him he’d won the lottery. “I understand.”

No questions about possible complications, no concerns, nothing. Just that sunshine smile beneath his full beard. I can’t help but study him.

What’s wrong with him? Is he hiding something behind that beaming smile?

But what could it be? And why?

"Cool," says Kayla, drawing my attention to her. "So it'll always beep when I go through airport security, right?"

A strange thought for such a little girl. "Do you fly often?"

She lifts her chin proudly. "All around the world."

"Wow. Even to Africa?"

"How long will it take before she can go home after the surgery?" her dad asks before the little one can answer, stepping up beside her bed.

He should be overjoyed that the accident turned out so lightly. That his daughter's wounds are healing and will leave barely any scars. He should hug her, engage with her, ease her worries. Instead, he cuts off her stories.

Why does he do that?

"She'll be able to get up again soon, but she'll need physical therapy and crutches for a while," I reply, letting him see in my eyes that I mean no harm to him or his daughter. "And a lot of affection," I add, because I simply can't help myself.

For a split second, he freezes, then pulls up the corners of his mouth. "Don't worry, I know what my daughter needs."

I find that hard to believe.

"Can we put stickers on the crutches, Daddy? Please, please, I want horse stickers. With glitter." She folds her hands pleadingly, then looks at me. "When will I get the crutches? And can I have ones that are pink?"

"That's stupid," her dad replies coldly before I can respond.

Whatever problem he has, it must be enormous. My eyes flick to him; his expression is blank.

Kayla pushes out her lower lip. "No, you're stupid."

"Absolutely, we can get pink ones," I say quickly.

"When is Mom coming?" the little one wants to know now.

Her father shoves his hands into his pockets. "As soon as she can."

"That'll be nice." Completely unfazed by her father's dismissive behavior, Kayla reaches out her hand to his, causing him to tense up.

The sight breaks my heart, which I let David know with my expression. But he doesn't seem to understand my signal—or he just doesn't care.

I can't help but scrutinize him closely. What's going on with him? "Any more questions?"

He shakes his head, grins affectedly. "Not at the moment. Let me know as soon as the surgery is scheduled."

It doesn't even occur to this David to thank me—again. Instead, he pulls out his phone once more. Confused, I turn to leave. Before I close the door, I glance back one last time.

"Reach out anytime if you need anything," I say as I slip out into the hallway.

Chapter Four

TAY

Looking for a quiet place, I walk through the hospital corridor, past a play area with balloons on the wall, the small couch by the window, and a few green plants.

Thirty-nine hours have passed since Kayla's accident. Two thousand three hundred forty minutes that have felt like hell on earth.

She's in the hospital and needs surgery. It was an accident, but the guilt is eating me alive, even as I smile on the outside, because that's just what I do.

Pretend that everything's perfectly fine.

The expression on the red-haired doctor's face haunts my thoughts. How she looked at me yesterday with her deep green eyes, so warm-hearted, even though she had absolutely no reason to be. On the contrary, she should have fought back, but she didn't want to fight me, no matter how many times I lashed out at her.

Yesterday, this behavior gave me a queasy feeling in my stomach, and now it's no different. There was something strange about her.

I look around, spot a room labeled as a cleaning room on the door sign, and step inside.

No one is here, so I lean over the sink and splash water on my face. When I raise my eyes, I see a stranger in the mirror: David.

David has shaggy hair, a thick full beard, old-fashioned glasses, and always wears a baseball cap. He's damn unattractive—and he has to be. No one looks closely at people like that. Every time I'm him, I automatically become invisible.

Unlike Tay, David doesn't have to constantly play the confident golden boy. He's allowed to be grumpy and rude sometimes, and that feels good. But every time I'm him, I also see in the mirror the man I would have been if I hadn't worked so hard on my career.

The career that could soon lie in ruins.

The career without which I can't breathe.

Suddenly, there's that buzzing again, the one that's been building up inside me for weeks. My heart beats faster, and I struggle to breathe.

I breathe against the tightness in my chest and pull my phone out of my pocket. Every part of me resists, but I have to finally inform Chloe.

"Kayla hurt herself while playing, we're at the hospital," I type in a message to Chloe.

A minute later, a video call from Chloe pops up. I automatically pull up the corners of my mouth and answer it.

"What happened?" she asks, her expression shocked, without acknowledging my David disguise. Behind her, I can see a hotel lobby.

I lean casually against the door. "Her shin is broken, it needs surgery." Her mouth falls open, her expression accusatory, and I know the words she's about to hurl at me will hit hard. So I cut her off and calmly explain what happened. "She'll need crutches for a while, but in a few weeks she'll be fine," I finish shortly after.

"The one time I leave you alone with our daughter and she ends up seriously injured. You should have watched her more closely." Deep worry lines crease her forehead.

"She's seven, she's allowed to play on her own."

She stares at me, outraged. "If she suffers any permanent damage, it's your fault."

Oh God, just the thought of that tears a deep hole in my soul. "She's going to be okay," I say instead of responding to words that strike precisely where everything's already in turmoil. "Listen, I need a nondisclosure agreement."

Yesterday, the head nurse Dr. Parker made it unmistakably clear during admission that no amount of money in the world exempts me from a clinic's legal obligation to collect patient data. At the very least, I'll have to tell her who Kayla and I are.

"I can get that. Anything else?" She reaches for a notepad.

Internally, I breathe a sigh of relief, but outwardly I remain composed. "The press mustn't find out about the accident."

She scribbles on the notepad. "It's bad enough they found out about the canceled contract for your next film."

That's the last thing I want to talk about right now. "The fact that we've always kept Kayla's face out of the media is working in our favor now. I'm David until we leave the clinic." That shouldn't be a problem—we've done it this way plenty of times before. "Only the head nurse will know, and I'll contractually bind her to confidentiality."

"I'll include extensive clauses, don't worry," she replies

firmly. Ever since the flop of that film, she's been acting completely irrational toward me, but in these words I finally recognize her again—this is the tough-as-nails lawyer I married.

"Afterward, Kayla and I will return to Inner Sambro Island, and from then on everything will go back to plan."

That's what she wants—what we both want.

"Hopefully," she replies dryly.

"I need to check on Kayla now."

"Give her your phone so she can call me. I really want to talk to my little darling," she replies and ends the call.

I put the phone away and take a deep breath before leaving the room. Out in the hallway, I run into Kayla's doctor of all people, who is just saying goodbye to a pair of parents.

The tall woman wraps her arms around Autumn's shoulders. "You're an angel, thank you so, so much."

Autumn's expression is full of bliss. "It was my pleasure," she says, running her hand over the woman's back.

Now Autumn lifts her eyelids, our eyes meet. There's so much warmth radiating from her that, just like yesterday, I imagine for a moment that I can feel her, even though we're meters apart.

It's crazy.

Crazy—and completely unnecessary.

I quickly turn away, and as I walk down the hallway, it feels like with each step I'm bringing myself a little more to safety. Which is ridiculous, because for years now, no one but me has had any say in whether I'm safe or not.

Chapter Five

AUTUMN

I peer at Mom over the rim of my coffee cup. I've noticed she hasn't touched her maple pie. She has no appetite. I look more closely. Has she lost weight?

Maybe. But at least I don't see any dark circles under her eyes, her blonde hair is freshly washed, and so are her clothes.

"How are you?" I ask as casually as possible.

Her smile looks a little tired against the lively atmosphere of the hospital cafeteria, but at least it's genuine. She places her hand on mine. "Don't worry, sweetheart, I'm fine."

Of course I'm worried. "Don't you feel lonely in our house? It must be very quiet." Even as I say the words, a sense of worry creeps up inside me. It was a mistake, I shouldn't have moved out. She's lonely.

"I enjoy the peace and quiet. Besides, I have a lot to prepare." Mom leans forward over the bistro table, her expression affectionate. "The exhibition is starting soon."

Her paintings. Being allowed to present them at the

community center means the world to her. "It's going to be great." I automatically wonder if her smile is genuine, if she's truly happy or just pretending. "Have you thought about my suggestion?"

She tugs at the ends of her blonde hair, her gaze drifting outside, where from the tenth floor the Halifax Harbor lies at our feet. "A dog isn't for me."

But it would keep her company, she'd be less lonely, and I can see that's exactly what she needs. If she doesn't want a dog, then I'll keep her company.

"You know, I don't really like the shared apartment, it feels so unfamiliar there," I say, and it's even partly true. "Maybe it would be better if I moved back home."

Shaking her head, she reaches for her fork. "You'll be thirty next year, Autumn," she says.

"So what? We'd be a multigenerational household." To set a good example, I shove a big piece of my brownie into my mouth. "It's totally trendy right now and I'd save on rent."

"Besides, it would take you an hour and a half to get to work, and you already have so little free time." She sets her fork down again without having eaten.

I lean back in my chair. "I could use that time to read, so it wouldn't be wasted."

Mom knows that I still have to familiarise myself with a lot of topics if I want to have my own clinic one day. Health policies, regulations for staff, clothing and equipment. And of course, the financing of such a facility. The intensive interdisciplinary care—the heart of my clinic—will be expensive.

A gentle smile flits across her face. "And when do you live?"

"I love my work." I nod, as if to confirm it. "That's all I

need in life," I add earnestly, even though it's not true. But I have to come to terms with the fact that I'll remain single for the rest of my life. After all, it would take more than a miracle for a man to love me. "Helping children makes me happy." That way, my life has meaning, even if I never have a family of my own.

She nods with a gloomy expression. My shift starts in five minutes, I should get going, yet I feel that I shouldn't leave her alone right now.

"Just yesterday, on my first day, I treated a little girl with a broken leg." Right on cue, Kayla's father appears in my thoughts. There's his aloof gaze, his expression switching between combative and recklessly smiling. "Her father couldn't properly take care of her. If I hadn't been there, she would've been left alone with her worries."

Once again, I feel the confusion that had gripped me yesterday. The thought of this David and the question of what's wrong with him haven't left me all night. Maybe something's weighing on him, or maybe I'm just imagining it.

"You're a wonderful doctor," says Mom with a gentle glow in her eyes, and I know that right now she's happy—even if only for a brief moment—because she sees how deeply I'm immersed in my work.

"After that, I met a boy for whom pediatrics is unfortunately something like a second home." I don't mention Brian's name or any other personal details, since I'm bound by doctor-patient confidentiality. Still, I tell her that he's battling a congenital heart defect, has undergone countless surgeries, and that I took the time to have a long conversation with him. "When I said goodbye to him, he pulled me into his arms and didn't want to let go."

It's moments like these that keep me alive. That let me

know that—even if I'm a monster—I'm at least loved for what I say and do.

As I tell my story, Mom's expression has grown increasingly joyful. Now she even looks as if there were no shadows in her life at all.

She blinks. "Your dad would be so proud of you, sweetheart."

"I think so too," I say wistfully, thinking about everything that would be different today if he hadn't picked me up from Henry's that day.

I roll the window of our Ford Explorer down a little further. The wind rushes against my cheek and tosses my hair, the hum of the engine grows louder. For a moment I close my eyes, smiling to myself.

"Did you have a nice afternoon?" I hear Dad ask from the driver's seat, and my smile deepens.

"Mhm," I murmur, my thoughts drifting to Henry and the way he looked at me when our fingertips touched. The warmth in his gaze before he lowered his eyelids. How he bit his lower lip, how hard my heart was pounding.

How he slid his fingers between mine. How I held my breath, as if I didn't need to breathe anymore when he touched me. As if he and that touch were what kept me alive.

"You didn't study, did you?" Dad flicks on the blinker. It clicks three times, and with each click, his grin grows wider.

I shake my head, feeling my cheeks flush at the thought that the most popular boy in school—the captain of the hockey team!—is in love with me.

"Mom and I were sixteen too when we met," he says, eyes fixed on the road.

And they still love each other today. I turn to him, the seatbelt pressing into my shoulder. "Did you know right away that she was the one for you?"

"The second I met her." His tone is full of longing.

I want that too. One day, when we're old, I want to lean on Henry's shoulder, look back with him on this afternoon and all the years we've shared. On a whole life, just like Mom and Dad.

Dad steers the Ford onto the highway, the old car rattling loudly over the bumps. I close the window, and suddenly I catch a sharp, hoppy smell that I hadn't noticed before.

I glance sideways at Dad. "Have you been drinking?"

"Just one." His eyes are sad.

"You never drink," I say, even though that's not true. You only drink when you don't know what else to do *would be more accurate. Like six months ago, when Mom lost the baby in her belly.*

He stays silent, and I fidget with my summer dress. A strange mood settles between us.

Again I glance at him. His eyelids look heavy, just like the corners of his mouth. There are lines on his forehead, deep lines.

"Do you want to tell me?" I ask him in the same way he does when he notices something's wrong with me.

He exhales slowly, his fingers gripping the steering wheel tighter.

So it really is that bad. I quickly grab his forearm, which is resting on the armrest between us. "You know I can only help you if you tell me what's going on."

Now he smiles wistfully, probably because he recognizes his own words in mine. "I know, sweetheart, I know."

For as long as I can remember, my dad and I have had this special connection. We only have to look at each other to feel how the other is doing. "Is it something with Mom?"

He answers my question with a shake of his head.

But if it's not about Mom, then what is it?

I squeeze his forearm to show I'm here. "Dad, I'm sixteen, almost an adult. You can tell me."

"Almost an adult, huh?"

I pull my shoulders back. "Why the beer?"

Silence spreads, Dad overtakes a truck and merges back into the right lane. "Today my boss told me the company is going to file for bankruptcy. Next week we'll all be getting laid off," he says, and I see him fighting back tears.

"You'll definitely find a new job quickly." Who wouldn't want him? There's no carpenter in the world who makes furniture as beautiful as he does. "And if not, I can work after school. Maybe even Mom—well, she's doing better, so maybe she could too..."

"Mom is still recovering," says Dad before I can finish the sentence. "She's doing well, but not well enough."

I think of Mom, how she stares out the window in the morning while Dad makes her coffee. How she absentmindedly turns her cup, her shoulders slumping forward as if she's already tired again just after getting up. But also how I hug her and how she hugs me back. How she at least wishes me a good day. And how she even did the laundry again the other day.

He's right, she's doing better. But not well enough.

"I'm here, Dad, don't worry, I'll help."

"Mom mustn't find out until I have a new job, you hear?" His tone turns serious. "It could set her back, now that she's just starting to stabilize."

Of course I know that, even much smaller problems throw Mom off balance since the miscarriage. "No problem, I'll keep it to myself."

"Thank you, sweetheart." He lifts his hand off the steering wheel to stroke my head. "Will you promise me something?" His gaze shifts to me for a moment, there's so much love in his eyes. "Promise me that nothing and no one will ever extinguish that light in you. Promise me that you'll always make the world a warmer place."

Even though I'm not entirely sure what light he's talking about, I nod. "Promise."

My heart leaps when I see Dad smile again. A split second later, I'm slammed into my seatbelt.

Brakes screech.

A scream.

The world turns upside down, my head slams against the roof of the car. Again and again.

There's my summer dress.

Red stains on white fabric.

The smell of hops.

Glass shatters.

Instinctively, I curl up.

The world falls still again.

"Dad?"

No answer.

I smell gasoline.

I feel heat.

I breathe smoke.

My eyelids grow heavy, my vision blurs, I look to the left.

"Dad! Are you okay?"

He's still silent.

My head feels like it's about to explode, but still, with trembling fingers, I reach for Dad's arm.

There it is.

"Dad, say something," I beg him.

A faint whimper escapes his lips. It's barely audible over the crackling, but it's there.

Tears fill my eyes.

In the distance, signal horns blare.

"Everything will be fine," I tell him. "You just have to hold on a little longer."

I unbuckle his seatbelt. Flickering flames dance across the shattered windshield, reaching for me, pouring their poison into the car's interior. Mesmerized, I stare at the fire, press myself deeper into the seat to escape the flames, but they draw closer.

Closer and closer.

And still closer.

Instinctively, I grab the door handle, yank at it, but it won't open. I pull harder, brace myself against the door.

Nothing moves.

Now the flames reach out for me, growing larger, more intense.

Hotter.

A scream escapes my mouth and a second later I'm engulfed in flames.

Even today—thirteen years later—the memory still makes me flinch. I smell the smoke, feel the heat on my skin, even in the places where the fire robbed me of all sensation years ago.

"If only that accident had never happened." Mom's voice brushes softly against my ear.

I feel her pain, feel how she starts to retreat into her shell. Back to where she was after the accident. Back to where she tried to follow Dad.

I quickly get up and hug her. Talking about the accident makes her sad. It hurts her to think about it, and it hurts me too, because since that day, my life hasn't been the same.

I look at her lovingly. "Remember how he absolutely had to try the steep slide at the pool and almost lost his swim trunks when he hit the water?"

"Good thing only you were nearby." She smiles, a sad smile, but at least she smiles, so I continue, and together we remember the funniest, most emotional, and most beautiful moments with Dad. I can't help but think again and again of David, who probably never had such moments with his daughter. At the same time, my guilt grows because I moved out and left Mom alone.

"You really should get going now, sweetheart," Mom says a few minutes later.

I look at the clock—she's right, I'm definitely running

late. "Listen, tonight I'll ask my roommates if I can get out of the lease. Just in case, if…"

"You're staying in Halifax. I'm already painting a picture for your room in the flatshare," she says, cutting me off before I can finish my sentence.

When she paints, she's stable. That's good, but I'm still worried. I pull away from her and look at her intently. "But only if you promise to tell me right away if you need me."

She smiles gently. "I already promised that."

I know. Still, I need to hear it again. I raise my eyebrows expectantly.

"I promise," she says, and I scrutinize her closely. There's nothing to suggest she's lying, yet I can't believe it. After all, I thought she was fine back then after the accident too, even though in truth she was too desperate to go on living.

Chapter Six

TAY

The sound of colored pencils, as Kayla draws a picture, fills the silence of the hospital room. She hums softly to herself while I scroll through the latest tabloid headlines on my phone, searching for my name.

This is how much the renovation of Tay Lawson's villa costs.

Harmless. I keep scrolling.

Tay Lawson – after the last movie flopped, is his career now failing too?

Four weeks have passed since the movie premiere, and it hasn't stopped. I watch a video featuring none other than Scott Pears. Of course, he smugly claims that he was originally supposed to play the role but turned it down because he realized the film would flop at the box office.

Bullshit. He wanted the role—desperately, in fact—but the producers chose me. That's how it was.

And of course he hopes to see me on the big screen again soon, but adds that unfortunately it's probably rather unlikely.

Asshole.

I close the video, keep scrolling through the headlines, and see myself smiling from the screen in a thousand different ways. It's not the first time I wonder how easy it is. That all you have to do is lift the corners of your mouth to make people believe everything is fine.

In my search, I find no indication that Kayla and I are in Nova Scotia, no speculation that there are problems in my family.

At least that.

I look over at Kayla, who is still focused on her drawing. "What are you drawing, Picasso?"

Grinning with the pen in her hand, she looks at me. "Nanny Mina, Mom, you and me eating ice cream." She holds up the sheet so I can see it. She's drawn a big sun whose rays touch all of us. "And there's Autumn with my crutches too, see?" she asks, pointing to the two pink lines next to the chair where the little girl with dark hair and glasses is sitting. Standing next to her is her doctor, smiling broadly. She's the only one looking at Kayla—Mina, Chloe, and I are just staring at our ice cream cups.

"Why is your doctor there?" I ask, and once again that strange feeling runs through me when I think about how Autumn has been looking at me over and over since our first encounter yesterday. When we pass each other in the hallway, when she checks Kayla's condition, when she asks if she can help. It's as if she sees something no one else does. Something no soul is allowed to see.

My daughter shrugs one shoulder. "Because she's my friend and she likes ice cream too, she told me. Vanilla is her favorite. So I said she can come along if Mom is there and we go get ice cream."

I shouldn't keep letting her believe Chloe would be here

soon. It should be easy to tell her, but like so often when I'm not playing a role, I don't have the right words for emotional topics.

"Mom's not coming," I tell her stiffly.

Kayla puts her pen down and pushes out her lower lip. "Why not?"

"We talked about how I'm David so the press doesn't find us here at the hospital," I remind her matter-of-factly.

She nods, her hair falling into her face. Clumsily, she tucks it behind her ear. "But Mom could be Mary like always."

She could. If we could breathe the same air for more than two seconds without tearing each other's hair out. "Mom's on a promo tour. If she cancels that to come to Halifax, then..."

"...then they'll find us," Kayla finishes my sentence, looking terribly unhappy. "And if Mina comes, then they'll find us too."

"Exactly. Your nanny's also on vacation and we won't be here long, we've got this." I see the watery sheen forming in her eyes, know that a good dad would comfort her now, but I don't know what a good dad would say. So I make a funny face. "Unless you'd like to move in here, then we'll sell the villa and live at the clinic from now on."

For a moment she looks at me questioningly, then exhales sharply. "You're dumb."

"No, you're dumb." I wink at her, glad that at least we have this one thing that helps me function as her dad.

My phone beeps, and a message from Chloe pops up on the screen. The non-disclosure agreement. Finally.

"I have to take care of something. Will you draw another picture for Mom in the meantime?" I'd like to add without Autumn, but I hold back. If Kayla asks why she's not allowed to draw Autumn, I won't have a good reason.

"Okay. Of us in our new house and the aquarium I'm getting," my daughter replies, grabbing a blank sheet of paper. "There are little Nemos in it and some Dories. And a sunken ship."

A relieved sigh escapes my lips. "Great idea."

She picks up a pen. "And Autumn is there too."

No, she's not!

Luckily, she gets to work so eagerly that I don't have to respond. On my way to the door, I check the fit of my fake full beard and adjust the black wig sewn into the cap. Then I slip into the hallway and head toward Dr. Parker's office. As I turn the corner, I spot Autumn standing with her boss next to a potted plant. Instinctively, I stop.

"That won't do, Dr. Hall," Dr. Parker says sharply. "In your interview, you emphasized your oh-so-big heart for children, and now you show up late on your second day? What exactly were you doing that made you forget everything around you? Fooling around with an orderly in the locker room?"

My gaze flicks to Autumn, who's chewing on her lower lip. "I'm sorry. It won't happen again."

"Of course not, that goes without saying. But unfortunately, that's not all." Dr. Parker places her hand on Autumn's shoulder. "Sandra said you were also inefficient."

Autumn takes a step back so her boss can't touch her anymore and hurriedly brushes her hair over her shoulders. "In what way?"

"In the way that you're doing things that aren't your responsibility." She raises her eyebrows. "Maybe I wasn't clear enough during orientation, so let me say it again:

parents provide care, nurses assist, doctors treat. It's not that hard to understand, is it?"

I lean against the wall, watching as Autumn gives a barely perceptible shake of her head. The conversation she had with Kayla while examining her leg pushes into my thoughts. She was so empathetic, took her time with my daughter. She gave Kayla something I can't give her. What her boss calls inefficient was actually good for Kayla.

"You stitch wounds, decide on treatment methods, maintain patient records, monitor emergencies." Dr. Parker's tone is now insistent. "And when you're done with that, you rush off to the next patient—without too much pointless chatter."

"I think talking to someone is useful too, sometimes it even helps more than dressing a wound," Autumn replies, almost apologetically.

Dr. Parker rolls her eyes toward the ceiling. "Dr. Hall, please, don't pretend to be dumber than you are."

Bam. A punch to the chin that landed. It was obvious she'd react that way.

Autumn stays silent, her eyelids lowered toward the floor. I can't help but wonder about her. Yes, Dr. Parker is her boss, but Autumn doesn't even try to defend herself. It's like she's stepping into the boxing ring and instead of raising her fists in defense, she just offers up her cheek.

"This is a healthcare facility with limited resources. We don't have the time or the money to concern ourselves with our patients beyond medical treatment," Dr. Parker continues.

Now would be the right moment for Autumn to pull her shoulders back, lift her chin, and strike back. *Don't worry, I've got everything under control,* she should say.

"I understand that this is important to you. You have to

make sure this department runs properly. That's certainly not easy," she says instead.

My jaw nearly drops. What is wrong with this Autumn?

"Good, then we're in agreement. You stick to doing your job and save the sentimental nonsense for your free time."

Autumn smiles politely, as if her boss hadn't just knocked her out cold. "Alright, I'll get to work then."

"Go ahead, don't let me stop you." Dr. Parker steps aside to clear the way for Autumn. "And don't forget to make up for the time you were late."

"Will do," Autumn replies and starts walking in my direction. As she passes me, our eyes meet and in hers I see something I never would have expected: gentleness.

Her boss just knocked her out in a single round and she's not aggressive? Or upset? Or annoyed?

"David." Now she's smiling at me too! "Can I help you? Does Kayla need anything?"

She wants to help me? Why, when it's clearly her who needs help? Still stunned, I shake my head.

How does this woman even survive in this world?

"Okay, I'll stop by later to see how your daughter is doing," she says, turning to leave. A delicate scent of strawberries is all that remains of her—and there it is again, that strange feeling I can't quite grasp.

I shake it off and hurry away—after all, the confidentiality agreement still needs to be signed. "Dr. Parker? I'd like a quick word with you," I call after Autumn's boss, who immediately turns around to face me.

Chapter Seven

AUTUMN

Whether I like it or not, Dr. Parker is right. She has to keep this department running, and she's doing her best—just as I want to do mine. Still, our conversation and the inner conflict it stirred up weigh heavily on me as I examine ten-year-old Kendra in the butterfly room, who's suffering from acute bronchitis.

But that's not all. David and the shocked expression he just gave me in the hallway also haunt my thoughts. Every time I see him, he confuses me more. With each encounter, more questions arise.

First and foremost, why does he keep others at a distance—sometimes with his combative manner, sometimes with that fake smile—that might not be fake at all. Maybe I'm reading too much into it. Still, he's undeniably distant with Kayla, and the fact that his wife still isn't here is strange too. Isn't it?

"Breathing is easier."

I flinch, realizing how lost I was in thought, and quickly turn to my patient. Although Kendra is smiling at me, I can tell by the way she's tugging at the bedsheets that something's on her mind.

"Your respiratory rate and oxygen saturation are good, that's great." I point to the monitor covered in butterfly stickers.

According to Dr. Parker, I should leave now. Medically speaking, the patient is on the mend and there's nothing more I can do for her at the moment. Besides, I wanted to check on Kayla, and there's a whole stack of medical records waiting for me in the doctors' lounge.

"Is there something I can help you with?" I ask anyway, because I simply can't help myself.

Kendra lowers her eyelids, still tormenting the blanket. "The inhalation therapy," she murmurs so quietly I can barely hear her.

I sit down on her bed and look at her with empathy. "You can tell me anything, no matter how unimportant you might think it is."

Her gaze flicks to me, and I know it takes a lot of courage for her to trust me, so I give her time. Eventually, she tells me about her fear of medical equipment and the panic she experiences during every inhalation therapy session, when she has to wear the mask and breathe in deeply.

I should have been with my next patient long ago, but this is important. If I help her gradually overcome her fear, it will have a profound impact on her entire life. So I stay with her, talk to her, ease some of her worries, and promise to be there for her next therapy session—even if I'm not on duty.

When I leave the room twenty minutes later, it's not just Kendra who feels a little happier—I do too—until I spot Dr. Parker, deeply engaged in conversation with a few colleagues. It's unmistakably about the new head surgeon, my roommate Sonora's boss.

"Ethan Stone is the most handsome man I've ever seen. An absolute treat. I'm telling you, you won't believe it—he'll leave you speechless," she jokes with amusement, and after briefly seeing him yesterday, I know she's not exaggerating.

Still, I shake my head. Earlier, she confronted me about my inefficiency, and now she apparently has time for gossip. Her rules clearly don't apply to herself.

I check my hair and pull my T-shirt up higher, then slip past the boss, who, as so often, is lost in inappropriately intimate speculation, and head toward the teddy bear room. The thought that I might run into David there makes my stomach churn.

Peppa Pig flickers silently across the TV when I enter. Kayla isn't watching; she's playing with the ends of her hip-length hair. There's no sign of her father. Earlier, he was still in the hallway and looked at me in shock when I asked about his daughter. Where did he go?

"Hey, Kayla, I have a surprise for you," I say, because there's a preliminary surgery date for her. And what's more, Sonora will be performing the procedure, which means I'll have an ally in the OR—a definite advantage.

She looks up at me. "I don't want a surprise."

Something's bothering her, that much is obvious. I quickly step up to her bed. "May I?" I ask, pointing to the edge of the bed. Kayla nods with a joyless expression, so I sit down and pull out the stethoscope. "I'd like to listen to your heart."

"Okay." With a tired motion, she brushes her hair back.

I place the stethoscope's chest piece on her chest, pretending to listen. "Your heart sounds sad," I then say. "Do you know why it's so sad?"

Tears form in her bright blue eyes, and my heart breaks in more ways than one. Not just because she's feeling down, but because she's going through it alone. Is that why David disappeared? Because he doesn't know how to deal with his sad child?

"Wait, let me listen more closely." Gently, I move the chest piece a few centimeters to the left. "I think it's scared."

Wrinkles crease her forehead, and for a moment she stares blankly past my shoulder. "Maybe."

"Of the surgery?"

She shakes her head.

"Afraid of what happens after the surgery?"

A tear rolls down her cheek.

I set the stethoscope aside, pull her into my arms, and rock her gently. "We'll get through this together," I whisper in her ear, and she bursts into sobs.

Sniffling, she nestles against me. "Brian from the airplane room said I'll never be able to walk properly again."

Brian—the boy with the heart defect who's been in and out of the hospital for years. It's easy to imagine that his illness feels endless to him, that he's gotten his hopes up too many times only to be let down. He probably just wanted to spare Kayla a similar disappointment and forgot that their situations are completely different.

"My leg will be ruined forever, I'll limp like Quasimodo and everyone will laugh at me," she adds now, and in that moment, I feel not only her pain but also my own.

I know what it's like when everyone is afraid of you. When they don't know how to deal with you, when they're disgusted but try not to show it, and their only solution is to keep their distance.

I know what it's like to be a monster.

I know what it means to feel lonely, always watching from the sidelines something you'll never be part of.

I squeeze Kayla a little tighter and wish for nothing more than to spare her what I had to go through. "Your leg will heal, but do you know what's just as important?"

"Hm?"

"That your heart gets healthy too, that it's not sad anymore," I reply and gently push her away from me a little to look into her eyes. "And do you know how that works?"

She wrinkles her button nose. "Can you patch it up with plates and screws too, like my leg?"

Her idea brings a smile to my lips. "No, your heart gets lighter when you give away a little of what makes it sad."

"And how do you do that?" she asks, frowning.

"By telling me how it's doing, what's worrying it and what it's afraid of—no matter what it is." Nothing will ever be too small or too unimportant, not for me. It took so many years for my heart to heal, Kayla shouldn't have to go through that. "What do you think, should we give it a try?"

A faint flicker appears in her eyes. A bit of hope among all the tears. "That's dumb," she suddenly says.

Startled, I study her. "Excuse me?"

She nods vigorously, adjusts her glasses, leaving fingerprints on the lenses. "And you're dumb too—totally dumb."

Wait a second, wasn't that what her dad said to her the other day? In a situation just as inappropriate as this one?

Maybe it's something like a code. Something the two of them say to each other while meaning something entirely different.

"Not as much as you," I reply experimentally, since she reacted the same way to her father's words the day before yesterday.

Her grin stretches from ear to ear, and it even seems

genuine. So it really is a code. But what does it mean? Still confused, I get up from the bed.

"You'll let me know if you need anything, right?" I ask, just to be sure.

"Yup." She reaches for the remote on her nightstand and turns the TV volume on.

I watch her for a moment longer, then sling my stethoscope around my neck and stand up. I've barely turned around when I spot David. He's leaning against the doorframe with his arms crossed.

Our eyes meet. Even though the baseball cap casts a shadow over his eyes, I see—for the first time—a flicker of emotion in them: fear.

So I wasn't wrong—something is weighing on him. Something that wants out, but he can't let go of. Something that's consuming him, with everything he's got, turning him into this cold person he doesn't have to be. What is it he doesn't want to show?

Without breaking eye contact, I walk toward him. The closer I get, the more closed off his expression becomes. It's as if he's building a wall to hide his fear behind. But now that I've seen it, I can't just unsee it.

"Can I help you?" I ask. "Whatever it is…"

"Is there already a date for the surgery?" His words sound aggressive. He massages his temples as if my question is giving him a headache.

"The day after tomorrow, three in the morning—provided the swelling continues to go down as well as it has so far. Dr. Sonora Wells will perform the surgery, she's an excellent surgeon." As I speak, I can't stop wondering why he doesn't just admit he's afraid. What does he think would happen? Or does he just not want to say anything in front of Kayla, trying to play the strong dad, not scare her even more?

"Very nice," he says with an exaggerated smile, without addressing the unusual time of the procedure. Only a few clinics perform routine surgeries at night; maybe he already knows that things are different at Halifax Harbor Hospital —or he still thinks I'll believe that he doesn't care about anything, not even his daughter.

I search his face for clues to the truth he's hiding deep inside, but I find none. He stares at me unrelentingly, the fake smile unchanged on his lips, but that doesn't fool me— not anymore. As soon as the opportunity arises, I'll confront him.

In the background, I hear Kayla giggling. "Oh no, George fell down again," she calls. "Daddy, Daddy, come, you have to see how Peppa Pig comforts him."

He adjusts his horn-rimmed glasses. "Kayla needs me."

She definitely does, but not in the way he's behaving toward her.

Promise me that you'll always make the world a warmer place. Those were the very last words Dad said to me before he died, and that's exactly what I try to do every day, even when it's hard. He taught me that everyone needs warmth —especially those who seem made of nothing but cold.

So I give David a compassionate smile. "I'm here if you need me," I say, and head off to my next patient.

Chapter Eight

TAY

The neon lamp above me flickers, a soft buzzing fills the deserted waiting room of the surgery and threatens to echo in my head.

It's driving me crazy.

I spring up from the uncomfortable wooden chair, walk to the window, and look out into the night. The lights of the neighbouring high-rises reflect in the ocean; not a single star shines in the cloud-covered sky. The minute hand of the wall clock ticks forward with a click. I glance at it.

Three o'clock.

It's starting. Right now, in this very moment, Kayla is being cut open.

"Dr. Sonora Wells will operate, she's a brilliant surgeon," I hear Autumn in my head, and as so often in the past few days, I see her before me—her compassionate gaze, the loving green eyes, the delicate smile.

Even when we first met, her presence felt unsettling, but what happened two days ago in Kayla's room was downright dangerous.

Not just because of the way she handled my daughter's fear and how effortlessly she found the right words, as if the best screenwriter in the world had written the script for her. But even more because of what watching the two of them did to me.

That flicker of warmth in my chest, right where the cold has lived that's protected me for years. For a crazy split second, it felt like something good.

I bury my hands in my pockets, take a deep breath, and want to look at the clock again. But I don't get the chance, because Autumn enters the room. Today without a lab coat, instead in jeans and a high-necked black long-sleeve shirt. Her fiery red hair is, as usual, worn loose, and her bangs are so long they almost cover her eyes.

"Hi," she says, raising her hand.

Faced with her warm expression, I tense up immediately. "What are you doing here?"

She walks toward me, either unaware of the effect her presence has on me or deliberately ignoring it. "I couldn't sleep. I kept thinking about Kayla's surgery."

She barely knows my daughter, knows nothing about her, has only spent a few hours with her. Still, she seems to care. "Go home."

Yeah, that wasn't exactly friendly, but it's hard enough to bear the thought of Kayla's surgery—I don't want anyone around me right now. Especially not someone who radiates so much... I don't even know what it is she gives off.

She shakes her head, and a tense silence settles between us. "You're afraid," she says suddenly into the quiet of the waiting room. "Why are you trying to hide it?"

She can't know that—she can't even begin to guess. I lift the corners of my mouth confidently. "I'm sorry to disappoint you, but you're wrong."

Her intense gaze locks onto me. "I saw it. The day before yesterday, in Kayla's room—the fear was written all over your face."

Why won't she drop it? "Get your eyes checked—something's clearly wrong with them," I reply coolly, but that, too, seems to bounce right off her.

She just keeps looking at me with that understanding expression. "It's okay to be afraid."

No, it's not, but instead of telling her that, I burst out laughing like she just told a joke. "Listen, I really don't know what kind of drugs you're on, but you should stay away from them."

Finally, she lowers her eyelids and I start to feel a little more confident. Time to end this conversation.

"Excuse me, I have to call Kayla's mom," I lie, pulling my phone out of my pocket.

"Does she even know that Kayla was all alone on the playground when she fell off a climbing frame that was clearly way too high for her?" Although Autumn's voice is full of caution—or maybe because of it—her words hit me.

It was a stupid accident, for fuck's sake, and I already feel guilty enough. The last thing I need is an overzealous doctor who doesn't know a damn thing but still thinks she can blame me.

"Kayla is seven, the area was safe, the frame wasn't even twice her height, and I was watching her from the house," I snap, my hand already on the door handle. Damn it, that sounded like I was defending myself—as if I even had to.

"Sorry, I didn't mean to… Based on what Kayla told me, I thought maybe you had…"

"…acted negligently?" I finish her sentence, fully aware that I'm about to win this fight. She lowers her gaze, and I slip my phone back into my pocket. "Looks like you were wrong," I continue coolly, glad to have regained control.

Now would be the right moment for her to leave, but instead she pulls a chair over and sits down. "You have a wonderful daughter." There's nothing but love in her words.

I know.

"Kayla loves you very much."

I know that too. What I don't know is how to respond to it, so I glance at the clock.

Twenty past three.

Autumn won't leave, that much is certain.

"How long did you say the surgery will take?" I ask, just to make her stop digging through my scarred heart with her words.

Chapter Nine

AUTUMN

He avoids me. Again. Does he think I won't notice how he keeps trying to steer the conversation away? Does he think I don't sense that, for whatever reason, our talk makes him uncomfortable, even though he pretends every single word of mine just bounces off him?

"So, how long will the surgery take?" he repeats his question, this time more urgently, and runs a hand through his scruffy beard.

He already knows, after all, Sonora explained the procedure to him. "About two hours," I answer anyway.

Still standing by the door, as if trying to keep an escape route open, he stares at the clock. He's probably wishing it showed something else. The waiting is driving him crazy—any parent would feel the same.

"Kayla is already in deep sleep, the surgeons have opened the operative field and are working to reposition the bone fragments to their original place." Although he doesn't ask, I sense that this is what he wants to hear.

"And what happens next?" he asks, controlled.

I explain to him how the surgeons use plates and screws to fix the bone. I deliberately keep my descriptions factual, since he clearly struggles with emotional topics.

"Then Dr. Wells will carefully check that everything is in the right place. To be absolutely sure, she'll take an intraoperative X-ray."

Out of the corner of my eye, I see that he now sits down as well.

"They'll check for bleeding and suture the wound." I'd like to keep talking—it seems to help him—but unfortunately, there's nothing more to say.

"What complications can we expect?" he asks, as if he were a university professor testing me, not a father deeply worried about his child.

Still maintaining a neutral tone, I go through everything with him, even though he surely already heard all of this during the pre-op briefing.

"In about an hour, we'll know more," I conclude my monologue a short while later, glancing at the clock.

With his forearms resting on his thighs, he stares at the floor. "Thank you," he says tonelessly, and something about that word feels as though it came straight from his heart and touched mine directly.

Whatever is wrong with him, whatever makes him this reserved person—in this moment, it loses a bit of its power, I'm sure of it.

Now he looks over at me, I smile. "You're welcome."

He doesn't return my smile; on the contrary, his expression hardens. "Why are you here?"

Because my nightmares wouldn't let me sleep. Because I wanted to be with Kayla when she wakes up, since her father isn't able to. And because my boss suggested I take care of "sentimental nonsense" in my free time.

"For the same reason you are," I reply.

From his expression, I can tell he doesn't understand how his daughter could matter so much to me that I'd be here on my own time.

"Sometimes we all need someone to stand by us in hard times," I say, because that's exactly what I had wished for back then. To have someone who's there for me.

There's a flicker in his eyes, first warm, then fearful, then it fades. A blink later, he puts on that smile again, the forced one I recognize even beneath the thick beard. "Who are you? Mother Teresa?"

Since Kayla was admitted, I've been trying to be there for her—and for him. I understand something weighs on him, I see that the person he shows me isn't who he really is. Still, I swallow hard at his words. "That hurt."

His expression turns deeply shocked, then he quickly looks away. "Sorry," he murmurs quietly, turning the wedding ring on his finger.

In my mind's eye, a woman appears beside him. I wonder if he's just as distant with her. How can he even maintain a marriage when he's so clearly incapable of showing his emotions? Maybe that's the reason she's not here.

"How long have you been married?" I ask, because part of me wants to know more.

Out of nowhere, he shoots up from his chair. "I'll get some coffee. Want one too?"

Chapter Ten

TAY

Autumn stares at me like I just suggested we commit murder together. “Um… no, thanks.”

“Something else?” I turn toward the door, just wanting to get out of there.

“Herbal tea, please.”

With a brief nod, I leave the waiting room. Only after I close the door behind me can I relax—at least a little.

Whatever she’s doing, she throws me off balance. Just one word from her, one intense look, one warm smile, and the defenses I usually maintain so effortlessly begin to falter. And yet, she doesn’t even do anything—she doesn’t attack, she doesn’t strike—still, she hits me. As if she’s fighting with weapons I don’t recognize and can’t defend myself against.

Why is she asking me all these unnecessary questions, and why—the hell!—is she laying her soul bare as if it were invulnerable?

That hurt. Those words just left her mouth like that. Doesn’t she realize how crazy that is, how vulnerable it makes her?

On the way to the vending machine, the memory of the conversation with her boss that I observed a few days ago inevitably forces its way into my thoughts. Even then, she made herself far too much of a target, was too soft, too vulnerable.

What is she hoping to gain from this?

And what am I actually hoping to gain by asking myself all these pointless questions?

Shaking my head, I walk down the hallway and try to focus on my surroundings. The neon lights, the dull gleam of the floor, the smell of disinfectant, the muffled laughter of employees in the distance.

Still, Autumn stays on my mind.

We all need someone by our side during tough times sometimes, she whispers, just to top it all off, as I reach the machine and pull my wallet from the chest pocket of my plaid shirt.

No idea why I can't control my fingers as they search for the right change. I take a few deep breaths, insert the coins, and press the button for herbal tea.

The hum of the machine is drowned out by the ringing of my phone. This time, I don't answer Chloe's call as a video call. She mustn't see me like this, no one should see me like this. So… all over the place.

"We agreed that I would call when the surgery was over," I say after a brief greeting.

"I haven't forgotten that, don't worry," she replies coolly, and for the first time since the conversation began, I feel solid ground beneath my feet. No matter what Chloe says, it can't touch me.

"You know how it is. As long as the procedure is ongoing, family members don't get any information." The herbal tea is ready. I set it aside, toss in some coins, and choose a black coffee for myself.

"Yes, I know, that's not why I'm calling." There isn't a trace of warmth in her tone. "I had a meeting with RPR Productions today."

Every muscle in my body tenses. "Did they make me an offer?"

"That's right." There's pride in her voice. "It wasn't easy to convince them, but they want to meet you."

I cover the microphone with my hand and exhale in relief. The scent of coffee drifts into my nose, and hope floods my chest.

"Are you still there?"

"Of course." I clear my throat. "What's the role?"

"You'll play a surgeon in a drama about forgiveness, morality, and the limits of human perfection. It's going to be the film of the year—the focus group went wild when they heard the script."

Something in my chest loosens. I could soon be back in front of the camera, finally letting out all the emotions that have built up inside me over the past few weeks.

I'm will do again that which means the world to me.

I need this role.

Absolutely.

"Just the announcement that I'm involved will steer the press in a new direction," I say, deliberately calm so Chloe won't notice the turmoil inside me.

"And the best part: the role is so challenging that you've got a shot at the Oscar," she adds.

Now she suddenly believes I could win an Oscar? Just a few days ago, she believed the tabloids when they said I had no talent. But I don't mention that—otherwise, she might think she hurt me with it.

"What's the offer?" I ask instead.

"We're not that far yet. First, they want to meet you at

an audition." I hear paper rustling in the background. "They're asking if you can meet them in New York in three days."

And I'm supposed to leave Kayla here alone? Of course Chloe thinks that wouldn't be a problem for me. She doesn't know me, knows nothing about all the feelings I keep locked inside, and I intend to keep it that way. So I begin to plan the trip in my head, heavy-hearted. I'll probably be gone less than eight hours. Kayla is in good hands with Autumn, and I don't even have to ask her to look after my daughter. She'll do it—I'm sure of that.

I already picture Autumn again, sitting by Kayla's bed, listening to her heart and explaining how she can take the sadness out of it. What will she think of me when I leave Kayla here alone?

I shake my head in confusion—what a stupid thought. I couldn't care less what's going on in Autumn's head.

"Sure, I can fly out." I let my gaze drift down the empty hallway. "Are you booking the flights?"

For a moment, there's silence on the line. The hum of the coffee machine behind me has long since faded.

"You'll have the tickets in your inbox tomorrow." Chloe's drive is unmistakable. "Use the time until then to do some research at the clinic. This audition could save your career."

No, it can do so much more than just save my career. It can save me. I have to get the role—nothing can go wrong.

Right on cue, that buzzing starts up in my head again—the one that's been with me since the failed film. "I'll call as soon as Kayla's awake," I say quickly, before the buzzing starts creeping into my chest.

"Absolutely, I'm always reachable." There's warmth in

her voice, but it's not meant for me—it's for Kayla, and I know it.

We say goodbye, and I take the second cup from the machine. My eyes fall on my wedding ring, which gleams dully under the neon lights.

Earlier, Autumn stared at it. She looked wistful, as if the ring held some deeper meaning.

How long have you been married? she asks again in my thoughts, and once more I'm flooded by that feeling of losing control, along with the memory of the moment my marriage fell apart.

"Don't you want to understand that your career is hanging by a thread, or are you just incapable of it?" Chloe snaps at me. Anger dominates her face, the red of her cheeks glowing against the subtle white of our kitchen cabinets.

It's been like this for days. That damned film and the way the press is pouncing on it—this whole thing is a nightmare. I feel like I'm standing at the edge of a cliff, her hands pressing into my back, pushing me forward, wanting me to fall into the abyss.

I can't breathe. Can't sleep. Can't think.

Just the thought of leaving Hollywood—this world where anyone can be whoever they want to be, and no one ever looks behind the façade—terrifies me to the core.

I fought for so many years to be here, to feel safe like nowhere else, and to live my dream of acting at the same time.

"My career isn't hanging by a thread," I reply, adding a tone of amusement to my words.

"Just once, I want to see that you have feelings, for fuck's sake," Chloe shoots back, far too emotional. "No one can be like this."

As if she had any idea what it's like to live with a heart that doesn't beat right.

She doesn't know shit—and that's a good thing.

I set the dish towel aside. "My training's waiting," I say, turning to leave.

"I want a divorce."

In the middle of my movement, I stop. "Since when?"

Her fingers dig into the edges of the kitchen island, her knuckles turning white. "Doesn't matter."

"So it's been a while. Why are you bringing this up now, of all times?" Does she think that now—when the press is tearing me apart—is the right moment for this?

She shakes her head.

"What about Kayla?" I ask, trying to stay composed.

"Oh, so now you care about her feelings?" she snaps. "Interesting."

"That's not the point. We need to discuss how to proceed," I counter.

"Of course." Suddenly, I see a single tear slip from the corner of her eye. "I'm not going to break my little girl's heart. You'll tell her—after all, this is all your fault." She wipes her cheeks with her hands. "Then we'll make it public."

A wave of fear rises in me. The press won't back off, and Kayla will be all over the newspapers. We've managed to keep her away from the reporters for so long, but our separation will change everything. Even though there mustn't be any photos of her, the speculation will explode and reach into her private life.

I have no idea how to protect Kayla from this. How to keep her heart from breaking under everything that awaits her.

Chloe's expression hardens. "You have two weeks."

How generous. "I'll take Kayla away," I suggest, because that will be best. "That way, we won't have to spend more time together than necessary, and I can go through everything with Kayla in peace."

"We'll give the nanny time off in the meantime, it's long overdue anyway." She nods grimly.

I'd rather have Mina with me—if Kayla reacts badly, at least she'd find the right words, because I definitely won't. "All right," I reply anyway. "We'll travel incognito."

"That's probably best. I'll come up with an excuse for the press." With a shaky breath, she lets go of the kitchen island and smooths down her blouse.

"Are you still my agent?" I ask, because that's something else we need to settle.

Her gaze locks with mine. "As long as you can still afford me."

Lost in the memory that brought me here to Halifax in the first place, I walk back into the surgery's waiting room. Kayla still doesn't know any of this, and I have no idea how or when I'm going to tell her. When I open the door and see Autumn sitting there, with her open expression and that lovable smile, it happens again.

For a split second, I lose control—and wonder how Autumn would react if she knew all of this about me.

Would she tell me it's my own fault? What a lousy father I am, that I should never have married Chloe, let alone had a child with her?

Or would she see how broken I am, scarred all over my heart? Would she ask why I built this kingdom of castles in the air that others call my life? Would she look at me the way she does now, in this moment when she becomes aware of my presence—full of warmth?

Would she try to heal me?

Bullshit.

Like hell she would.

She doesn't even know who I am underneath my disguise. Besides, she's just someone who happens to be Kayla's doctor. Nothing more.

A bit too forcefully, I press the herbal tea into her hand. "Any news from the OR?"

"Not yet," she replies in a far too empathetic tone, looking at me in a way that makes my stomach turn. "I'm sure everything's going well."

She can't know that, so she shouldn't say it. I take a sip of my coffee and feel her still watching me.

"I'm sure," I mutter, because it's better not to go any deeper into the topic.

Suddenly, Autumn stands up, walks over to me, and places her hand on my upper arm. The touch feels warm and gentle. Warm, gentle, and dangerously close. "No matter what happens, I'm here for you."

I don't want to believe her, and even less do I want to look at her, yet it happens. My eyes find hers. "No matter what happens?" I hear myself ask, and I no longer understand myself.

What the hell is wrong with me? Why am I responding to her overly emotional nonsense?

Instead of answering, she just nods. Her thumb brushes my upper arm for the briefest moment, but even that, combined with the way she looks at me, scares me.

My heartbeat speeds up.

I should leave, right now, but I'm frozen in place.

"We can do this," she whispers now.

She doesn't know Kayla and knows me even less. Her words shouldn't touch me—on the contrary, they should roll off me like raindrops on a windowpane. Instead, they slowly seep into my soul like water into parched earth and awaken something that died a long time ago.

Unable to look away, I search for something that could rescue me from this situation, and at the same time, I'm not sure I even want to be saved.

The door swings open.

A doctor with long dark curls enters, and suddenly it's no longer about whether I want to be saved or not. It's happening, and it feels bittersweet.

Chapter Eleven

AUTUMN

A mischievous grin plays on Sonora's lips. Her gaze brushes over my hand, which is still resting on David's upper arm, and I realize how this must look to her.

There's nothing I should be embarrassed about, yet I suddenly feel unbearably hot. I quickly put some distance between David and me. He steps aside and fiddles with his baseball cap.

Fortunately, Sonora now turns to David with a professional expression. "Mr. Meiers?"

He crosses his arms in front of his plaid shirt.

"How did the surgery go?" I ask for him, since he clearly can't. "How is Kayla? Were there any complications? When can we see her?"

Confused, my roommate pushes her wild curls out of her face. "We were able to successfully stabilize the fracture, there were no complications, and your little one tolerated the anesthesia well." As she reports, she alternates her gaze between David and me, as if she's unsure whom to address.

I exhale in relief. "That's wonderful, thank you, Sonora."

Out of the corner of my eye, I notice David's jaw clenching. "What happens next?"

That must be his code for when can I see my daughter? Why doesn't he just say it out loud? What is he afraid of?

"Your daughter is in the recovery room and should be fully responsive again in no more than two hours. You may go see her now, if you'd like." Sonora gestures toward the door. "I can take you there."

"Absolutely." Only after the words leave my mouth do I realize that I've taken away David's chance to respond himself. Our eyes meet briefly. I'm not sure, but I think I catch a glimpse of panic behind all that control in his eyes.

Sonora raises her eyebrows, and I signal to her that we'd better get going. The three of us leave the waiting room and step into the empty hallway.

Sonora marches ahead briskly. "As soon as the little one is awake, her vital signs are stable, and there are no immediate complications like bleeding or circulatory issues, she can be transferred back to pediatrics," she chatters cheerfully, as if trying to fill the silence emanating from David.

"So maybe this afternoon already?" He sounds like he's scheduling a business meeting.

"That's quite possible." Sonora smiles, her dimples showing. "Dr. Hall will take care of everything else; you're in the best hands with her," she adds, giving me a very inappropriate wink.

I clear my throat. "We'll monitor the wound healing, manage Kayla's pain, and regularly check the leg."

"When can we go home?" David's voice falters briefly as he says the words home, as if something about that place troubles him.

"That depends on how things progress and how well she responds to physiotherapy, but typically it takes about a week," I reply.

His expression remains objectively neutral.

"Here we are." Sonora, out of breath, heads toward a white double door and opens it.

We step into the dim light of the recovery room. Sonora leads us to a sink where we wash and disinfect our hands. Then she hands us protective gowns, hairnets, and shoe covers.

"I don't need that," David says, glancing at the hairnet.

"Oh yes, you do," Sonora replies firmly. "You also need a beard cover, and the cap has to come off."

He reaches for his headwear, which he apparently wears twenty-four hours a day, pulls it lower over his forehead, and shakes his head decisively.

It's just a hairnet. While I put mine on, he throws his into the trash can.

Sonora's questioning gaze finds me.

"Thank you, Sonora, I'll take care of the rest," I say quickly, even though I have no idea how I'm going to get David to wear the hairnet.

"Alright, I have to move on anyway, the patient files are waiting." She spins around and heads to the door. "Page me if there are any problems," she says to me and slips out the door.

I give David a pointed look. "I'm sorry, but without the hairnet, I can't let you see Kayla." The hygiene regulations exist for a reason. "You don't want to risk an unnecessary infection, do you?"

He presses his lips together, looking as though he needs to think, even though this really isn't a difficult decision.

"What's going on? What's the problem?" I study him

intently, but in the dim light, I can barely make out anything in his eyes. "We can talk about it, I'm sure we'll find a solution."

He reaches for a fresh hairnet. "I'll put it over the cap."

So he wouldn't take it off for anything in the world. I automatically think back to when he changed his shirt after the coffee spill. Even then, he didn't take off the cap. Is there something under that baseball cap? Something no one's allowed to see?

Yes, that's the only logical explanation.

What if he's not just hiding his fear behind his sometimes tough, sometimes fake-smiling facade, but also something entirely different under his cap?

Something ugly, perhaps. Maybe we have more in common than I previously thought. Maybe life has left its mark on him too, maybe he also has scars he hides from the world.

The thought sparks a warmth in my chest that makes me search his face for clues to confirm exactly that.

"What's that supposed to mean?" A crease forms between his brows, his eyes flashing, ready for a fight.

Of course I know what he means by *that*—the way I look at him. "What do you mean?" I ask anyway. I want to know what's hiding behind that wall he's showing me. I need to find out if we truly have something in common.

"I want to be alone with my daughter," he replies and quickly walks around the corner, where Kayla is sleeping in one of the beds.

Confused, I remain by the sink. I should respect his wish, yet I can't bring myself to leave the room. Instead, I do something that's completely out of character for me.

I open the door and let it shut again so he'll think I've left. Then I crouch by the wall and peek around the corner.

Holding my breath, I watch him step up to Kayla's bed. He doesn't look at her; instead, he stares at the readout on the monitoring screen.

In the beam of the lamp beside the bed, I can see him much more clearly than before. His nostrils flare, his chest rises and falls rapidly. He slams his clenched fists hard against his thighs.

Now he blinks rapidly and presses his lips together, then finally lowers his gaze to his daughter.

"Oh God," he bursts out suddenly, without warning.

His tone carries the answers to all the questions I've been asking myself over the past few days.

He loves this little girl, lying before him in deep sleep, more than anything else in the world. Why he can't manage to show her that, why he pretends with her and with everyone else, is a mystery to me.

With both hands, he takes hold of her fingers and sinks to his knees beside Kayla's bed. I hear him exhale shakily, see his muscles give way, feel his façade crumble, and recognize the person he truly is—his heart is full of emotion, full of love, but also full of pain.

His head sinks onto the sheet, his glasses pressing into his skin. "Kayla. I'm so sorry. Forgive me, please, forgive me!" he pleads with his sleeping daughter.

Unable to do anything else, I watch him drown more and more in his pain. Until tears well up in my eyes.

"I should have taken care of you." He presses his lips to the back of Kayla's hand.

The image of the two blurs before my eyes, and suddenly David becomes my dad, and instead of Kayla, I'm the one lying in that hospital bed.

Yes, you should have, and you shouldn't have driven drunk, I think, feeling a familiar anger rise in me that I don't want. You did this to me, you made me a monster and left me alone with it.

"I should have been there and kept you safe." Endless sorrow resonates in his words, burning deep into my soul.

That he couldn't be there for me wasn't his fault. It was an accident, his death, and everything that happened afterward was fate. Still, the anger over everything that happened tightens my throat.

"I'll make it right, no matter what you need, you'll get it, I promise!" I hear someone say, and I can no longer tell whether it's David or my dad.

How are you going to do that? Thick tears roll down my cheeks. You're dead, damn it, how could you die when I needed you so badly?

I fight against these thoughts, against the chaos they stir inside me. They're wrong, no matter how right they feel in this moment.

"Promise me that nothing and no one will ever extinguish that light in you. Promise me that you'll always make the world a warmer place." Dad's voice is everywhere inside me. It reminds me of what matters in my life, even when it's damn hard sometimes.

Only thanks to this do I manage to tear my eyes away from David. On tiptoe, I slip out into the hallway before my anger makes me do something I never wanted to do again.

Chapter Twelve

TAY

I bury my face in Kayla's hands. The guilt that has built up in me over the past few days, the feelings I locked away behind my wall, the fear—all of it pushes its way out. It overwhelms me uncontrollably, and I don't even understand what's happening to me in this moment.

This isn't who I am.

Years ago, I trained myself to appear invulnerable on the outside. Nothing can hit me hard enough for anyone else to notice. No one will ever know when they hurt me. And yet here I am, on my knees, in the half-light beside my daughter's bed, even though someone could walk in at any moment and see my true feelings. With the beeping of the monitors in my ears, the smell of disinfectant in my nose, and fucking tears in my eyes that have no business being there.

"No matter what happens, I'm here for you."

Those were Autumn's words earlier, and that wasn't all. Her presence, the way she looked at me, the warmth, the sense of safety, the openness. Everything about her threw me off balance.

And when I saw my daughter lying helplessly in front of me, it suddenly happened. The scars on my heart tore open, turned into gaping wounds, bleeding out all the feelings that had been trapped there for years.

I never wanted children, and I didn't want Kayla either. Chloe and I should never have had her. Just six months after our first kiss, Chloe placed a blue-and-white plastic thing on the breakfast table, and I knew instantly what it meant.

I knew I couldn't be a father, but Chloe already loved the baby growing inside her far too much not to have it.

Nine months later, I held a little girl in my arms, her wrinkled face scrunched up before she opened her eyes and looked straight at me—and in that instant, I knew I had to protect myself more than ever before.

There was this delicate being who didn't yet know how to hurt others. Who was so pure and so honest and so beautiful that with a single breath, she slipped past my scars and into my heart.

For seven years, I've kept my love for this child locked in my heart, never showing anyone how terrifyingly vulnerable she makes me, how much I worry about her.

Now she's lying in the hospital bed in front of me, and I'm completely at the mercy of my emotions.

Because of Autumn's disarming nature, because of everything that's come crashing down on me in the past few weeks. And not least because I haven't been in front of a camera for far too long. My emotions had no outlet, no way to escape, and now they've broken through.

"No!" I clench my fists, knowing I have to fight against it.

Kayla will get better, and I will go back to work. Because only then will I be okay again—in the only way that's possible for me.

Chapter Thirteen

AUTUMN

I run to the bathroom, where I wash my face and tug at my hair until I look like I always do. Only my slightly reddened eyes still show signs of my outburst, but even those will fade soon. I brace myself against the sink, look at my reflection in the mirror, force the corners of my mouth upward, and think of David with his thousand different ways of smiling, all of them fake.

"Now what?" I ask my reflection. Go back to David and pretend I don't know that he's drowning inside in all those feelings he so stubbornly hides?

I can't do that. My heart has seen his and recognized itself in it. He suffers in silence, and then there's still the mystery of what's under his cap.

I feel a kind of hope I haven't had in so long. Are we really more alike than I thought?

I shouldn't hope for that, and yet the thought that it might be true is just too beautiful. Because if it were, maybe he could look past my scars and, who knows, maybe I could still find happiness?

"Even if he could, he's married," my reflection reminds me, snapping me back to reality.

He is, I know that, and besides, there are no miracles, no matter how much I wish for one. So I should get these fantasies out of my head as quickly as possible.

I quickly make my way to pediatrics, where my shift starts in half an hour anyway.

Over the next few hours, it gets easier by the minute to be myself again. I laugh at Brian's jokes, the boy with the heart defect who, thanks to our conversation a few days ago, now understands that he unnecessarily scared Kayla. During my lunch break, I accompany Kendra to her inhalation therapy, and afterward I treat a boy in the emergency room who swallowed three red Lego bricks. I'm in my element—even if not quite as efficient as Dr. Parker would like—but I cherish every smile from my little patients, every high five.

At noon, I give one of my patients a firm hug before finally discharging her from the hospital. "Are you excited to go home?"

She nods against my shoulder. "To see Minki."

Her cat, which she told me about during rounds yesterday. Dr. Parker gave me a stern look, but I still chatted with the little one while checking her vital signs. It wasn't a waste of time—I combined two tasks.

"I'm sure Minki is incredibly excited to see you too," I say now, releasing my patient from the hug.

She slings a lion-shaped backpack over her shoulder, and her parents thank me profusely. A wave of warmth rises in me. I can still do this—I can make others happy. Just not David.

We step into the hallway together, and I wave after my patient until she disappears into the elevator with her parents. With a wistful smile on my lips, I turn toward the doctors' room, where a stack of medical files is still waiting —and spot David.

Of all people.

"I… uh…" I stammer, suddenly self-conscious in the face of the truth I've discovered beneath his rough exterior.

He looks at me with that nothing-in-the-world-can-touch-me expression. "Is there a problem?"

Images of him from this morning flash before my mind's eye. Of his pain, his true self he refuses to reveal at any cost. "No, everything's fine."

"Kayla is being transferred now, she's stable," he says flatly, and if I didn't know she meant the world to him, I'd honestly think he didn't care about her at all. It's fascinating how good he is at pretending in front of others.

I check my pager. No messages, even though the team should have contacted me for the handover. "Are you sure?"

He lifts his chin. "Of course, there were no preoperative complications."

I can't help but wonder if he'll ever show me his true self. Why he's chosen to act as ugly as he already is under his cap.

"Is something wrong?" he asks.

"It's called postoperative, preoperative means before a procedure," I reply absentmindedly, because the questions just won't leave me alone.

He adjusts his horn-rimmed glasses. "That's what I said —post-op-er-a-tive."

His expression is so confident that I start to doubt whether I misheard him. I wave it off, because in the end, it doesn't matter. What matters is Kayla and that she's okay. "Yes, sorry, I should…"

"The surgical team said it would take about twenty minutes," he interrupts me matter-of-factly.

Now that I know how much pain he's in, I understand him so much more—and yet so much less. Anyone could understand that he is deeply weighed down by worry for his daughter. So why does he do everything he can to appear carefree on the outside? What happened to him that broke both his body and his soul?

While I'm still searching in vain for the answer, my pager vibrates. It displays the message from surgery that I missed earlier. "Wonderful, Kayla's handover can take place."

He leans casually against the wall. "What handover? What do they do before they hand over Kayla?"

"Transfer," I correct him automatically. "I get the surgical and anesthesia reports, information about her medication and aftercare. That's how we make sure there are no gaps in communication."

He taps his chin, which is hidden beneath a scruffy beard, with his index finger. "Interesting. Can I come along and listen?"

I probably look at him in disbelief. Since when does he want to be near me voluntarily? "Why would you want that?"

He lifts the corners of his mouth, revealing perfect teeth—a stark contrast to his otherwise wild appearance. "I'm just curious how it all works."

Could that be the truth? I briefly think back to when I explained to him what was happening in the OR during Kayla's procedure. He wanted to know, but he hadn't asked

—it was more like those clinical facts were the only thing he could bring himself to talk about.

Is he afraid he'll lose his mind while waiting for his daughter? Does he feel like he needs to be there for her, but doesn't realize that it means nothing to Kayla as long as he remains so emotionally distant?

I study him, but his expression reveals no discernible emotion. "Family members aren't allowed during handovers. Wait here, I'll be back soon with Kayla."

"I'm coming with you." He pushes himself away from the wall, and I see the pleading in his eyes. Suddenly, I feel sorry for him.

Because he apparently thinks he has to hide his feelings, even though nothing is harder for him than being here in the hospital, and on top of that, he probably doesn't even realize what he's doing to his daughter. Automatically, I think of my dad, wonder like so often what he would think if he could see me today. About my scars, about what that one day turned me into, and about what I made of myself. But deep down, I've known the answer for a long time: he would be shocked.

Chapter Fourteen

TAY

Oh man, what's going on with Autumn? Why does she look so sad? A queasy feeling rises in me. Is it because of me? Whatever, she just needs to stop. Right now.

"Well? Are we finally going?" I ask curtly, because anything else would be unthinkable.

She blinks, and suddenly something happens that's even more uncomfortable than watching her distressed expression: she catches my gaze with hers. Through the green of her eyes, I can see straight into her soul—and there's sorrow. A deep, dark kind of sorrow that makes it hard for me to breathe.

God, why is she silent? Why is she just standing there, looking at me like that? What does she expect to get from it?

This would probably be the moment when anyone else would ask if everything's okay. But how could I, when I'm sure she'd give me an honest answer and not make up an excuse.

Usually, I'm the one who wins staring contests and

shows the other person who's in control. But now I lower my eyes.

My God, she's doing it again, right now. She's making me do things I never do. What is it with her?

"Fine, then I'll go alone." With those words, I march off toward the elevator.

Halfway down the corridor, I hear footsteps behind me—Autumn catches up. To my surprise, she doesn't remind me again that I'm not allowed to be present during the transfer. Instead, she stands silently beside me as we wait for the elevator.

She remains silent, her gaze fixed on the elevator doors, just like mine. Still, I feel her presence—I hear her breathing, catch the faint scent of strawberries in her hair, sense the tension radiating from her.

The chime of the arriving elevator feels like a release, but as soon as we step inside and the doors close again, that strange atmosphere returns.

It's as if a cloud of unspoken questions hangs between us. As though we're communicating without saying a word. There's blame, there's worry, and a kind of heaviness that settles on my shoulders.

Holding my breath, I watch the numbers on the display count down far too slowly.

Sixth floor.

A wave of uncomfortable warmth spreads through me.

Fifth floor.

I notice that she's stopped breathing too.

Fourth floor.

She tugs at her hair.

Third floor.

I desperately need to catch my breath, but I can't.

Just one more floor, then I'll be free.

The three on the display disappears, I stare at it, waiting for the saving two – but before it appears, the elevator suddenly stops.

"What…?" I automatically look at Autumn, whose hand is on the stop button. She's halted the elevator. "What are you doing?" The panic is barely audible in my voice, yet Autumn might have picked up on it. Fuck. "Undo that right now."

Her eyelids flutter, she keeps running her hands over her lab coat. Now her expression turns intense. "We need to talk."

She knows something. Or doesn't she?

Yes, I see it in the knowing way she studies me. My God, has she figured out who I am?

Suddenly I feel like I'm trapped in this elevator with her. A cage with locked doors, and I can't escape. "I don't see what we need to talk about," I reply firmly. "Let the elevator keep going, Kayla shouldn't have to wait for us."

A sad smile flickers across her face. "Kayla has been waiting her whole life – for you."

Ah, so that's what this is about. "Move aside." I step toward her and reach for the stop button, but she blocks my way.

"I know you're scared, and that you're hiding your feelings." Her words are so gentle, but inside me they feel like a thousand tiny bombs, bringing my world to a halt.

"You have no idea, so stop assuming things about me," I reply coldly, bracing myself for her comeback.

She doesn't strike back. On the contrary, a watery sheen forms in her eyes, her brow furrows. She looks like she's letting down her guard, standing so defenseless in front of me that I could knock her out with a single blow.

She's risking me striking her down, and it doesn't seem to scare her in the slightest.

"I know you love your daughter – with all your heart – and that you have no idea how to deal with it." Pain dominates her expression.

I don't want this. Her closeness, this conversation, the openness, the emotions. I don't need any of it. All I need is for this damn elevator to start moving again.

"You don't know anything." Not even that beneath my disguise, I'm Tay Lawson. But in some crazy way, it seems like she's seeing right through David's facade to Tay, and straight into my heart.

This has to stop.

I step even closer to push her aside. The moment my hands touch her upper arms, an electric charge zaps across my skin, making me let go immediately.

Unfazed, she holds my gaze. "One day it'll be too late to show her your love." She stares at me, letting me see everything in her. I try to resist, yet I can feel this is something personal for her, something that hurts. "One day, you'll be nothing but an unpleasant memory to her. The father who never loved her."

Suddenly, I see an adult version of Kayla before me. A young woman who constantly wonders why her dad couldn't love her.

"Whatever's weighing on your soul, Kayla's suffering because of it."

I should protest, fight back against Autumn's words, push back. Instead, I just shake my head vigorously and feel relieved that I can at least manage that, while the wall inside me begins to crack dangerously. That's exactly how it started this morning in the recovery room. Soon it will collapse. If Autumn keeps going, it'll be reduced to rubble in seconds. Autumn will see all my scars, will see how broken I am, and that can never happen.

"It's not too late yet," Autumn says gently. "Think about it."

It's not that simple. I almost tell her that, and I can feel the sentence would leave my mouth full of sorrow. She doesn't know me, she doesn't know where I come from or what happened to me. No one does, and that's the only way it works.

That's just how it is in our world. There are rules we have to play by if we want to survive.

"Get out of the way already." The coldness in my tone makes me shiver.

With a disappointed shake of her head, she does. I stare at the red stop button longer than necessary, fully aware that it will save me. All I have to do is pull it, and I'll be free.

"I'm sorry," Autumn whispers beside me. "I shouldn't have been so direct, I just wanted… you have everything anyone could wish for. If you could accept it…"

No, no, no, that's not how this is supposed to go. She should be yelling at me, calling me the worst father in the world, furious. And she definitely shouldn't be apologizing for caring about my daughter—and somehow, apparently, about me too, even though I've been such an asshole to her.

"I'm sorry," she repeats now, with feeling.

I've never met anyone like her. Someone I can't distract from everything I've barricaded behind my behavior. Someone who gets far too close with ease and doesn't use what they see against me.

It's confusing, she is confusing. Everything about her radiates warmth and what do I do? I'm ugly and mean and spiteful to her, even though she stands there defenseless.

I turn my head, feel exposed under her gaze, but

somehow I endure it. "No," I hear myself whisper, "I'm the one who's sorry."

With a quick motion, I pull out the stop button, and as the elevator starts moving again, it feels like my world is turning once more—though slightly different than before.

Chapter Fifteen

AUTUMN

Ever since David and I left the elevator, he's been on my mind. The way he apologized to me before getting it moving again. The painful expression that took over his face as he did.

As if something inside him is even more broken than I thought.

I shouldn't be thinking about him, yet he lingers in my mind as I leave Halifax Harbor Hospital after my shift, strap my bag to the bike, and walk it home while calling Mom on the way. Today, I find it hard to focus on her stories. But the fact that she painted a new picture makes me happy. She really seems to be in a good phase, and there's nothing I want more than for it to last.

"That sounds great, I'll stop by this weekend and take a look," I say, relieved, though I don't want to get my hopes up too soon. "What are you planning for tomorrow?"

I think Mom knows why I'm asking, and I don't want to act like her babysitter, but I do it anyway, and she tells me about a hair appointment while my thoughts drift back to where they don't belong: to David and the question of why he hides his inner self so deliberately. Maybe there's something ugly about him too, but his heart is beautiful, warm, and lovable—I'm sure of that by now.

A bell rings. "That must be Lanie," says Mom on the other end of the line. "I have to go."

My aunt is coming to visit? Did Mom mention that? "Say hi for me," I reply absentmindedly and park the bike in the rack in front of our apartment building.

We say goodbye and I stroll upstairs to the flatshare, where I find June and Nyla in the kitchen. A big pot of pasta sits on the table between them, giving off a delicious scent of basil and sautéed vegetables.

"Oh, thank God, I thought no one else was coming." Nyla's doe eyes sparkle alongside her oversized earrings. "There are about ten portions of pasta left."

June brushes back her light blonde hair, turns to me and points at Nyla. "Because she basically just ate the vegetables again."

"Oh, come on." Nyla waves it off and gets up from her chair to grab a plate for me. "Come on, sit down. Sonora's asleep. Do you know where Olive is? Is she still on shift?"

I have no idea. Only a genius could keep track of our constantly changing and mismatched schedules. "No clue," I say, shrugging.

"You can have my seat," June says with a long yawn. "I still have some research to do."

"For your asshole patient?" Everyone in the apartment has heard about the guy June knows from high school who's now her patient. The fact that she has to diagnose his mysterious illness to land the specialist position in the diagnostics department is really getting to her.

"Mhm, yeah, that one." June absentmindedly tugs at her Barbie-blonde mane.

Strange. Considering she went on a full-blown rant the day before yesterday when we talked about him, she's unusually quiet now. I shoot Nyla a curious glance; she gives me a knowing grin.

"Have a nice evening, you two." June leaves the kitchen before I can ask her what's really going on with her.

I drop my bag, sit down in the now-vacant seat, and push the gossip magazines aside.

My eyes fall on all the flawless people on the covers, and suddenly I see all my scars again, in all their ugliness. But they also remind me that David and I might have something in common. That we're both damaged and maybe that's exactly why…

Stop, I didn't want to think about that anymore.

Damn it, what's wrong with me?

"Here you go." Nyla sets a plate down in front of me and places a fork beside it. "Enjoy."

Lost in thought, I reach for the cutlery as Sonora shuffles into the kitchen in a faded pair of pajamas. Her curls are in wild disarray, and a crease from her pillow is imprinted on her left cheek.

"This shift change is a nightmare," she says, yawning.

Nyla leans against the kitchen counter, fine lines forming on her forehead. "I thought you were still on the night shift for a while."

I thought so too, yet I barely listen to Sonora as she talks about a sudden change in the shift schedule. Instead, I picture David again, this time in the surgery waiting room. Nyla and Sonora are discussing Sonora's strange boss while I see David in front of me, returning with the drinks. For a moment, there was something in his eyes. Something... oh, I don't know.

"But that's not even the most interesting part." Someone nudges me. "Right, Autumn?"

I look up, and Sonora is grinning at me. "Hm?"

She takes a sip of her water. "Come on, tell us, what was going on in the waiting room today?"

Images of David and me flicker through my mind—again. My hand on his arm, us looking at each other, intense, ambiguous. My heart pounds with excitement. "What do you mean?"

Sonora's grin widens. "You and the dad of the little girl with the tibia fracture—there's definitely something going on."

"Ooh, now it's getting interesting." Nyla plays with her earrings. "Is he hot?"

Sonora taps her chin thoughtfully. "He really needs to see a barber before we can judge properly."

She's not wrong. The shaggy full beard, together with the horn-rimmed glasses, covers most of his face, and his hair probably hasn't been cut in months. Maybe he's hiding something not just under his cap, but also beneath his beard?

"Mhm, mhm," Nyla says. "So tell me, what exactly happened?"

I feel myself blushing, even though there's absolutely no reason for it.

"Well, here's what happened." Sonora turns to Nyla, who leans forward on her chair with anticipation. "When I came into the waiting room to report on the procedure, the two of them were standing really close together—her hand was even on his arm—and they were exchanging looks… oh boy, oh boy… things were heating up."

"And then? Did they kiss?" Nyla asks.

"Oh, they definitely would have if I hadn't interrupted them. They were just about to," Sonora replies, nodding confidently.

I shake my head. "That would never have happened, and besides, it was all completely different. The man is married." But maybe not happily, after all, his wife still hasn't shown up at the clinic, my heart adds unnecessarily, and I realize I've got a problem.

Sonora drops into the chair next to me and props herself up on the table. "Alright then, tell us—what really happened?"

Two pairs of eyes practically drill into my face. I search for the right words, but can't find any.

Yes, it was a strange moment, somehow, I don't even know. Still, I shouldn't read too much into it.

"He's my patient's father, we were talking about the surgery and the follow-up treatment." Which is actually true.

"Yeah, it sure looked like that," comments Sonora, prompting Nyla to laugh. "And the way you two jumped apart like startled rabbits when you noticed me, that was because…"

"…you flung the door open so abruptly, of course. Anyone would've been startled." I quickly take a bite of the pasta so I don't get tangled up even deeper in my excuses.

"I see." Sonora has no intention of letting me out of her sight.

Yeah, exactly like that—or not at all, who knows. In my desperation, I chew the pasta longer than necessary, then smile at Nyla. "How's it going with you, actually? Is the work between the ER and the ambulance service what you expected?"

"Yeah, it's all pretty much as I thought," she replies, but her expression suggests she's thinking about something very specific that's nothing like she imagined.

"Speaking of work." Sonora glances at the kitchen clock. "I'll be up for a few more hours—who's up for a few episodes of Emergency Room with me?"

Nyla laughs. "I've had enough Emergency Room in real life today."

Sonora fixes her gaze on me. "You're not going to bail on me, are you?"

I had actually wanted to read. "Of course not," I reply with a smile nonetheless, fully aware that she won't question me about David anymore once the TV is on.

Besides, I should stop thinking about that man anyway. Whether he's happily married or not, whether he's hiding something under his cap or not—under no circumstances should I hope for a miracle that won't happen.

I desperately need a distraction, and thanks to the TV series, I manage at least for a few hours not to think about him. Still, he creeps back into my mind as I collapse into bed late at night and reach for one of my textbooks on hospital management.

Chapter Sixteen

TAY

Crossing the living room of our vacation house, I run my hands through my hair, take a deep breath, and sink once more into the scene that I haven't managed to get right for hours. In my mind, I become Dr. Cross. I see my patient before me, despair etched across her face. I feel the burden of the bad news I have to deliver, feel what it does to me, feel my heart opening.

"The biopsy shows a deficient..." No, that can't be right.

I glance at my tablet and read the sentence again. "The biopsy shows a malignant neoplasm, we need to perform a histopla... no, histopatha... no, histopathological examination to determine the tumor type more precisely."

A heavy sigh escapes my mouth. Who can pronounce all these technical terms correctly? And besides, what even is that? Histopathological?

I tap the word, but the Wikipedia entry that pops up might as well be written in Chinese, and I wouldn't understand it any less.

Damn it, how am I supposed to slip into character for the audition the day after tomorrow if I have to focus so hard on pronouncing the medical terms correctly? Not to mention the routine procedures a doctor uses to treat patients.

Autumn, for example. How skillfully she handled Kayla's examination yesterday afternoon. Her movements were smooth and effortless, a gentle smile on her pretty face. I watched her intently—maybe even too intently—until she started throwing me skeptical glances.

Now I'm here at the holiday house, staring out at the sea with clenched fists, the water lying before me in idyllic calm at dawn, while a storm brews inside me.

I have to pull this off, I want this role—no, I need it.

I try again. "The biopsy shows a ma-lig-nant neoplasm, we need to perform a hipla…" Fuck.

There's nothing up there, get that through your head you failure, I hear Mike sneer in the middle of my strained attempt and can practically feel my brother tapping his finger against my forehead.

Harder and harder—until it hurts.

I bat his hand away. He hasn't had any power over me for years, and that's not going to change now. I need to focus, learn the lines, become a doctor.

Still, I sink into the past like quicksand. The memory envelops me, more intensely than should be possible, presses on my chest, wraps around my throat.

Pressing my fingers to my temples, I think hard. I know the word, I know it. It'll come to me any second now.

"Well, loser, what are you failing at today?" That was my brother, shuffling into our room. "Still haven't figured out it's a waste?" No sooner is he beside me than he leans on the desk.

Automatically, I cover the vocabulary notebook with my forearm. "What do you want?"

He snorts back the snot in his nose. "The yearlings are getting their branding today, you have to help hold them down."

Immediately, I smell burnt fur and hear the calves screaming. There's no way I'm going to show my little brother that just thinking about it makes me sick. "Can't, I have a test tomorrow," I say, trying to sound cool.

"So what? Me too, but I don't need to study for it," he replies with a shrug, then taps my forehead with his index finger. "You're gonna fail anyway. There's nothing up there, get that through your head, loser."

His words hit me like poison darts, and each time he says them, I believe them a little more, even though I know they're not true. "Get lost, Mike, I've got stuff to do." I grab my vocabulary notebook and flop down on the bed with it.

"You'll never amount to anything." His expression is full of disgust now, just like the man Mike got those words from: Dad. "And you're not cut out to be a cowboy either."

Definitely not. A cowboy is the last thing I want to be. But I will find something that lets me leave this goddamn place behind. I'll find something that feels right. And once I've found it, I'll never let it go. Never again.

With a cry, I hurl the tablet onto the living room sofa, run to the punching bag in the corner, and pummel it with bare hands until sweat beads form on my temples.

The headlines from the past weeks dance before my eyes. A loud buzzing fills my ears.

Movie flopped – is former superstar Lawson facing the end of his career?

I draw back and slam my fists into the punching bag, one after the other. My knuckles ache, but I keep going. Still, a future begins to take shape before my mind's eye—one that tightens around my chest like a vice.

I see myself in front of the camera, playing the shallow Hollywood pretty boy, stuck in a meaningless role with no depth.

Gasping for air, I hit harder. Faster.

I see myself choking on my emotions because there's no way to let them out anymore.

Dizziness overwhelms me.

I see the thing that keeps me alive slipping away from me. And I see myself falling apart, becoming that little boy from Montana again—the one with no future.

Fuck.

Panting, I collapse to the floor, bury my face in my fists, feel the sting of split skin on my knuckles, and hear that damned buzzing in my ears—but that's not what scares me.

The fact that my heart feels like it's bleeding—now, after all these years when my career made it invincible—that's what's truly terrifying.

The buzzing moves from my ears into my head, then into my forehead, down my neck. It travels through my back, tightens my chest, knots up my stomach.

I fight against it, breathe, focus, cling to the last shred of control I have left in me.

This has to stop. Whatever has been happening to me over the past few weeks, it needs to end. I need this role—it's my only chance to get my life back on track. Whatever I have to do for it, I'll do it.

An hour later, I pull my baseball cap low over my forehead and enter the pediatric ward of Halifax Harbor Hospital, knowing there's one person who can help me save my career—and with it, my life. And that person is, of all people, the one who's stirred up so much in me these past few days. Autumn.

She can show me what I need to do to be a doctor. How I need to talk and move. She can explain the medical terms to me. If I ask her for help, she'll give it. Because she's a kind, generous person. Because she gives so much more than others deserve—including me.

The fact that I not only give her nothing in return but also hide from her who I really am feels wrong. Still, it's better this way. Safer—for Kayla and for me.

As I suspected, I find Autumn in my daughter's room. Their shared laughter reaches my ears as I press down the door handle and step inside.

"Daddy!" Kayla's doll-like eyes sparkled behind her glasses, and she opened her arms as if she wanted me to hug her.

Immediately, Autumn's words from yesterday echo in my mind. One day you'll be nothing more than a painful memory to her. The father who never loved her.

I swallow hard, step up to Kayla's bed, and hug her in the same stiff, distant way I always do—and for the first time in my life, I'm ashamed of what I am: someone who doesn't show emotion. Someone who strikes first before the other person can. Always in fight mode, relentless, addicted to control. A damn iceberg who now offers his daughter the same pathetic greeting ritual—fist bump, high five, fist bump.

No one wrote the role of Kayla's dad for me, and without a role, I'm just me. "Did you sleep well?" I ask woodenly.

"Yup." Kayla gives one last high five, her tiny fingers

brushing mine for just a moment. "Look what Autumn gave me." She points to the other side of the bed.

Pink crutches, covered with countless glittery horses in different sizes and colors galloping across the bright background.

"In a few days, I'll learn how to walk with them," Kayla tells me excitedly. "It's called physical therapy, I know that from Autumn."

Fascinating. Autumn managed to turn something that probably no one enjoys into something Kayla looks forward to like unwrapping presents on Christmas.

"That's great," I say hoarsely, glancing at Autumn, whose gaze is fixed on my daughter. So much warmth radiates from her, so much comfort, so much gentleness. Seeing Kayla so happy and excited seems to make her happy too, and she has no problem showing it.

I clear my throat. "Would you explain to me exactly what happens during therapy?" I ask Autumn.

Instead of Autumn, Kayla answers. Like a waterfall, she explains that she'll be learning exercises to help her leg heal quickly. Fortunately, all I have to do is nod and say wow from time to time.

"Will you come watch me, Daddy?" Kayla looks at me pleadingly.

Out of nowhere, an image flickers through my mind. It shows my daughter barely able to stand on her legs. Tears of disappointment stream down her cheeks as she realizes her body won't do what she wants. She tries to flee into my arms so I can comfort her. And there I am, frozen stiff with fear and broken by guilt, smiling brightly to push it all behind my wall.

"We'll see," I reply dismissively, feeling like the biggest asshole on earth.

Kayla crosses her arms over her chest in an exaggerated gesture. "You're dumb."

Relief floods through me, and I stick out my tongue. "No, you're dumb."

"You both are," I suddenly hear Autumn say, deadpan, which makes Kayla burst out laughing.

Her laughter is so contagious that Autumn and I join in. I dare to glance at Autumn and catch a glimpse of her wiping tears from the corners of her eyes. Where her hand touches her hair, a scar flashes beneath her bangs. A split second later, it's hidden again by her fringe.

Now she places her hand on my daughter's shoulder. "If your dad can't make it, I'll come with you to physical therapy," she promises Kayla, whose eyes light up with hope.

To the guilt I already feel toward my daughter, a completely irrational guilt toward Autumn now joins in. If her boss finds out that she's accompanying Kayla, Autumn will get another warning, that's for sure. I'll talk to Dr. Parker, insist that Kayla's doctor attend the therapy sessions, and pay for it if necessary. It's the least I can do.

But now I should finally ask Autumn for her help. "Can we talk outside?" I ask her.

She glances briefly at her wristwatch, then follows me into the hallway, where there's far too much commotion to have a proper conversation. Nurses dart along the corridor, doors open and close, visitors stream in and out, children laugh.

I look around searchingly, but both the play area and the waiting room are full of people.

"How can I help?" Autumn asks.

"Is there a place where we can be alone?" The thought of being alone with her makes my heart beat strangely fast. Is it the fact that I'm about to lie to her even more than I already have that's making me this nervous?

She slips her hands into the pockets of her lab coat. "Out in the hospital park?"

Five minutes later, the sliding doors open in front of us and we step outside. Relieved to leave behind the disinfectant-saturated air of the clinic, I inhale the salty sea breeze drifting over from Halifax Harbor. Then I square my shoulders and start walking with deliberate ease.

"I have a favor to ask," I say, just as I planned.

The sunlight makes Autumn's hair glow as she turns her head toward me. "Anytime."

That's the answer I'd hoped for—no, expected—because that's just how Autumn is: helpful and warm-hearted. Far too much so, really.

We step onto the gravel path that winds through the park, lined with shrubs and trees. "In my free time, I act in plays with an amateur theater group." I avoid looking at her, feeling the weight of my lie pressing heavily on my chest. "But now I've got the chance to be part of a more professional production, and I'm supposed to play a doctor."

"Wow, that sounds great," she says.

The gravel crunches beneath my shoes as I look up at the sky, where wisps of thin clouds drift like shreds of fog.

Maybe I should have had her sign a non-disclosure agreement too, then I could speak freely, but the fewer people at Halifax Harbor Hospital who know my true identity, the better. Trust is a luxury I can't afford, and Autumn, no matter how considerate she may seem, can't be an exception.

"The audition is the day after tomorrow." I clear my throat. "I want to make a good impression as a doctor, so I thought I could accompany you through your daily routine."

"What do you actually do for a living?" Autumn looks at me inquisitively; I catch it out of the corner of my eye.

"I'm a banker," I reply, as I always do when I'm David. A lie that has always come easily to me over the past few years. Today, I almost choke on it. I feel the urge to tell Autumn who I really am. In a strange way, I want her to know. "Pretty boring, right?"

"Every job is important," she replies.

A fresh breeze blows over from the sea, I take a deep breath, then I feel confident enough to look at her directly. "Would you help me with the role?"

Her hair whirls up in the wind and briefly brushes against my neck. She quickly smooths it over her head. "You're a good actor."

Yes. There's a reason my work is my whole life and everything I want. "Still, I have to fully immerse myself in every role."

She smirks, but she doesn't seem amused—more thoughtful. "And once you've done that, you can fool anyone, right?"

Excuse me? What's that supposed to mean?

A questioning expression dominates her face. "Why are you doing this? Why are you playing roles?"

Because without acting, I'd suffocate in my own emotions—but I can't tell her that. "So, can I look over your shoulder or not?"

She stops abruptly, and I mirror her. Once again, she fiddles with her hair. If she weren't looking at me so intently, I'd think she was nervous.

"You can, if you promise me you'll stop pretending from

now on." Her words sound gentle, yet they hit me like a shockwave.

Instinctively, I adjust my cap—it fits perfectly. My fake beard is in place too. "What makes you think I'm pretending?" I hear myself ask.

No one has ever unmasked me, because the truth is that people never really look at others. We're always wrapped up in ourselves, never looking past the façades others present, not even wanting to see what's hidden behind them. We prefer to stay in the world where we feel safe.

That's how it works, and that's how it should be.

Except, apparently, not for Autumn, whose gaze now grows more intense. "Does it even matter?"

Maybe. Maybe not. Instead of answering, I shrug—and once again feel far too clearly that I want to tell her about myself.

I don't even understand why. Maybe because of that stupid little voice inside me whispering that I can trust her. That she won't strike if I let my guard down.

"Yeah, I think so too," says Autumn, lowering her gaze to the gravel path, where she nudges a few pebbles aside with her shoe.

"What do you think too?" Once again, a question has left my mouth before I even thought about it. But instead of the usual tension, the bracing for battle that my body normally responds with automatically, something else happens: I remain calm, feel safe, even though my mind knows I'm not.

"That it doesn't matter. None of this will ever matter," she replies. Her eyelids flutter. "What matters to me isn't *what* you are on the outside, but *who* you are on the inside."

Yesterday in the elevator, she already managed to bring

the world to a standstill with her words. Now she's doing it again—and all without even looking at me.

Stunned, I study her face, find nothing but sincerity in it, know that I should explain to her now that my inner self shouldn't concern her, but the words won't come out.

"Why?" I hear myself ask from the depths of my heart, and I no longer understand myself.

Chapter Seventeen

AUTUMN

A spark of hope lights up David's face, warm and bright, and I feel myself sinking into it. The remoteness in his eyes is gone; at last, he lets me see what he usually hides behind it: fear. Of what, I don't know—only that it's there. A fear that seems bigger than any other feeling.

"Why doesn't it matter to you *what* I am on the outside, but *who* I am on the inside?" he asks again.

Because if only what we are matters, then I'm nothing more than a monster. Because it would mean that I'll be lonely and broken for the rest of my life, that I'll never be whole, no matter what I do.

I shrug. "Because I want to see the world the way I want it to see me."

A flicker of sadness crosses his face. "But what if the world isn't like that?"

The truth in his words hurts. I've experienced exactly that far too often—but that's not all. My gut tells me that he's been through the same. And suddenly, all the pieces that never made sense before fall into place.

Whatever he's gone through because of what's hidden beneath his cap, it's stolen his belief in the good in others.

"If it's harsh and cold and unfair, and the only way to survive is by becoming harsh and cold and unfair yourself?" I ask quietly, even though I already know the answer.

I can feel that this is what drives him.

He presses his lips together, his nostrils flare. It's a silent yes that touches me deeply, and the hope that we might have more in common than I first thought suddenly becomes certainty.

We are both disfigured and, in the eyes of others, nothing but ugly monsters. But if we looked at each other without our disguises, our hearts would recognize one another, and we would feel that we're no longer alone.

"What happened to you?" I have to know. I need to find out if he could be the miracle I've forbidden myself to believe in. That one person who can look past everything ugly about me because he knows what it's like to be ugly himself.

For a while, we just look at each other. A wild cocktail of fear, longing, and pain fills his eyes, and for a split second, I believe he's about to answer me. My pulse quickens, warmth rises inside me. But then, the distance in his gaze builds like a dam, holding back all those emotions. It rises higher and higher, and I know—he's not going to answer me.

"Where do we start? Technical terms? Or important techniques?" David tries in vain to lift the corners of his mouth into a smile.

"What kind of doctor are you pretending to be?" I ask, fighting off the disappointment I shouldn't be feeling. After all, I know David is married—of course he has no interest in me whatsoever.

"A surgeon." He grins mischievously, and a spark of passion lights up in his eyes—something I haven't seen in him before.

"All right, I've got time for one lesson before my shift starts." I nod toward the hospital.

Ten minutes later, we are back in the pediatric ward. People bustle past us, the beeping of monitors and the general chaos of the floor ever-present. We stand by the hallway cabinet where we keep the rubber gloves.

I grab one of the boxes. "If you want anyone to believe you're a doctor, you've got to be able to slip these on in your sleep."

He gives it a try but gets his fingers tangled in the glove. "These are too small. I'll never fit into them."

"Relax your fingers," I say, stepping closer to help him.

As I take his hand to adjust the glove, I feel the warmth of his skin. Our fingers brush, and even though it lasts only a moment, my heart skips a beat.

His eyes drift to mine. "Okay, I've got this," he says quickly. He tries again, but is so clumsy that the latex tears. "Told you, it's too small."

Sandra, who's walking past us at this very moment, throws us a suspicious glance.

"Just let me help, then you'll see." I take his hand, and once again, a flutter of nervousness stirs in my stomach.

It shouldn't be happening, but suddenly the air between us feels heavier, and I realize we're standing far too close. Every time my fingers brush against his hand, a tingling sensation spreads across my skin. My shoulders graze his, and I find it increasingly difficult to focus on the gloves.

Does he feel it too?

As soon as the glove fits perfectly over his hand, our touch comes to an end. "See? It fits perfectly," I murmur, confused, fully aware that I should be putting some distance between us.

"Thanks. I guess you were right after all." His voice sounds oddly strained.

So he felt it too. What does that mean?

It takes effort, but I manage to take a step back—yet I can still feel the warmth of his hand in mine. "Don't mention it," I say quietly, while he slips into the second glove much more deftly than before.

"There we go," he remarks with a composed expression. "Who do I get to treat now?"

Just as I'm about to reply that he certainly won't be treating anyone, my pager buzzes. "Rule number one." I pull the device from my lab coat pocket. "The pager always takes priority."

"Consultation 1 in the emergency room, infant with fever and shortness of breath," reads the message.

Shit.

He steps up beside me to read it too. "What does Consultation 1 mean?"

"That I need to hurry." I quickly slip the pager back into my pocket and take off. "We'll continue later," I call over my shoulder, then turn the corner and rush toward the elevator.

Chapter Eighteen

TAY

After her shift yesterday, Autumn handed me a stack of books—medical literature I should look through to learn more about the world doctors live in. Then, over coffee, she explained the routines on the ward, the responsibilities, and the codes used to ensure quick and efficient communication.

She stifled a yawn more than once, but the thought of going home didn't even cross her mind. And after we said goodbye, I was left with a strange feeling of emptiness.

I think about all of that now as I step into the cafeteria on the tenth floor of the hospital.

About all that, and so much more. About Autumn's gentle smile, for instance. The way she smooths her hair back, the sparkle in her eyes when she talks about her work. The way her lips curl every time she says *wonderful.* The way that *wonderful* makes my chest vibrate. The way it feels far less dangerous than it probably should—more like… beautiful, somehow.

With the same confusion we felt when we said goodbye yesterday, I now look around the cafeteria and find a secluded spot all the way in the back, next to the glass wall that overlooks Halifax Harbor. On the way there, I grab a plate and some cutlery—the food I brought with me.

An unprecedented nervousness grips me as I sit down and lay the reference books on the table. I spent half the night flipping through them, reading passages aloud, and watching documentaries about doctors. Everything depends on Autumn's judgment today. If she believes my performance, I'll be able to convince at the audition too.

And here she comes already.

"Hey, sorry I'm late." Autumn's gentle words wash over my rising panic. "It's just been so hectic."

"No problem, Kayla says hi—she can't wait for the next therapy session." At the thought of my daughter, I even manage to smile at Autumn despite the pressure weighing on me. "I hope you like curry?"

Her eyes fall on the food I brought. "Love it." She sits down. "How's the script coming along?"

"Good." But not good enough. I hand her a copy of the scene I have to perform tomorrow. "Would you read Emma's part?"

She places the script next to her on the table. "But I have to warn you, I didn't even make it into the drama club at school."

I catch myself wondering what else she did in school. What she was like as a student, whether she was already so strikingly beautiful as a teenager, and how many hearts she's broken in her life. Strange that I'm thinking about things like that, even though they don't matter, even though I shouldn't want to know anything about her at all.

I quickly clear my throat. "No problem, it already helps if you just read the lines and check whether I'm pronouncing everything correctly."

"Okay." Autumn takes a bite of her curry and closes her eyes for a moment. "Wow, where did you get this? It's divine!"

A smile sneaks onto my face unnoticed as I watch her enjoying the food. It's nice to see her so content and to know that something I did is the reason for it.

"Oh, sorry, I'm ready," she says suddenly, focusing on the script. "Scene: A small examination room. On the metal table lies an X-ray image of a patient, next to it a clipboard with notes. Dr. Elliot Cross, an experienced surgeon, holds the X-ray up to the light and examines it intently."

"We can skip that and go straight to the dialogue." I search for the first line. "We don't need to pay attention to the stage directions either."

Autumn raises her index finger to stop me. "Dr. Emma Bennett, an anesthesiologist and his longtime colleague, sits on a stool watching him, her posture a mix of concern and challenge. The room is filled with the tension between them, which goes far beyond the medical discussion." She looks up. "Wonderful, Dr. Cross, let's see what you've got then."

For a moment, I'm on the verge of getting lost in the warm green of her eyes, but I manage to pull myself back just in time. I quickly straighten up in my chair and focus.

"The tumor has infiltrated the inferior vena cava and affected the area around the retroperitoneal lymph nodes. The wall is perforated, and the continuity of the vascular structure is severely compromised. This requires an en bloc resection of the affected sections, followed by an autologous vein graft." The practice paid off—I didn't make a single mistake. Even though I don't really understand what I just said, at least I sounded like a doctor. Or so I think.

Autumn nods at me, then her gaze shifts to the paper. She's not supposed to pay attention to the stage directions, yet her expression turns skeptical, just as the script demands. "You know that could compromise the mediastinal circulation. And what about the postoperative hemorrhaging?"

"The hemorrhaging is minimized through transarterial embolization prior to the procedure," I say firmly, managing to get more and more into character.

"It's pronounced emb-o-lization," Autumn corrects.

I repeat my line—this time correctly—then she continues.

"But that's all theory, Elliot. The risks are too high. Is that justifiable?"

"If you question every risk, you lose control, Emma. And when you lose control, what's left?" As the stage direction requires, my voice softens. I feel the text, feel the inner conflict, the weight of the decision, feel what all of this is doing to me.

As if Autumn truly were Emma, she leans toward me. "Trust. And if you abuse that trust, Elliot, then what? Where does that lead?"

I lean toward her, look at her intently, open my heart. "This operation… I have to carry it out."

"I know you want to stay in control." Autumn props her head on her hand. "But what about the things you can't control?" she whispers.

Dr. Cross (his gaze intensifies, almost tender), I read in the script. I lift my eyelids, look at Autumn. She does nothing, just sits across from me, yet suddenly I forget my lines.

Shit.

"Um…"

"Okay, I think that's enough for now." Autumn sets her script aside and rubs her forearm as if she's cold. "That was incredible. So… emotional."

She studies me and I can't shake the feeling that she suspects something. Has she recognized me? But if she has, why doesn't she say anything?

Maybe it would have been better to let her in on it. I don't know, I just know that the thought somehow feels right.

"But as soon as technical terms come into play, you can tell you're focusing too much on the correct pronunciation," she continues now.

Her criticism is gentle and cautious, yet my throat tightens.

"Here, for example." As empathetic as she sounds, it doesn't help me in this moment, when I imagine myself failing at tomorrow's audition. When I picture my dream slipping away—and all of it feels far too real.

Shit, I didn't want to think about that anymore, but it still crashes over me, and I feel just as helpless as I did a few days ago, when guilt over Kayla overwhelmed me.

What. The. Hell. Is. Wrong. With. Me?

"The retroperitoneal lymph nodes—you stressed the wrong syllables on that one."

When she says the words, it sounds so easy. So natural, as if none of it were a problem.

And there it is again. That faint but menacing hum in the background, growing louder and louder.

I want this role—I need it.

But how am I supposed to get it? The damn audition is already tomorrow!

Something inside me tears open again, scars turning back into wounds. Just like a few days ago in the recovery room after surgery—only this time, it's bigger. More forceful.

More destructive.

My heart races as if it's trying to leap out of my chest, my breathing becomes shallow and rapid.

And suddenly, a wave of emotions crashes over me. Feelings that have been lurking inside me for weeks, now bursting out, unstoppable.

I can't breathe anymore.

Oh God, what's happening?

I shoot up from my chair. "Excuse me," I gasp, and rush outside.

But it's no better out there. The hallway feels narrow, and it's closing in more and more. It's like my lungs are too small, like there's not enough oxygen in the air—even though I know that's not true. But my body doesn't believe my mind. Every breath is a struggle.

I'm about to suffocate.

Arms wrap around me, pulling me along with them.

A soft voice.

The scent of strawberries.

My hands are trembling, my legs are weak, about to give out any second.

Elevator doors.

David's distorted reflection.

Red hair.

"Breathe slowly. In... out... nice and easy, you're safe."

I can't.

The room around me blurs, everything feels both incredibly close and impossibly far away. I try to focus, to form a clear thought, but my head feels like it's wrapped in cotton.

"I'm here, you can do this."

The doors slide open. Another corridor. Dark.

"Almost there."

My chest tightens, sweat breaks out—cold and hot at the same time.

I'm suffocating.

And then there's this overwhelming feeling. It's not just fear—it's like something inevitable is coming for me.

"Try to focus only on my voice. We'll get through this together, you don't have to face it alone."

There's no way out. No escape.

Light breaks through the darkness.

Cold through the heat.

"Breathe, David, breathe."

I breathe.

"That's it, you're doing great. One more time."

I draw in another breath. The pressure on my chest eases, and I keep breathing.

Breathe. Breathe. Breathe.

"Yes, just like that."

My muscles, which had been so tense just moments ago, suddenly feel limp and heavy. It's as if all the energy is draining from my body. My hands are still trembling.

"Sit down." Someone strokes my upper arm. "Everything's okay."

I lift my gaze with effort. I feel like I've been underwater for a long time and am finally breaking the surface.

There is the sky.

The sound of the waves in the distance.

Sunbeams.

Autumn's worried face.

I let myself sink back against the wall behind me.

"Everything's okay. You're okay," Autumn assures me, but as much as I'd like to believe her, I can feel that it's not the truth.

I haven't been okay for a long time—and maybe I never really was.

Chapter Nineteen

AUTUMN

I keep stroking his arm. David's muscles relax, and finally, my heartbeat begins to calm as well.

"Where are we?" he asks, frantically adjusting his cap.

"On the clinic roof." Thank God Sonora told me about this place. It's the perfect spot for David to come back to himself. "You had a panic attack," I explain gently as he looks at me with a mix of fear and confusion. "But it's over now, everything's fine."

"Oh God." He lets his head fall back against the wall that bordered the rooftop.

I sit down on the ground next to him. What has just happened was a clear sign. Whatever is going on with him, he is in a bad way. "Do you want to talk about it?"

He looks at me. The sunlight makes his irises glow behind the thick lenses of his glasses. There is no wall, only despair. Still, he shakes his head.

He doesn't trust me, thinks I can't understand what it feels like to do everything to stay in control, and still lose it.

I pull my legs up and wrap my arms around my thighs.

"It's like you're no longer in control of your senses. You know you're doing things that are wrong, but there's absolutely nothing you can do to stop it." I glance at him carefully—his eyes are fixed on the sky, his lips trembling slightly. "You lose control, whether you want to or not. You're not yourself anymore. You feel helpless and vulnerable and think it'll never stop."

My voice grows quieter and quieter until it finally beaks in the light of my own memory—because of pain, because of sorrow, because of shame.

"You do things you don't want to do. Things you don't understand, that don't make any sense." Even though I'd never had a panic attack, what I'd struggled with for years wasn't all that different. "You know it's breaking you, and you know you need help because you can't get out of it on your own. But…"

"That's never happened to me before." The words leave his mouth without sound. "It was the first time."

I wish I could tell him that the first time is the worst—but that wouldn't be true. At least, not for me.

The first time was the beginning of a vicious cycle that kept pulling me in deeper. For years, I was trapped in its grip, and to this day I wonder what would've happened if I hadn't bottled it all up. But I also know that doing so was what ultimately destroyed Mom.

But this thing with David is different.

He has the chance to avoid getting caught in that vicious cycle in the first place.

"Do you want to talk about it?" I try again, gently, so he doesn't feel pressured.

His shallow breathing fills the silence between us. I don't know what he's thinking or how he'll react, but I reach for his hand—and he doesn't pull away.

Chapter Twenty

TAY

For minutes we sit in silence, leaning against the wall. I look up at the sky, as if I might find answers there to questions I don't even know yet.

Autumn's fingers glide over mine. "I'm here. No matter how bad it is, I'm here," she says softly, and I believe her.

The shock of what just happened runs deep. So deep that I'm actually considering telling her everything. Showing her who I really am, beneath the disguise and deep inside. How broken I am. How would she react?

What would she do if she knew Tay Lawson was sitting next to her? Would she still be able to see past my facade into my heart? Or would she, like all the others in my life, be blinded by my good looks, my fame, my wealth?

"You don't have to talk about it. We can just sit here until you've recovered." There's understanding in her tone.

Once again she's being so selfless, giving far too much without asking for anything in return. And yet—or maybe precisely because of that—I want to give something back to her.

"Two months ago, my life was still fine. But then…" I can't go on, can't admit who I am and how much the thought that my career might be over has been weighing on me for weeks.

Silently, she strokes my hand. I look down, watch her slender fingers on mine and wonder if she realizes what she's doing right now.

What it feels like not to be pushed by her, what it means to me not having to fight. What the fact that it's not about who strikes first, who has the better defence, who wins or loses, does to me.

There's so much going on inside me that I can't share with her, but at least she should know something. "My marriage is over."

Autumn's movement falters briefly, then she touches my wedding ring. "Why are you still wearing it?"

"For Kayla."

"She doesn't know," Autumn says with understanding.

I shake my head, which feels unbearably heavy. "We're on holiday here so I have time to talk to her about it, but I…"

"You can't bring yourself to do it."

"My wife wanted me to take over," I continue, so I don't have to respond to Autumn's words.

She moves closer to me, her delicate scent enveloping me. "Why?"

I feel the warmth of her body beside me, feel a kind of safety I've never known before. Thoughtfully, I look at the dull silver metal of my ring, see the grooves time has left behind. They're superficial, just like my marriage—and the life I need to feel safe.

"Because I destroyed this marriage. It's my fault." Part of me can't believe I just said that and gave

Autumn a glimpse into my soul. But the other part feels liberated.

Her arm wraps around my shoulders. I exhale, wanting to tell her how nice it is to sit here with her, and that it feels like she's taking a bit of my burden away. But that would be too much, so I entwine my fingers with hers and gently squeeze her hand.

"I never loved her," I hear myself say tonelessly. "Marrying her was a mistake and now…" My voice breaks.

"…now you're afraid Kayla will suffer because of your separation," Autumn finishes my sentence, putting into words exactly what I can't bring myself to say.

I nod with my jaw clenched.

"Whatever happened in your marriage, the fact that your wife is leaving you to deal with it alone isn't fair."

She sounds convinced, but only because she doesn't know that Chloe thinks it wouldn't bother me to hurt my daughter. Because my wife is certain I don't have any feelings anyway—after all, I've made sure of that for years.

I turn my head to look at Autumn. "Nothing in this world is fair." That's the truth—one that hurts, but also one I must never forget. Not even when I'm near her.

A watery sheen forms in her eyes. "Yeah," she whispers.

So she's been through it too. She knows the pull life can have, how it takes everything from you and then spits you back out. How hard you hit the ground, how much it hurts. I reach out and touch her cheek, longing to feel, just for a moment, a little less alone with her.

Suddenly, a flicker of unease flashes in her eyes, and as my fingers move toward her temple, she pushes my hand aside. "Don't," she says, lowering her eyelids.

Our eye contact breaks, and I realize what just happened. My heart beat—not because fear or panic triggered it, but because of affection. That one beat cracked it open a little, and through that gap, a warm feeling slipped out.

I turn away, no longer understanding myself, unsure of what's happening to me. "I'm sorry, I didn't mean to…"

"It's fine, everything's okay." Her voice sounds strained.

Life taught me to block out other people's emotions, but now, in this moment, I want to know what's going on inside Autumn. I want to glimpse her soul, to find out what that would do to me.

But she pushes herself up from the ground. "Work's waiting."

It is, and no matter how heavy my heart suddenly feels, my mind knows it. Not just her work, but an entire life is waiting—my life, of which she only knows a fraction. With everything that is, unlike what just happened, real.

Chapter Twenty-One

AUTUMN

On my way to the door, I turn around and look back at David. My heart is still pounding like crazy; I can feel his hand on my cheek and his fingers slipping between mine. I feel his warmth, the trembling of his body, and his scent, which still clings to me.

"My marriage is over," I hear him whisper again and again. "I never loved her."

More than anything, I want to turn around, run to him, and sink to my knees in front of him. To take his face in my hands, gently pull it toward me, and press my lips to his.

We wouldn't have to speak, because we would feel something far greater than words—something that carried so much more meaning.

Still, I slip into the dark hallway and frantically smooth down my hair as I hurry toward the elevator.

Even though there were moments when I believed it might be possible, in the end, it could all just be a dream again—and that, I couldn't bear.

I step into the elevator, and my gaze falls on my reflection. The sight David knows. The one he just looked at so longingly, the one he touched, the one he wanted to caress. Instinctively, I imagine the worst-case scenario—what might have happened if I hadn't stopped it.

I picture his fingers reaching my temples and brushing my hair aside. How he would have felt the bulge there, how a small crease would have formed between his brows. How the smile would have faded from his face as he slowly uncovered the monster that I am.

How he would have looked at me—full of disgust, full of revulsion. And how, just seconds later, he would have turned away in a panic.

If he's like all the men before him, then it would have gone the same way.

And what if he's different? whispers a far too hopeful voice inside me.

There's nothing I want more than for it to be right. But how could I have taken that risk? It might have been the end, and I don't want it to end.

Not again.

I dial Henry's number, the ringing tone sounds. Downstairs, I hear Aunt Lanie washing the lunch dishes.

Mom is at the clinic. She seemed quiet during my visit. She only ate after I forced down a bit of the cake—for her sake, so she could see that it's okay to eat. That you can be sad and full at the same time, even if it feels wrong.

"Hi, Autumn," says Henry breathlessly on the other end of the line.

"I'm back home." The words home taste dull on my tongue. As if they're old and spoiled, no longer edible. "Do you want to meet in the park?"

His hesitation is brief, but I notice it. Since that one visit he paid me in the hospital, we've only spoken on the phone. He said he'd caught a virus and was lying in bed with a fever and chills. But Lucy told me he was at school. I understand that it was hard for him to see me so disfigured, so I played along. Now I'm home, still in shock from Mom's suicide attempt, but also longing to forget what happened for a moment —together with Henry.

To be the girl I was before the accident again.

He clears his throat. "A few minutes should be fine."

At least a bit of warmth returns to my chest. "I'll head out now."

He promises me he'll head out too, and I decide to put on the dress he likes so much. A little later, I'm standing in front of the mirror in the mint-green fluttery dress with spaghetti straps, tracing the burn scars that cover my entire décolleté with my index finger.

Henry knows they're there. He saw them when they looked much worse. He's probably happy about my progress.

My finger glides over a particularly thick ridge, and I try to get used to the thought that it belongs to me, that it's a part of me.

Maybe it feels hard for him today, but tomorrow it will already feel easier.

I force my lips into a smile and leave the house.

Henry is sitting on the wicker swing when I arrive. I walk toward him, wave and smile as he lifts his hand too. A gentle tingling spreads in my stomach—for the first time since the accident, I feel a little bit happy.

Am I allowed to feel that?

Am I allowed to be happy even though my dad is dead? Am I allowed to be happy when my mom is so unhappy?

I can't find any answers to my questions, so I arrive at Henry's place early.

"Hey," he says, his gaze fixed firmly on my eyes. He's almost staring, looks tense.

"Hey." I sit beside him on the wicker swing, we push off and let ourselves fall back. Lying next to each other, we stare up at the sky

above while the swing sways gently back and forth. He's strangely quiet today.

"How are you?" I ask eventually.

"Better."

"I'm glad." I stretch my fingers toward his, gently touch them. He returns my touch. "I missed you."

"Mhm," he says, then I see out of the corner of my eye how he turns his head toward me. "Autumn?"

I turn to him, look into his beautiful blue eyes, then let my gaze drift to his lips. The ones I'd love to kiss right now. The ones that could help me forget a bit of what's weighing me down. "Yeah?"

Clearing his throat, he places his hand on my cheek. "Lucy talked about your scars at school." Pity reflects in the depths of his eyes. "Everyone knows, they're going to stare at you."

A queasy feeling stirs in my stomach.

His fingers brush my hair back. "They call you a monster. And I, I am…" Desperation flickers in his eyes.

Then suddenly, I understand.

I understand why he stopped visiting me, why he was so distant on the phone, why he looked me so directly in the eyes earlier, as if he didn't want to see anything else about me.

"I'm a monster and you're the captain of the hockey team," I finish his sentence. He's the star of our school, the guy who could have anyone. The one who's already prom king, even though the prom is still years away.

He's the kind of guy who needs a queen by his side. And when he looks at me, he doesn't see a queen. Not anymore. When he looks at me, he sees a monster.

"It's just, I don't know, I can't…" he stammers.

"What can't you do?" I ask, even though every part of me doesn't want to hear the answer.

"I'm sorry, we can't anymore…"

I press my lips together to keep them from trembling.

"It's over between us." There's relief in his voice. So much relief that he's finally said it.

I knew it. I knew it exactly, and yet it hits me deep inside.

It's so unfair. If Dad hadn't had that accident, none of this would be happening. Everything would be different. I would be happy.

No, stop, I can't think like that. Dad didn't want this, it's not his fault.

"It's probably for the best," I force out. "Aunt Lanie will be going back home soon, and I want to be there for Mom." My voice trembles, and I struggle to hold back my tears. "I wouldn't have had time to see you anyway."

For a while, he looks at me with sadness. The swing moves in smaller and smaller arcs. "I wish..."

"Me too." I lower my eyelids.

His fingers brush my cheek, and he leans in closer, so close I can feel his breath on my lips. "I'm really sorry, Autumn," he whispers.

Something breaks inside me. I take his hand from my cheek and roll onto my back again. Out of the corner of my eye, I see him do the same. Shoulder to shoulder, we gaze at the sky as the swing slowly comes to a stop.

Not a single cloud marred the sky when Henry broke my heart thirteen years ago and then disappeared from my life even as a friend. Before the accident, we were perfect together—he loved me. But the monster the accident turned me into—that he could no longer love.

No one can. The new neighbor Louis couldn't, and neither could my classmate John. Aidan, Lucas, and James couldn't either.

Could David do it?

If he himself were scarred under his cap, maybe he could. He has to take it off for me, because only when I've seen his scars might I be able to overcome my fear and show him mine.

The elevator stops on the seventh floor, I enter the pediatrics ward and head straight for the nurses' station, where Sandra is sorting patient files.

She raises her penciled black eyebrows. "That was a long lunch break with Kayla's dad."

"Of course I'll make up the time," I say quickly, ignoring her insinuation. I still make it to my planned meetup with my roommates at the Halifax Waterfront Broadwalk on time.

"Mhm, mhm, that's exactly what I meant." With a knowing look, she hands me a file. "New admission in the digger room. P070424-067, gastroesophageal reflux."

"I'll go see how I can help then." I quickly take the patient file and hope that work will distract me a bit from the chaos of thoughts surrounding David.

Still, throughout the entire shift, I can't stop hoping that David is different from everyone before him. Because the idea of that is far too beautiful not to lose myself in it.

Chapter Twenty-Two

TAY

The limousine stops in front of the design hotel. Through the tinted windows, I look up, wanting to see the sky, but all I see are skyscrapers and neon signs. New York feels cramped today, and even though crowds are pushing along the sidewalks, there's a loneliness inside me that I've never known before.

Since I said goodbye to Kayla and Autumn this morning, I've felt it inside me, with me. But that's not all—my thoughts keep returning to Autumn, to her gentle smile, her soft voice, the warmth of her presence. And then there's this inexplicable longing to be with her again, even though she rejected me yesterday.

Would she have done the same if she knew who was hiding behind the not-so-attractive David? She still doesn't know *who* I really am, and this lie weighs heavier on my conscience than ever before, even though she knows so much more about who *I* am than anyone else in my life.

The car door opens. "Mr. Lawson?"

I blink and recognize my driver, who gives me an encouraging nod.

It's starting. The next hour will decide my future. With a queasy feeling in my stomach, I peel myself out of the seat. As soon as I put on my winning smile, the first camera flashes go off.

"Tay, where have you been the past few days?"

"What role are you auditioning for today?"

"Where is your family?"

Tay hasn't existed these past few days—being him again now feels strangely foreign. Still, I function. My body runs the program it's trained for over the years. I pose with a confident smile for the cameras, answer questions without saying anything, and all the while I automatically think of Autumn, for whom every word carries meaning. Nothing about her is superficial, while everything about my life is.

Until now, that was exactly what I loved about Hollywood. But right now, as I fend off the press with a fake smile and feigned ease, I'm no longer sure if it's really right.

"Everyone's talking about you, calling you a hollow pretty boy with no acting talent!" my wife's voice rings in my ears, and I know that all these people standing here pretending to admire me were saying exactly that just last week.

That I'm a failure. Someone who only succeeds because of his looks. Someone who's nothing more than a pretty shell.

They said that about something that means the world to me. Not because they believed it, but because they knew negative press makes a lot of money.

This is the world we live in. This is what people are like —only Autumn seems to be different.

"Thanks for coming, I hope we'll see each other soon," I

call out to the crowd, flash my best angle one last time, wait for the camera flashes to fade, and stroll toward the hotel entrance with deliberate nonchalance.

"Oh God, he's so hot," I hear a journalist sigh just before I slip through the revolving door.

Five minutes later, I'm in the penthouse suite, unsuccessfully trying to find a comfortable position in the futuristic-looking wicker chair. In my mind, I go over my lines again and again, while gray clouds gather in the sky beyond the window. The denser they get, the harder it is to breathe, and Chloe's incoming message reminding me how important this audition is doesn't help at all.

The double doors swing open, two men and a woman enter. I rise to my feet, my smile in place—despite everything, I'm a professional after all.

"Tay, how lovely you could make it." Through the lenses of her colorful glasses, which give her a catlike appearance, the woman sizes me up. She must be Sophie, Vice President of Production at the production company.

"The pleasure's all mine." I let my gaze wander to the two men. I already know the producer—we've worked together before. "Hi, Phil."

He brushes back his graying hair and holds out his fist to me. "Yo, Tay, cool that you're here," he says, pointing to the lanky guy who, with his sunglasses and shaggy black hair, looks like one of the Ramones. "That's my casting director."

Instead of a greeting, the man gives a slight chin nod, which I return. "Nice to meet you."

"We should get started." The cat woman glances at the face of her oversized watch. "Where's Sheila?"

Someone else is joining the hearing? Before I can ask, a

stunningly beautiful blonde stumbles into the room. "Sorry," she murmurs.

"Finally. Tay, this is your scene partner." With an affected wave of her hand, Sophie ushers us into another room.

We step through the door, Sophie and the men settle into the cozy chairs, Sheila and I take our positions.

Sophie clears her throat and lowers her gaze to the script. "Scene: A small examination room. On the metal table lies a patient's X-ray, next to it a clipboard with notes. Dr. Elliot Cross, an experienced surgeon, holds the X-ray up to the light and studies it intently. Dr. Emma Bennett, an anesthesiologist and his longtime colleague, sits on a stool watching him, her posture a mix of concern and challenge. The room is charged with a tension between them that goes far beyond the medical discussion." After reading the text, she sets the script aside. "And… action," she says, sounding not only a bit like a quarrelsome cat, but also staring at me just as intensely.

I look at her a moment longer than necessary.

Now I have to deliver, otherwise…

Fear creeps up inside me.

Fear that could turn into panic.

Panic that I must not allow, because it could overwhelm me, just like it did yesterday.

I quickly grab the script and pretend it's the X-ray. I immerse myself in it, trying to become the doctor I need to be today if I don't want my career to go down the drain.

Only when I feel myself merging with the role do I raise my eyes to Sheila. "The tumor has infiltrated the inferior vena cava and affected the area around the retroperitoneal lymph nodes." I manage the mix of professional tone and inner emotion. "The wall is perforated, the continuity of the vascular structure is severely compromised. This requires an en bloc resection of the affected sections, followed by an autologous vein graft." Yes, that was good. Internally, I relax, outwardly I show nothing.

"You know that could endanger the mediastinal circulation. And what about postoperative hemorrhaging?" she purrs, completely inappropriately.

"The hemorrhaging… will be minimized by transarterial embolization before the procedure." Shit, there was a pause, a tiny hesitation. I clear my throat. "You should know that," I force out, even though that's not in the script.

My colleague looks at me, puzzled—I need to get back on track.

Right now.

"But that's all theory, Elliot. The risks are too high. Is that justifiable?" she asks.

"If you question every risk, you lose control. And if you lose control, what's left?" The moment I say my line, I know it wasn't good.

Now my heart starts racing too. I'm breathing, but I can hardly get any air.

"I'm here. No matter how bad it is, I'm here," Autumn suddenly whispers, and it feels as if the voice is coming from my heart.

Her words give me strength; I imagine Autumn standing in front of me, imagine how her warm soul outshines my cold fear.

"The trust. And if you abuse that trust, Elliot, then what?" In my imagination, it's Autumn smiling at me instead of the blonde. "Where does that lead?"

As the stage direction demands, I move toward her, and suddenly it's no longer hard to let go.

"This operation… I have to do it," I say with feeling,

and I'm no longer myself, but this doctor who's desperate for redemption.

"I know you want to stay in control." Autumn looks so understanding that I relax even more. "But what about what you can't control?"

I lean toward her, feel her warmth, sense the safety she radiates. "What would that be?"

"You can't fix everyone, Elliot," she breathes, and by now she's no longer Emma or Sheila or anyone else. She's Autumn—and she's holding me up.

Like yesterday, I reach out to her, gently touch her cheek. "Sometimes trying is all we can do."

Longing flickers in her eyes. "And what if you destroy yourself in the process?"

I move my hand over her temple, brush her hair back, and this time she lets me. My heart beats faster. "And what if it's different?"

Autumn moves closer, her hand touches my chest. I fixate on her lips, which say something I barely catch, but it doesn't matter, because my lines are done.

Only one stage direction remains in the script. Dr. Cross kisses Emma. But that's not what's happening now. Tay—not the fake David, but the real Tay—kisses Autumn, that's what's playing out in my head. I let my feelings run free, feel something I've never felt for a woman before.

"And… cut!" The woman's voice shrills in my ears like a siren.

Autumn pulls away from me, her red hair turns blonde, the green eyes turn blue. Autumn is Sheila again, and I become the Tay who forces one of the thousand smiles from his repertoire onto his face. My feelings retreat at lightning speed to where they're safe.

"Thanks, Tay, we'll be in touch," says Sophie from the production company and gestures toward the door.

Phil's expression is neutral, the casting director jots something down in his notes. I play the confident golden boy, say goodbye to the casting crew, and stride to the door as self-assuredly as if I were convinced I'd landed the role.

In the hallway, I run into Scott Pears. Of all people.

"Lawson! Don't tell me they invited you to the audition?" he says, raising his brows in feigned surprise. His hair has grown longer since our last encounter, and he's sporting a three-day beard. Trying to look like Dr. Dreamy—which, unfortunately, he does. "Your wife really pulled some strings there."

His dirty grin leaves me cold. "Nice to see you." I smile at him with slick politeness. "I'd love to chat, but my plane is waiting."

He waves it off. "Sure, I don't have time anyway. Gotta snag the role of Dr. Cross so my Oscar gets some company soon." As he passes by, he places his hand on my shoulder, trying to push me down, but I hold my ground. I don't budge an inch.

I pretend not to notice what he's trying to do. "Good luck."

"Only people without talent need luck." *Someone like you*, his look says.

There's no way he can know how much those fake news got to me. "And what's your excuse if you don't get the role?" I reply with a wink, as if he just made a joke, and brush his hand off my shoulder. "Think about it. See you around."

"Hopefully not," he mutters just loud enough for me to hear, then enters the penthouse and I head back to the airport.

Chapter Twenty-Three

AUTUMN

Sitting on a plain chair at the edge of the therapy room, I watch Kayla. Her dark hair is a wild mess as she sits up on the mat after the isometric exercises that keep her muscles and joints active.

"That was great, Kayla," says the physical therapist gently, placing one hand lightly on the girl's back. "Are you ready for the crutches?"

Kayla glances at me briefly. A flicker of uncertainty flashes in her eyes, and in that moment, I see David in her expression. I give her an encouraging nod, and she turns her gaze resolutely to the therapist while my thoughts drift.

At yesterday's meeting with June, Nyla, Sonora, and Olive at the Halifax Waterfront Broadway, I couldn't think about anything but David. This morning I could barely breathe when I ran into him in Kayla's room before my shift.

We didn't talk to each other, not really—after all, his daughter was in the room—but we exchanged glances.

Mine were probably anxious and longing at the same

time, his questioning. When we said goodbye and I wished him luck for his audition, I could see how much this role meant to him. Still, it was hard for him to leave Kayla alone. I wanted nothing more than to hug him, to take away his inner conflict. But as so often, he was distant, so I just raised my hand in farewell. That must have looked totally ridiculous.

"And now hold your balance," the therapist instructs.

I pull myself together and focus on Kayla—after all, I'm here to support her. With the therapist's help, she leans on the crutches.

I feel a lump in my throat as her therapist lets go and the little one stands on her own, relieving the injured leg, just like she's supposed to. Her eyes shine, I clap my hands softly to show her how proud I am.

If David could see her like this… maybe the moment would be big enough to make him show Kayla how he feels. Just like he showed me yesterday on the roof.

"Very good, Kayla, time for a break." The physical therapist helps Kayla into the wheelchair and pushes it over to me. "I'll be right back."

I signal to her that I'll stay with the little one. The therapist leaves the room, Kayla takes a deep breath next to me and brushes a strand of hair from her face.

"Did you see that, Autumn?"

"Of course, that was awesome!" I reply, scooting closer and raising my hand for a high five.

She slaps my hand. "Next time, can you make a video for Daddy so he can see it too?"

"That's a great idea." I reach for my phone in the lab coat pocket. "We can send it to your mom too, if you'd like?"

"Mhm," she murmurs, suddenly looking sad.

"Is your heart feeling sad?" I leave my phone in my pocket and place a comforting hand on her shoulder. "Tell me about it."

With her gaze lowered, she plays with her fingers. "Mom's not here because she doesn't love Dad anymore."

Oh. I freeze for a moment. David said Kayla had no idea. "How do you know that?"

"Whenever my nanny's gone and they think I'm already asleep, they fight." Kayla tucks her hands under her thighs. "Mom calls Dad an iceberg—sometimes that makes him mad, but most of the time he doesn't care."

In my mind's eye, the scene Kayla just described plays out. I imagine his wife as a grown-up version of their daughter.

"Daddy tries to calm her down, but she doesn't listen," Kayla continues, looking at me with tears in her eyes. "He's kind of weird sometimes, you know. He makes a lot of jokes when he doesn't know what to say, but Mom never laughs."

Hearing that almost breaks my heart. His daughter has long since seen through him. She knows he's wearing a mask, that he struggles to show his true feelings.

Now she grips the armrests of the wheelchair. "Lately, Mom gets really angry."

I pull her into my arms and rock her gently. "That must be hard for you."

"Then she yells at him, when she should just make a joke and everything would be fine." She sounds convinced, clearly thinks she has to protect David. Because she senses how vulnerable he really is.

I struggle to hold back my tears. This little person in my arms reminds me far too much of myself.

"Then he leaves and Mom cries," she says quietly. "I

pretend I had a nightmare and scream really loud so she'll come and hug me."

Without even realizing that in that moment, it's not her that's comforting her daughter, but the other way around. Kayla isn't just protecting her dad, but her mom too. She's carrying far too much on her small shoulders, and that's not good for her.

I stroke her hair. "Why don't you tell them you hear them fighting?"

She wriggles out of my arms and looks at me, distressed. "It's like with Christmas."

"What do you mean?" I rest my head in my hand, frowning.

"That's just logical." She seems very busy now, spreading her arms wide. "Mom believes Santa Claus brings the presents. But Santa doesn't exist, I've known that for a long time." She lifts her chin proudly. "But if I tell Mom the truth, she gets sad."

I'm starting to understand. "You think that if Mom and Dad know you hear them arguing, they'll get sad."

"Mhm." Her big round eyes stare at me intensely. Suddenly, her expression changes, turning guilty and fearful. "You can't tell Dad, Autumn. Please, promise me, this is our secret, okay?"

In my mind, I see David's pain-stricken face as he confessed to me that he only wears his wedding ring for his daughter's sake. Even though he didn't confirm my suspicion that he's been trying for days to gather the strength to tell her the truth, I'm certain that's exactly what's happening.

The way the little one protects her dad while he's so afraid of what she already knows isn't just twisted, it's also bad for Kayla. She shouldn't have to carry that kind of responsibility at her age. Still, I can relate to both of them, understand what drives them—that desire to protect the other. Because it's the same thing that's ruled my life for years.

In the past few months, my life has taken on a new order. Bit by bit, things have settled into places I once thought they didn't belong, but there they are now, and I'm getting used to it.

Even today, I hide the monster under a high-necked shirt before heading downstairs. Not only are my classmates grateful for it, it's better for Mom too. Seeing my scars reminds her of the accident, and that makes her sad.

Mom is sitting at the breakfast table. As so often, her head seems heavy, she picks at her roll and stares out the window.

I slide into the chair next to her and reach for her forearm. "Want to stroll through downtown a bit this afternoon?" I ask, and once again, I feel like I'm the mom and she's the daughter.

"That would be nice." She always says that, but when the time comes, she doesn't want to anymore. Then she's tired, needs to rest.

"Okay, I'm looking forward to it," I say, forcing a smile. "Did you take your pills?"

She nods, but I still glance over at the pill dispenser I fill every week. The compartment for today is empty.

"Do you need anything before I go?" I ask, automatically starting to clear the table. My gut tells me she won't manage it on her own.

"Today would have been our anniversary." The words slip from her lips tonelessly.

My heart grows heavy. I think of what Dad told me about how they met, how happy they were together, how he could make her glow. And there it is again—that terrible helplessness that's had such a hold on me since Dad died.

The helplessness that must not stop me.

On the day of the accident, I promised that nothing and no one would ever dim my light. And I know I have to fight for that now too.

For everyone, but especially for my mom.

"Do you want to look at the photo album together?" I ask her—after all, the therapist said it would help her to remember the good times with Dad and to process her grief that way.

She smooths the tablecloth. "Later."

"Later" means it hurts too much.

"Later" means never.

All I want to do is scream. To get rid of the burden the accident has placed on me, to be a carefree teenager again. "Okay." I kiss her forehead and hug her one last time. "I'm coming home early from school today, gym class is canceled."

The fact that gym class has supposedly been canceled for weeks now doesn't seem to register with her. I don't yet know what excuse I'll come up with for the gym teacher today—I just know I don't want to change in front of the others. I don't want to hear them gasp, don't want to see them awkwardly look away, don't want to feel their uncertainty about how to treat me. I don't want to feel that I don't belong.

Everything would be different if the accident had never happened.

I swallow hard at the thought. But the anger is still there. It sits in my stomach like a stone, slowly corroding everything. I sense that one day it will be everywhere inside me.

"I never liked gym class," I hear Mom say.

She tries to sound casual, but she doesn't quite manage it. She's sick and she's lost the love of her life—no wonder, really.

"But you have other talents," I say with forced cheerfulness, even though it's hard. "Will you do a bit of painting today? The light's good."

Mom's gaze drifts to the easel I set up for her in the sunroom. The canvas has been blank for weeks. "That's a lovely idea, I'll do that."

I wish that were true. "Great, I'm looking forward to seeing it."

My eyes drift to the kitchen clock—I'm running late, but it's still hard to leave. Mom needs me, and even though her therapist says it's time for her to actively take control of her life again, it's too soon—I can feel it.

"How's Lucy doing, anyway?" Mom asks, to my surprise.

"She's with Henry now," I tell her, and immediately feel a sharp pang in my chest when I picture them strolling down the hallway. His arm casually draped over her shoulders, her head resting against his chest. The way she looks up at him. The way he leans down and kisses her forehead.

She has everything I've lost.

"I'm sorry to hear that." Mom's eyes fill with tears. "Are you okay with it?"

No. I haven't just lost Henry, I've lost my best friend too. Not even she knew how to deal with me. With a monster who has no father and a sick mom. It hurts, but I have no choice but to accept that she wants nothing to do with it. I don't want anything to do with it either, but I'm stuck.

In this life.

In this monster body.

But I can't tell Mom any of that. She shouldn't have to worry—especially not now, when she's already struggling so much.

"If you're not feeling well, I want to know. I want to be there for you, sweetheart," I hear Mom say amidst my thoughts.

And I want nothing more than for her to actually be able to do that. For me to be able to share a bit of my burden with her. "Everything's fine, the two of them are a great couple."

"You have such a big heart." A smile spreads across her face. A wonderful, proud, warm smile that gives me hope.

I hug her. "See you this afternoon."

"Have a nice day." She reaches for her coffee cup and gets up from the chair. For a split second, she looks like a completely normal mom saying goodbye to her daughter, and in that moment, I know it's right to protect her from everything that's tormenting me.

"You too," I say with a smile that stretches to my ears, simply because it makes me happy to see her like this.

Since the accident, I've always been by Mom's side. No matter how off-kilter my own world was, she and her well-being were more important. It wasn't easy, but I never doubted that it was the right thing to do.

"So, will you promise me not to tell Daddy?" Kayla's voice pulls me out of my thoughts.

I see her sitting in her wheelchair, see the hope in her eyes.

What's happening here with her and her parents is different from what happened in my family. Her parents are healthy, they can fulfill their responsibilities. Kayla doesn't have to protect them—on the contrary.

"Having a secret like that doesn't feel good, does it?" I murmur absentmindedly, thinking of all the things I still protect my mom from to this day, to keep her from relapsing.

Kayla puckers her lips into a pout. "Don't know."

"I think you should tell your dad. We could do it together." It will free her from a burden she shouldn't have to carry. For the blink of an eye, I imagine what it would be like to let go of the responsibility, to protect my mom less, to let her go more. But then I realize that Kayla's situation isn't comparable to mine.

I quickly focus on the little one, who looks at me uncertainly. I can practically see her weighing the pros and cons.

At that moment, Kayla's physical therapist reenters the room.

"You don't have to decide right away, but promise me you'll think about it, okay?" With these words, I hold out my pinky to Kayla.

She hesitantly hooks hers around mine. "Okay."

"Thank you." I signal to the therapist to begin. "And now we'll make the video for your dad. Are you ready?"

"Ready."

My shift is almost over and David still hasn't returned from his audition. I shouldn't be wondering where he is or how he's doing, whether we'll see each other today and what it'll be like when we do. Still, I can hardly think of anything else —I'm nervous, anxious, and excited all at once.

Only my little patients manage to distract me for brief moments. So I'm all the more grateful to be standing next to Sandra at the bedside of the five-year-old boy who's staying in our elephant room after a bout of pneumonia. His breathing is steady, his oxygen saturation stable. Sandra is hooking up a new IV while I take his temperature.

"Very good, the fever's continuing to go down," I say quietly, glancing at the thermometer so as not to disturb his light sleep.

"Yeah, he's making good progress." Sandra checks the IV line with practiced ease. "Speaking of progress… what's going on with you and Kayla's dad?"

Startled by her change of topic, I flinch. "What do you mean?" As if I needed to check our patient's vitals, I focus on the monitor covered with elephant stickers.

I still catch Sandra's mischievous grin out of the corner of my eye. "Well, you're spending a lot of time with him. There's already a betting pool going on the ward."

Oh dear. "Since when?"

"For a while now." She shrugs. "Dr. Parker bet ten dollars that you're hitting on him because he's loaded."

"She thinks I'm that kind of person?" Outrage wells up

inside me, and I clear my throat, fiddling with my stethoscope to calm myself.

She shrugs again. "Brenda even upped the bet by five dollars—she said with how unattractive he is, his money must be the only reason."

Because you can't love unattractive people. That's just how it is. "He's my patient's father. Of course I'm spending time with him," I reply, ignoring the nervous flutter of my heart.

Sandra wags her finger. "I saw you two in the cafeteria. You were… getting along pretty well." With that, she tucks the medical file under her arm.

I cast one last glance at our patient. "Sleep well," I whisper, and head off with Sandra.

As we step through the door, she buries her hands in the pockets of her scrubs. "Anyway, I bet twenty dollars that he's the love of your life."

I never took her for such a romantic. "That's not…" I begin, but she cuts me off with a mischievous laugh.

"Oh, come on, Autumn. There's something there, isn't there? You have to admit, he doesn't look at you like just any doctor."

Maybe that's true. For now. Until he finds out that nothing about me is as beautiful as he imagines.

Possibly.

Or maybe not.

Damn it, I don't know.

Torn inside, I pull the door shut, my eyes automatically darting down the hallway.

No sign of David.

"He's the father of my patient. That's all there is." I don't even understand it myself, only that I can't stop hoping David might be able to handle my scars, even though no other man ever could.

Sandra raises her eyebrows. "Mhm. That's all there is. Sure."

I just shake my head and smile, unsure of what to say to that. "Which patient is next?"

"The acute bronchitis in the Butterfly Room is waiting for her discharge approval."

The acute bronchitis is a person, so we should treat her like one. "The little one's name is Kendra." And she handled her inhalation therapy so brilliantly despite her fear that I could burst with pride for her.

Sandra tilts her head. "Tell me, isn't it exhausting to constantly sacrifice yourself like that?"

It is, and the fact that there's so little left for me often makes me sad. "It's worth every effort," I reply, because that's true too, and I head off to see Kendra.

Chapter Twenty-Four

TAY

In the elevator, I press the button for the seventh floor, where the pediatrics department is located. Being David again feels liberating. My breathing is calmer, my muscles more relaxed, the corners of my mouth lift. And not just because no one expects anything from David and I'll soon be with Kayla again, but also because I'll see Autumn.

Once upstairs, I step into the hallway, immerse myself in the hectic activity of the children's ward, and look around for the woman without whom I wouldn't have survived the audition. She wasn't even present, yet she saved me from my fear.

It's crazy, and I don't understand it, just like I don't understand this longing that fills me completely, driving me further and further down the hallway, and the disappointment because I don't see Autumn anywhere.

She knew roughly when I'd be back. Is she avoiding me on purpose? Because I got too close to her on the roof yesterday? Because she senses what she stirs in me and at the same time knows it's not the same for her? Or does she suspect that I'm not who I pretend to be?

When I enter Kayla's room, I feel that I can't keep lying to Autumn and get closer to her at the same time. I have to decide, but I don't know how, especially since I don't even know where this is supposed to lead. All I know is that her presence does something crazy to me.

"Daddy, Daddy, finally!" My little girl beams at me, and not for the first time, my stomach knots when I think about how she still doesn't know about her parents' separation.

I walk over to her and hug her—in the same stiff way I've always done throughout her life. "Hey, you."

We go through our greeting ritual—fist bump, high five, fist bump—then she starts talking a mile a minute. She tells me every detail about her day, and with each word, my pride swells. She's so brave, so positive. I can't help but smile, and not just because she keeps mentioning Autumn.

"She made a video. You have to find her, Daddy, so she can show it to you." Her deep blue round eyes plead with me. "Then you'll see how good I already am with the crutches. It won't be long before I'm walking with them."

"I'm afraid Autumn's already gone home." There's disappointment in my voice.

"No, she wanted to wait, you have to look for her, Daddy, she's definitely still here." She nods so vigorously that her glasses almost slip off her nose. Busily, she pushes them back up. "Really, she promised."

And what Autumn promises, she keeps. "Okay, I'll see if I can find her."

My heart beats faster as I leave Kayla's room. At the nurses' station, I run into Sandra, the nurse who's been checking in on Kayla from time to time over the past few days. In her hand, she's holding one of those odd pens that apparently every employee here has—hers has a green tassel.

Just to be safe, I pull my cap further down over my face. "Excuse me, I'm looking for Dr. Hall. Do you know where she is?"

A strangely knowing smile flashes across her lips. "You're looking for Dr. Hall? I see."

Automatically, I square my shoulders, tense my muscles, and fix her with an unyielding stare. "I need to speak with her. Immediately."

She taps her pen against the medical chart in front of her while eyeing me. "What do you need from her?"

"Listen." I lean over the counter toward her, instinctively trying to impose my presence. "I'm paying a fortune for the best possible treatment for my daughter. If I want to speak with her doctor, you don't question it—you find her."

Faced with the sharpness of my words, she recoils. "Take it easy, I'm already paging her," she says, getting to work.

Not a minute later, Autumn hurries down the hallway toward us. Her coat flaps behind her, and her red hair swings in rhythm.

"We have a Code Yellow?" she calls out. Sandra points at me with her index finger, and Autumn's alarmed gaze lands on me. "What happened?"

With her flushed cheeks, she looks even more attractive than usual. "Everything's fine," I say to ease her concern. "Kayla wanted to see you." And so did I—much more than I'd realized until now.

Her hair is tousled from running, and I have to restrain myself from reaching out to smooth the strands.

She smirks. "I think I know what this is about."

"Exactly that," I say, enjoying the knowledge that we're

both talking about the same thing without having to name it.

"I guess that means I've won," Sandra murmurs happily. Whatever she means by that doesn't matter right now, so I ignore her.

"Well then, let's go." Autumn slips her hands into her lab coat pockets and gives me an expectant look.

Together, we stroll over to Kayla's room. "What's Code Yellow?" I ask, still thinking about her intense reaction from earlier.

"Relative out of control." She gives me a sly grin.

"It wasn't that bad." I have to laugh, she joins in, then asks me about the audition.

I'd love to tell her everything, but I force myself to stay vague. It feels wrong, and when she smiles blissfully, I can barely hold back. I want to tell her that she's the one who saved me. Tell her what this role means to me, so she understands how much she's done for me.

Luckily, we reach Kayla's bedroom door before I lose control. My little girl squirms around in bed and squeals with delight when Autumn pulls her phone out of her coat pocket as she enters.

"I want to watch too," she shouts, prompting Autumn to sit down beside her on the bed and signal for me to take a seat on the other side.

I sit close to my daughter, and as Autumn starts the video and my girl stares at the screen, completely captivated, I manage to gently wrap my arm around her without tensing up. Her shoulder is so small, it disappears entirely in my hand.

I already see Kayla sitting on a bench. "I want to keep going," she says bravely to the therapist, who then hands her the crutches. I can't help but smile. She must have inherited that unshakable will from me.

I watch as Kayla gets ready. Her gaze grows focused, she takes a deep breath, then braces herself on the crutches.

"Here it comes—you're going to be amazed. No one does it as fast as I do, that's what the therapist said," my daughter bursts out.

On the screen, Kayla struggles to her feet, sometimes with a focused look, sometimes uncertain, until she's standing supported by the crutches. A bit wobbly, but she balances with great pride.

Seeing that takes my breath away, and hope begins to grow in me that soon she'll be running around carefree again like she did before her fall.

"It's really dumb, right?" Kayla looks up at me. Embarrassment clouds her expression.

"No," I say hoarsely. "Not dumb, but incredibly amazing."

Her eyes widen, but Autumn's reaction to my words is even more intense. A mixture of pride and longing floods her face.

"Did you hear that, Autumn?!" Kayla asks, chin lifted. "My dad thinks I did a great job."

"Of course I heard that," Autumn replies, looking only at me.

Kayla snuggles up to me, and for the first time in years, I don't tense up. "Thank you, Daddy."

The thanks belong solely to the woman with the red hair, sitting less than half a meter from me on the bed. I still don't understand how she did it, but she changed something.

I silently mouth "Thank you," knowing full well it's not

enough. She waves it off like it's nothing, even though now more than ever it feels like it's everything.

Behind Kayla's neck, I reach out to her. The very second I touch her shoulder, she flinches. She doesn't shake me off, but I can clearly see her tense up.

A knock at the door keeps me from asking her what's wrong.

The door swings open. "Dinner," a staff member chirps, juggling a tray over to Kayla's bed.

Autumn stands up, nervously tugs at her hair, smooths down her coat, then goes back to fussing with her hair.

Something is wrong.

With anyone else, I wouldn't care, but with her it's different. I don't want to see her like this—I don't want her to be nervous or afraid.

"Yeah, pasta with tomato sauce," cheers Kayla, who apparently hasn't noticed the tension that suddenly fills the room.

The hospital staff member leaves the room, and Autumn also heads out. "See you tomorrow," she says, disappearing through the door faster than I can respond.

"Will you be okay on your own?" I ask Kayla, who already has the fork in her hand.

She rolls her eyes. "I'm a big girl, you know that."

"Of course I know that." We give each other a high five. "Be right back."

With those words, I rush outside, where I see Autumn's red mane disappearing around the corner.

I quickly catch up to her. "Wait!"

She turns to me with a tense expression.

"What was that just now?" I ask as soon as I catch up to her. "Why did you take off so fast?"

She bites her lower lip, as if unsure how to answer my question. "I wasn't needed anymore."

"You're always needed." My voice naturally takes on a warm undertone, which Autumn seems to notice as she looks at me wistfully.

"Is that so?" she asks quietly. A flicker of longing and pain flashes in her eyes for a brief moment.

"How could it be any different?" I wouldn't ask a single soul in this world that question, because I wouldn't care about the answer in the slightest.

But with her, it's different, everything is different, I am different.

She doesn't answer, just shakes her head nervously, wants to keep walking, and I know I shouldn't stop her. Whatever this is between us, it's built on a lie. She thinks I'm David, a banker from New York, and no one knows what would happen if I told her the truth.

I should let her go—for my own safety—yet I hold her back.

"Would it really be so bad? If we needed you? If I needed you?" I ask, not recognizing myself. It's because of Autumn, and it feels right, that's all I know. Feeling safe near her, telling her what I feel, is so easy in this moment. So natural.

I have to finally show her who I am beneath this disguise. If I explain it to her, she'll understand, and then we'll figure out where whatever this is between us might lead.

She takes a deep breath, her expression torn. "If you need me, then only because…"

I reach for her hand, and at least she lets me hold it. "Because?"

"Because you don't… I can't…"

If she can't, then why doesn't she just turn around and leave? Why is she standing here with me, so close I can feel her breath on my neck, holding my hand?

"What's wrong?" I gently squeeze her hand.

Almost imperceptibly, she returns my touch. "I…" Once again, she seems unable to find the words.

"Did I overstep?" I was so fascinated by her, so addicted to her warmth. I've never felt anything like this in my life—maybe it made me see things that weren't really there.

"No." Autumn's desperation brings tears to her eyes. "It's complicated…"

I could accept her answer, be glad she doesn't want to talk about it, walk away and try to forget. But I don't want that. I want us to show each other everything we are.

My own thought frightens me.

How is that possible?

What is this woman doing to me?

"Let me go, please, it's better this way." What she says isn't what she means. Instinctively, I think back to when we were stuck together in the elevator. How she practically forced me to listen to her.

She did it for me, and that wasn't the only time she stood by my side.

Autumn was there for me in moments when everyone else I've ever known would have left me alone. She was there, and she didn't judge me. On the contrary, she understood me, caught me when I fell.

Now it's my turn.

"I'm here for you. No matter how bad it is, I'm here." These are her words that I now speak, and I feel they come from the depths of my heart.

Chapter Twenty-Five

AUTUMN

Just a few hours ago, I wanted nothing more than to be alone with David. To find out if we're both wounded in the same way.

But now that the moment has come, I'm nothing but fear. If it weren't for that one spark of hope, I wouldn't let him pull me from the crowded hallway into the storage room.

He closes the door behind him; only a little light filters into the room through the small window. A single arm's length away from me, he leans against the wall. Together, we breathe into the silence of the space, and I don't know what to say.

"All my life, I never wanted to know what was really going on inside other people." His quiet voice breaks the silence between us. "I didn't want to see their hatred or their ugly souls."

The way he says it, it sounds like he truly believes every person has an ugly soul.

"But you." He turns his head toward me. "You never

asked for permission—you showed me your innermost self, and there was no hatred, no ugliness."

Because I'm ugly somewhere else, I should reply, but the words catch in my throat.

"You never judged me, never turned your back on me, no matter how shitty I acted—and I did, way too often." His expression is full of warmth. "I understand if you don't want to tell me what's going on."

"You don't understand…" My heart grows heavy.

He moves a little closer. "Then explain it to me."

The same questions that have haunted me for days take hold of me again. What if I show him? Would he stay? Or would he—no matter whether he's broken too or not—run away on the spot?

I bite my lip. "I can't."

"Why not?" Determination is written all over his face, and I can feel that he won't back down.

A burning pain shoots through my chest. "Because I don't want it to be over," I whisper soundlessly, because that's the truth. I still want to hope a little, just dream a tiny bit of something that's actually impossible. Of that miracle—that he could love me despite my scars.

Shaking his head, he reaches out to me. "What's supposed to be over?"

I allow him to touch my forearm. His fingers rest warm and gentle on the fabric of my shirt. There's nothing I'd rather do than pull him into my arms. Kiss him, forget for a moment what I am—together with him. At the same time, I know it would only make things worse.

His cap casts a shadow over his eyes. I have to know, and if it's what I think, if it's what I'm hoping for, then maybe I can overcome my fear.

"What are you hiding under your cap?" I ask.

He presses his lips together.

"There's something, isn't there?" The words leave my mouth without a sound. "Something no one's supposed to see."

For a moment, his fingers tense on my arm. "Yes."

"Take it off," I ask him. My heartbeat quickens. "Take it off and I'll answer every one of your questions."

His intense gaze finds me. "Why is it so important to you?"

"Because it could change everything." The words come straight from my heart, where the hope for a miracle burns.

He looks at me so intently that I can see straight into his soul. There's worry there. "I…"

For the first time since my accident, I want to believe that love is possible for me too. That I don't have to spend my life alone.

"Take off your cap." My voice trembles, my breathing is shallow.

His left hand still resting on my arm, he reaches for the cap with his right. "First, you have to promise me something."

My God, it's true.

He's like me!

Warmth floods my chest, tingles through my stomach, and paints the world in the most beautiful colors. "Anything you want."

"Promise me you won't tell anyone." He moved a little closer, the scent of his skin surrounding me. "Not a single soul can find out."

"Your secret is safe with me." Just like I'll be safe with him. And once we've shown each other how broken we are, we can be whole together.

He nodded, his thumb brushed along my arm, then he exhaled slowly.

I stared at the cap he pulled from his head in slow motion—along with the shaggy hair.

So that isn't his real hair.

Holding my breath, I watched as chestnut-brown hair gradually came into view.

No scarred scalp.

No marks.

Just hair.

Now he pulled the cap off completely, let it fall to the floor, and started fiddling with his beard.

So that's not his either.

A faint crackling fills the room as he removes the fake beard. I wait for the scar, the ugliness, the thing that connects us—but there's nothing.

Why…?

Now he takes off the horn-rimmed glasses too, and in that moment, I realize I was wrong. He and I have nothing in common. He's no monster—on the contrary, he's perfect.

Perfect, perfect, perfect.

The jawline, the dark eyes, the lips… Wait a second, is that…?

Oh. My. God.

I clap my hands over my mouth.

That's…

Tay Lawson!

While my head struggles in vain to process this knowledge, my heart begins to break—in a way it never has before.

He twists his attractive, flawless, far-too-perfect face into an apologetic smile.

Unable to say anything, I stare at him.

He takes my hands, pulls them away from my mouth, and touches my lips with his thumbs. "Hi, I'm Tay."

Yes, he is Tay—the Beautiful.

And I am Autumn—the Beast.

Whatever happened in the last few days, it wasn't real. And it never will be.

Not in any existing world.

Not in any life.

"You're Tay Lawson," I stammer, and he gives a crooked smile.

"I'm sorry for all the secrecy. There was no other way."

To hell with secrecy. The fact that he lied to me about who he really is doesn't hurt in the slightest.

What hurts is that the two of us are nothing alike. What hurts is knowing he'd be disgusted by me if he saw my scars. But what hurts most is that I was foolish enough to hope for a miracle, even though I should have known it doesn't exist.

"I couldn't let the press find me," he says.

The press.

Of course. He's a star. Always in the spotlight. Constantly in the media. The last thing he needs is a monster at his side.

"I can't do this," I force out, placing my hands on his chest to push him away.

He doesn't move. Instead, he gently takes hold of my wrists. "Please, don't."

What else am I supposed to do? Stay here until my heart is nothing but broken pieces?

"Tell me what you're thinking," he pleads, his voice barely audible.

What do I think? Nothing at all, but I know all the more: I know that he and I have absolutely nothing in common. I know that someone as perfect as he is will never understand what it's like to be me. I know I don't belong in his light. And I also know that I need to end this as quickly as possible. "I think we'll both save ourselves a lot of pain if I leave now."

Tears burn in my eyes as I push past him. And as I leave him behind in the storage room, a familiar rage crawls from the wreckage of my heart.

That damn accident.

That shitty day.

It ruined everything, destroyed my life, my chance at a happy future.

It destroyed *me*.

Ruthlessly, the rage takes control, devours everything good in me, threatens to extinguish the light I must never lose, forces its will upon me.

There are only ugly thoughts left, tearing me apart inside.

I breathe against the tightness in my chest, but it's useless. A nearly forgotten cocktail of anger, hatred, and self-loathing floods me with full force.

I don't want it, yet I feel myself losing control over my thoughts. Becoming the person I don't want to be.

It hadn't happened in years, everything had been okay —*I* had been okay.

I have to get out of here.

All I want is for my anger to stay locked in the storage room as I slam the door shut. I storm down the hallway, but it's still inside me. I feel it searing into my soul, draining every last bit of hope, and I know there's only one way to end it.

Don't want to do it.

But I have to.

Frantically, I rush down the hallway, reach the supply room, and lock myself inside.

I find a scalpel.

With trembling fingers, I pull it out of its plastic sheath.

I unzip my jeans and let them fall to the floor.

I press the blade to the inside of my left thigh, push it into the skin, feel the burn, breathe in the pain.

This pain, greater than my anger at the world.

Blood wells from the line I draw with the blade. Small drops that grow larger and flush out what I need to get rid of.

The darkness. The selfish thoughts. The rage. It hurts—and at the same time, it feels incredibly liberating.

I soak in this unique kind of relief I was addicted to for years. The feeling I thought I no longer needed intoxicates me more intensely than ever before.

Another cut.

The darkness leaves my body.

And another one.

Deeper.

Oh God, that feels good.

I close my eyes, savor the emptiness spreading inside me, and fill it with the right thoughts and feelings. Fill it with the light I must not lose.

That I became this monster is a fate I cannot change. Just like the fact that Mom is sick and I have to be there for her.

I accept my fate, acknowledge that the David I imagined doesn't exist, and that I have to forget Tay. Soon he'll leave Halifax, he won't play a role in my life anymore.

Over and over I drill these sentences into my head, and as long as the blood flows, they're almost true.

Chapter Twenty-Six

TAY

Her delicate scent of strawberries still lingers in the air, our touches still tingle on my skin, her words burn in my chest.

I think we'll both spare ourselves a lot of pain if I leave now.

That she's shocked is understandable. But what were those words supposed to mean?

With both hands, I run through my hair, trying to clear my head, but I still don't understand anything.

No woman has ever reacted to Tay Lawson like that—on the contrary, as soon as they saw me, they wanted more of me. Who I really am, what defines me, what I'm afraid of, what I dream about, what hurts me—no one ever cared about that. They wanted to possess me, show off with the beautiful shell, and that was exactly right for me. In that superficial life, I was safe.

I never showed Autumn that flawless shell, she only knew my broken soul—and she stayed. Just now, she saw the only beautiful thing about me for the first time—and fled with a look of disgust.

There are too many emotions inside me that I can't grasp. I only know one thing: they need to come out.

In my desperation, I clench my fists and punch first my thighs, then the doorframe, until my knuckles bleed.

Panting, I stare at them, follow the red trail running across the back of my hand, feel the burning, exhale wearily, still full of unanswered questions.

I don't know how to find the answers, but I feel all the more strongly that they won't let me go until I have them. That I can't go on like before, that I can't pretend Autumn hasn't changed something in me.

I bend down for my cap and pull it on, glue the beard to my face and put on the glasses. Then I open the door and go looking for Autumn. She needs to explain what she meant when she said we'd both be spared pain if she left.

I don't find her in the hallway, the play area, or at the nurse's station. Only Head Nurse Sandra crosses my path, and she refuses to page Autumn again.

"Listen, it hasn't even been twenty minutes since she was with you." She furrows her drawn-on eyebrows. "I get that you two… whatever you've got going on, but Dr. Hall's shift ended half an hour ago."

That may be, but she's still here. "I just saw her, and there are a number of medical questions she needs to answer for me. Tell her I'm waiting for her in Kayla's room," I reply firmly.

"Ah, love must be a beautiful thing…" Sandra shakes her head ever so slightly, then smiles at me. "I'll gladly let her know, if I see her."

With a brief nod, I turn away and march toward Kayla's room. A flicker of hope burns inside me that Autumn might already be there.

That she has processed the initial shock and is ready to explain to me what she meant by her remark.

But when I enter Kayla's room, it's only my daughter there, her cheeks smeared with tomato sauce.

"For dessert there's chocolate pudding. I'm giving it to you," she tells me, pushing her hair behind her ears.

So much love for her flares up inside me. "That's really sweet of you." I sink down onto the edge of the bed. "We could also share it, if you'd like?"

"Really?" she says, eyes shining, as she hands me a spoon and the pudding bowl. Suddenly, she furrows her brow. "Are you okay, Daddy?"

Automatically, I look at my hand. Not just because I know what my daughter is referring to, but also because Kayla's concern fills me with guilt. "It's just a scratch, don't worry, everything's fine."

For a while, I hear nothing but her breathing. "You're silly," she says eventually.

I lift my eyelids. "Yes, I am." As incredibly silly as this game that developed between us over the years because I wasn't able to show her my love.

I wish I were a little more like Autumn. Warm and open, kind and loving. But those scars inside me remain, and the thought of making myself vulnerable in front of Kayla still hurts.

"So what about the pudding? Don't you want it anymore?" she asks.

My gaze flits to her, lingers on the small nose, the pretty eyes behind the glasses, the dark hair framing her face. This child is a part of me—no, not just *a* part, she is the *best* part of me. That's exactly what I should tell her, she needs to know it.

"Why are you looking at me like that?" She wrinkles her nose.

I quickly shake my head and stick the spoon into the pudding. "Because you're looking at me like that," I reply helplessly.

She presses her lips together, and I realize I've just left a small scar on her heart. That I've been doing exactly that for years. That I'm just as lousy a father as mine was.

While we eat together, Kayla tells me once again about the physical therapy, which seems to be occupying her mind a lot. "Autumn was with me the whole time," she finishes the story and hands the spoon back to me. "When I grow up, I want to be like her."

"You want to be a doctor?" Absentmindedly, I scrape the last bit of pudding from the bowl.

"Pfff, no, Daddy." Kayla's amused giggle fills the room.

I pause mid-movement. "Then what?"

"I want to be able to smile like her, so it makes people feel all warm inside. And I want to speak in a way that feels like a hug." She props her chin in her hands. "I want to be someone everyone just has to love."

Because she thinks that's not the case right now. Because she believes her father doesn't love her. The thought sears into my chest, makes it hard to breathe. Searching for the right words, I hand her the last spoonful of pudding.

She looks me over. "That's dumb, isn't it?" she asks sadly and puts the spoon in her mouth.

"No, it's not." It's anything but that. The words are inside me, but they won't come out—damn it, why can't I say them to her?

Kayla's mouth twitches, and I realize that even though I haven't said everything, I've said so much more than usual —and I know exactly who I have to thank for that.

Autumn.

Gently, I brush Kayla's hair from her forehead. "Should I steal another pudding for us?"

"Oh yes!"

"Okay, but first we'll clean your cheeks." On the way to the sink, my thoughts return to Autumn and the question of what comes next. How anything can come next at all.

Lost deep in all sorts of possible and impossible scenarios, I wet a paper towel with water. My fame doesn't make anything easier—that much is clear. As I turn off the faucet, my phone beeps in my pocket.

First, I hand Kayla the towel, then glance at the screen.

It's a message from Chloe. Does she already have news of the decision about the role of Dr. Cross?

Is this the reassurance I so desperately need?

Involuntarily, I hold my breath as I open the message—fractions of a second later, her words hit me like a bomb.

Chapter Twenty-Seven

AUTUMN

After the blood comes the guilt.

Anger, blood, guilt—a vicious cycle I had long since broken free from.

With tears in my eyes, I search the aluminum shelves in the storage room for cloths and bandages.

Why did I do it?

The question consumes me as I clean my hands and dress the fresh cuts. The bandage, with its innocent white, covers what I don't want to see, and as long as it stays there, I can pretend there's nothing terrible underneath.

But beside it—on the right, the left, above and below—traces of the past run through my skin like silent witnesses to the ugly truth.

I shouldn't have done it again—and it will never happen again. I quickly pull up my jeans, take several deep breaths, and wipe the tears from my cheeks.

"It's okay – I'm okay," I say over and over, but I still can't believe it.

Everything is spinning in my head.

Tay Lawson.

Damn it, how could I have fallen in love with Tay Lawson? There's no man in the world less suited to me than him. And how could I have fallen in love again at all, even though I knew it would end in disappointment?

Once again, tears stream down my cheeks, as if part of me refuses to accept the truth. But things are the way they are, and the sooner I get used to the idea, the better.

Just a few more days, then Kayla will be discharged and I'll never see Tay again.

Just a few more days, then the wound that now feels as if it will never close will begin to heal.

It always does. My job is to make sure this wound leaves as few scars as possible. I won't let my heart be damaged.

One last time, I wipe the salty drops from my cheeks. "Your patients need you," I remind myself, even though my shift is technically over, and finally the tears stop flowing.

I linger for a moment, then tug my bangs down over my forehead and leave the supply room. I absolutely don't want to run into Tay, so I grab the patient files I still need to finish and barricade myself with them in the doctors' lounge.

Before I start work, I send Mom a quick message to see if she's doing okay. She replies immediately, seems completely absorbed in preparing for her vernissage, and I'm glad that at least everything's fine with her.

Just as I open the first file and pull the pen with the ridiculous tassel from the breast pocket of my lab coat, my boss enters the room.

Fully aware that my eyes are still puffy from all the crying, I lower my head so that my hair covers my face.

"Ah, Dr. Hall, have you wasted too much time with the

patients again today, or is that why you're working overtime?" She walks over to the kitchenette and opens the upper cabinet.

"It was busy," I answer evasively and update Brian's chart with today's lab results.

Porcelain clinks, the coffee machine hums, and the rich aroma of coffee fills the room. "When I was a resident, I once fell in love with a patient's father," Dr. Parker suddenly says. "Let me tell you, he was incredibly hot, seriously ripped, and an absolute virtuoso in bed."

Heaven help me, can't she respect boundaries just once? I don't want to know things like that about her. Besides, she only told me a week ago how important efficiency is at work, and now she's making time for a conversation like this? I avoid looking at her and focus solely on the chart.

She lets out a long sigh. "We screwed like crazy..."

Oh God. She's my boss!

"We had three unbelievable weeks where I barely slept," she babbles on. "Then suddenly his wife showed up."

She falls silent, I can feel her gaze on me and suddenly the air between us feels far too thick.

"You do know he's married, right?" she asks seriously. "The man has a family, Dr. Hall."

He doesn't. At least not really, but of course I don't tell her that—he confided in me, after all. Besides, that's completely irrelevant.

I shift around in my chair, unable to find a comfortable position. "I really don't know..."

"Oh come on, don't pretend—you know that. Everyone here knows that," she cuts me off. Then she sits down next to me. I glance over at her and see the deadly serious expression on her face. "Be careful. He's not who he pretends to be."

Excuse me? Dr. Parker knows who's hiding behind David's disguise? How?

"Ohhh, so he's already taken off his cap for you. Pillow talk and all that, yeah yeah, things got steamy, sure." She leans in toward me. "I get it, Dr. Hall, he really is a tasty treat, quite the looker."

Yes, he is—my God, he's a Hollywood star!—but that's not the point at all. "How do you know…"

"Don't look at me like that, I know everything that goes on in this facility." With a proud expression, she sips her coffee. "Whatever's going on between you and Mr. Supersexy, you do realize it's not real, don't you?"

"There's nothing," I reply so weakly that even I don't believe myself.

"Enjoy the sex for all I care, go as wild as you like. But let one thing be clear…" She eyes me closely, a serious expression on her face. "When he and his family leave the hospital and your life, I expect you to do your job properly."

I nod.

"For the kids, you know," she adds with a wink.

Does she really think I'd let my patients suffer because of my broken heart?

"Of course, don't worry." While the words leave my lips automatically, for the first time I wonder whether it wouldn't be better to confront her.

Because of the intrusive way she brought up the topic, because she's probably already talked to half the department about it, and because of the prejudices she throws around so carelessly. Until now, I've always come up with excuses for her behavior, didn't want to accuse her of anything, didn't even want to bring it up. I've been protecting her.

If I tell Mom the truth, she'll be sad, I suddenly hear Kayla's voice whispering inside me, and again I feel how wrong it is that this little girl protects her parents so much. This morning during physical therapy, her words made me think of my mom, and I was sure that Kayla and I were similar, though our situations were completely different. And they are, when it comes to my mom—but what about all the other people in my life?

What about Dr. Parker? Why am I protecting her from criticism that is entirely justified?

"Well, we'll see about that." Chin raised, she scrutinizes me.

David—Tay or not—would never stand for this. He wouldn't back down an inch; he'd fight, though far too fiercely.

"We won't, because you already understand how important my patients are to me and that there's no reason to accuse me of anything," I hear myself say, driven by emotion, and I'm surprised by how firm I sound. "Besides, my private life is private, and I ask that you respect that in the future."

"Well, well, strong words—I'm impressed." She raises her eyebrows. "Then back them up with action. Chop-chop, get to work; those medical records won't fill themselves, will they?" She pats my shoulder. "And wash your face. Otherwise, you'll scare our poor sick little ones so badly they'll drop dead."

The thought alone makes me swallow hard. "Don't worry, I'll do that right away," I say, desperately hoping she'll finally leave me alone.

Too much has already happened today. Everything inside me feels shaken, raw, broken. Deliberately, I turn to my notes, prompting her, thankfully, to get up from the chair.

"Oh, and don't forget the condoms, or this'll end in a tragedy even Shakespeare couldn't have imagined more tragically," she throws over her shoulder on her way to the door.

It already is, I think, disheartened, and notice how the text I just wrote begins to blur before my eyes.

Chapter Twenty-Eight

TAY

They know.

Damn it, they followed me after the audition in New York, found out where I flew to.

That's what Chloe wrote to me last night, and the consequence is obvious: the paparazzi are on their way to me.

Tense, I stare out the window into the breaking dawn while Kayla slumbers peacefully in her bed. Pediatrics is on the seventh floor, and the flat roof above the entrance blocks my view.

Are they already down there, lying in wait for me? Or are they still roaming the city in search of clues? They'll question every taxi driver who made trips from the airport to Halifax yesterday, follow every lead.

They're a pack of wolves, and after failing to catch me for more than a week, they're starving.

If I stay here, they'll find me—and they'll find Kayla. They'll easily figure out that Kayla got injured while in my care, call me a lousy father, pin God knows what on me, just to throw it all in my face in front of the whole world. I should run with Kayla, just like Chloe suggested in her message last night. We need to disappear and finish the treatment at another clinic.

But leaving now would also mean never seeing Autumn again. Never finding out what was going through her mind yesterday when I let my mask slip. I haven't seen her since she fled the storage room. Is she busy, or is she avoiding me?

Maybe she doesn't have any feelings for me—neither for David nor for Tay. Maybe I was the only one who felt something every time she looked at me with all that warmth. I thought she looked at only me that way, even though she does it with everyone.

It's just her nature, it doesn't mean anything.

All the more reason it should be easy to turn my back on Halifax—yet it feels wrong. So wrong that I haven't replied to Chloe's messages yet.

Nearly twelve hours have passed, she's followed up twice, urged me, reminded me what's at stake and that this is the worst possible time for bad press. She wrote all that, and I know she's right with every word—my God, this could cost me the role of Dr. Cross! My future would be ruined, my dream, my life, everything could fall apart.

Once again, I read her messages while the hallway outside slowly comes to life. Carts rattle past, bright laughter rings out, followed by a jumble of voices.

There's no doubt—the smartest thing would be to leave Halifax immediately.

Autumn's face appears before my mind's eye, with all the inner turmoil she showed me yesterday, even before I revealed who I am. Something is hurting her, deeply. It's making her unhappy, consuming her life—completely independent of the fact that I'm Tay Lawson.

Maybe she doesn't feel the same way about me as I thought I felt for a moment. Maybe she doesn't need me the way I need her.

Still, I can't leave until I know for sure. If I clear things up—today, once and for all—and if she tells me again to go, then I'll be gone tomorrow.

Kayla's blanket rustles, and she lets out a soft sigh. I step up to her bed, see her sleeping peacefully, and kiss her fragrant forehead. "Be right back," I whisper to her, then head outside.

I have to find Autumn. No matter what happens next, everything starts with her. I glance briefly at the clock—it's still early, but she's probably already here. I begin my search at the care station, then move on to the doctors' office, the play area, the visitor section. I even check the supply closet and the storage room, but there's no sign of her.

A wave of nervousness rises in me as I leave the ward and head toward the cafeteria. The scent of coffee and fresh pastries greets me—and I spot Autumn at the register.

She hands the cashier a few coins, grabs a paper bag, and turns to leave.

It takes only a split second for her to spot me at the entrance. Her expression reflects a wild mix of emotions that makes it impossible for me to guess what she's thinking.

I step toward her and raise my hand. "Hi."

"Hi." She fidgets awkwardly with the paper bag, avoiding eye contact. "Is Kayla okay?"

Together, we leave the cafeteria. "She's sleeping peacefully." I smile at her, trying to ease some of the tension that's been clinging to her all day. "Do you have a moment for me?"

Suddenly, she stops and lifts her gaze; our eyes meet.

"No one will hear anything from me, if that's what you're worried about."

"That's the last thing I'm worried about." She would never hurt me. "But there's something else I'm far more concerned about."

Her breathing quickens. "Unfortunately, I don't have time."

I'm not letting her brush me off that easily. "Your shift doesn't start for another thirty minutes."

Nibbling on her lower lip, she looks at me. "There's a patient I need to see before…"

"Fine, then we'll talk later." Whenever that may be, but it has to be today. The clock is ticking, the danger is getting closer. "When's your lunch break?"

She shrugs. "I really can't say—might have to work straight through."

That was clear enough. She doesn't want to talk to me. A wave of resistance rises in me. "Fine, then suggest a time and I'll make myself available. What works for you?"

Suddenly, the movement of her chest stops, as if she's holding her breath. "I…"

It's unmistakable that she feels cornered by me, yet I take another step toward her, getting so close I can smell the scent of her hair. Gently, I touch her upper arms.

"I know you're scared," I say softly, because that very emotion now dominates her expression. I deliberately choose the exact words she used in the elevator a few days ago. The words that stirred something in me I had thought impossible until then.

Her lips tremble. "You don't know anything."

I lean in toward her, my cheek brushing against hers. "You're the most generous person I know. You're there for everyone, you give your love and warmth with both hands." And she keeps nothing for herself.

She exhales in short bursts.

"You always want everyone around you to be happy, but what about your own happiness?" Admittedly, it's a shot in the dark, but it might be true. The way she lets her boss walk all over her. The way she turns the other cheek even after taking a hit. How she sacrifices herself for her patients, even in her free time.

Who's there for her? Who holds her when she falters, who catches her when she falls?

Me, my heart whispers, and in that moment I know this is about so much more than just finding out why she reacted so strangely yesterday.

It's about her and me. It's about how she makes me feel like I can heal, and how I only want to do that with her.

I pull back a little, looking at her intently. "Have dinner with me tonight. Please, Autumn."

Her eyelids flutter, and suddenly a longing sparkles in the green of her eyes. "That's not a good idea."

"Why not?" I'd love to stroke her cheek, but she's already recoiled sharply from that more than once. So I settle for letting my thumbs glide over her upper arms.

"Where is this supposed to lead?"

We'll find out—have to find out. "There's a good chance I'll leave the city tomorrow," I reply. "Do you really want us to part like this?" With all the unspoken questions between us. With all the tangled feelings, with everything that could have been?

If she doesn't want me, she should say so. But she doesn't. Instead, despair dominates her expression as she keeps looking at me.

"No, I don't want that." Her voice is so quiet I can barely hear it.

Hope stirs inside me. "Let's meet at seven at the harbor. Berth 5, Pier 3," I say quickly. "Please."

A hesitant smile flickers across her face, just for a split second, but it's there. Whatever it means, it could be something good. "Okay."

Rarely in my life have I been so happy about an "okay." In my euphoria, I press a kiss to the back of her hand.

She doesn't pull her hand away, and once again I feel that there's something between us—something I didn't imagine. Whatever's holding her back, tonight I have to find a way to convince her to give what we have a chance. Because if she doesn't, there won't be any more chances.

Chapter Twenty-Nine

AUTUMN

On one of the boats gently rocking in the waters of Halifax Harbor, Tay is waiting for me—disguised as David, as always. He waves at me, a soft smile playing on his lips. The last rays of the setting sun reflect on the water, bathing the world in a warm light.

Coming here was a mistake. I should've stayed home, buried myself in my books, and kept working on the concept for my own clinic. Because the man I'm running toward now is Tay Lawson. He lives in a world ruled by beauty. Just the thought that he could love me is completely insane!

I know that, and I also know I need to guard my heart —but I agreed to this meeting anyway. There was something in his eyes that made me forget all my resolutions. It mattered so much to him. *I* mattered so much to him—he actually fought for me.

With trembling fingers, I straighten my blouse and greet him as soon as I'm within earshot.

He gestures toward the boat, which is probably just one of thousands of luxury items in his life. "Please, come aboard."

"I thought we were going out to eat." Is he planning to take me out on the water instead? Toward the sunset?

"We are." There's something mysterious in his expression. Now he reaches out his hand to me. "Let me help you."

So we're going to have dinner on the boat, just the two of us. That's… romantic. My heart skips a beat as I take his hand and step onto the swaying boat. Tay leads me toward the back.

He gives me a crooked grin and steps up to the helm. "Have you ever piloted a watercraft before?"

"I'd rather leave that to you," I reply, eyeing the many buttons on the cockpit. I'm already nervous enough—what if I bump into the dock?

Following his instructions, I untie the ropes and pull in the buoys dangling along the boat's side, while he starts the engine. In the light of the setting sun, we chug out onto the ocean, seagulls accompanying us on our way.

I glance over at David-Tay, see the contented smile on his face, smell the scent of his skin mingling with the ocean air, and wish for nothing more than to hold on to this moment, where we're just David and Autumn—not the beauty and the beast.

He turns his head toward me. "Wanna try now?"

Curious, I step closer, grab the wheel, and let him slip in behind me. His hands touch my sides as he steers the boat with me.

Every part of me longs to let go. To forget what's holding me back. To simply enjoy.

"It's wonderful, don't you think?" His voice is right by my ear.

Is he talking about steering the boat or about how comfortable I feel near him? "Yes," I say softly, because it's the right answer to both.

"I think we can drop anchor."

Automatically, I glance back—the harbor and the skyline of Halifax behind it seem far away. "Okay, how does this work?"

Together, we bring the boat to a stop and drop anchor. Then Tay leads me to the front of the boat, where a set table awaits us.

The small torches he now lights bathe the scene in warm light. A basket of bread and an elegant-looking bottle sit secured in holders beside it. I'm not used to someone taking such care of me. I blink away tears of emotion.

"Sit down." He gestures to the wooden chair with the blue-and-white striped cushion. "I hope you like this non-alcoholic Hugo. You can have wine too, but I have to steer the boat, so…"

"Gladly, thank you." My attempt to sound composed fails. I should finally ask him what he's trying to achieve with this meal, but my lips remain sealed.

He pours our drinks and clinks glasses with me. As he does, he looks so deeply into my eyes that a tingling begins to spread through my entire body—even in places where the fire destroyed so much that I thought I couldn't feel anything anymore. My heart melts, blinded by Tay's disguise, thinking David, an unremarkable man no one knows, is standing before me. My stupid, stupid heart.

"Thank you for coming," he says and takes a sip. The soft light of the setting sun reflects in his glass.

I don't know what to say. That I'm glad I came? That I don't even understand myself why I did?

At that moment, he reaches for his cap to take it off.

"No," I blurt out before I can think. "Keep it on." As long as he's David and not a Hollywood megastar, I can pretend there's still a future for us.

Yes, it's completely crazy, but I can't help it. Just thinking about how different our lives are, how little we fit together, how there's no future for us, is too painful.

He stops immediately. "Why?"

I look at him over my glass, once again searching for the right words for something that's essentially unspeakable.

"You like David more than Tay, don't you?" he asks, removing his hand from the cap.

I lift my shoulders apologetically.

Shaking his head, he studies me. "Do you even realize that you're the only person in the world who feels that way?"

With a deep breath, I set down my glass. "What are we even doing here?"

"We're continuing what you so abruptly ended in the storage room," he replies. "Why did you run off?"

"You're Tay Lawson." And with that, everything is basically said. "You're a star, you're on the covers of glossy magazines, you're every woman's dream."

A crease forms between his brows, as if he doesn't understand what I'm getting at. "So you are mad that I kept it from you."

"It's… well…" My God, now I'm stammering too. Why don't I just say it, damn it?

"Okay, cards on the table." His expression grows more intense. "Yesterday in the storage room, you said you didn't want it to end, and I thought you had feelings for me."

I do—far too many, in fact, and I'm sure he can see exactly that in my eyes now.

"No, Autumn, that's not how this works. You can't go silent now—I want you to say it." He takes my hands. "Tell me you don't feel anything for me. Tell me to leave. Tell me I'm the last thing you need in your life—and I'll go."

He is. He's the last thing I need in my life—but at the same time, it feels like he's also the first. My God, why is this so hard?

For a while, we just look at each other. His eyes reflect a flood of emotions, but most of all, that same unshakable determination I saw this morning.

"So I wasn't wrong." His words are nothing more than a longing whisper.

Locking my gaze with his, I shake my head.

"What are you afraid of?" His hands gently press mine, and I know it's time to be honest with him. However he reacts, he deserves to know the truth. It'll hurt when he turns his back on me afterward, but he won't understand any other way.

"I..." I reply, my voice thick. "There's so much you don't know about me."

His expression turns understanding. "Tell me about it."

If I do, everything will be over. It will be anyway—I should just spit out the words—yet I can't bring myself to do it.

"Should I start?" He lets go of one hand and reaches for his glass.

"You have secrets?" He hid even more from me than just his true identity? "Big secrets?"

He nods absentmindedly, the soft lapping of the waves against the bow filling the silence between us.

"What kind?" I ask, knowing full well it wasn't fair.

Yesterday, I promised him I'd answer his questions if he took off his cap. He did, and I broke my promise. That wasn't okay, and I can't let it happen again today.

If he answers my question now, I'll have to do it too. It will hurt more than almost anything before. It will be the end. The last hope for a miracle in my heart will burn out.

Still, I owe him that much.

Chapter Thirty

TAY

The sun has already sunk into the sea; only the light of the torches on the table illuminates Autumn's face, which is filled with both fear and hope.

She has just wanted to know what secrets I have managed to hide from the world so far.

"Where I come from, for example," I reply. She doesn't ask further, seems hesitant, so I tell her about my childhood in Montana. About what my father and brother did to me, how small it made me feel, and how I started to protect myself from all of it.

I tell her more than I've ever told anyone before. Not even Chloe knows these details. She would've definitely used it against me one day, but Autumn wouldn't. She's different, with her I'm safe.

"So that's where your supposedly cold heart comes from." Tears shimmer in her eyes. "That's awful."

"As soon as I turned eighteen, I ran away without saying goodbye." A shiver runs down my spine when I think back. "I made my way to Los Angeles, left everything behind, and haven't had any contact with my family since."

She shakes her head. "You don't know how they're doing? If they're in trouble? If they miss you? If they regret what happened?"

"No." And I don't want to know either. I take a sip of my drink. "I don't even know if they're still alive."

"Wow, that's… intense. I thought your parents died young and you grew up in an orphanage."

"That's what I made everyone believe." My gaze drifts briefly past Autumn's shoulder to the horizon, where the distant lights of the coast shine.

Clearly struggling to keep her composure, Autumn tugs at her bangs. "How is that possible?"

Carefully, I set the glass down on the table. "A new name, a non-disclosure agreement with exorbitant penalties that Chloe forced on my parents and brother without much questioning, and a story that sounds far better than the truth."

"A story the press is happy to believe," Autumn says absentmindedly. "So that's how this works."

"You give them something to work with. Something they can sink their teeth into. And they won't ask any more questions." All they want is to sell their rags, and nothing sells better than the stories people want to read. "Over the course of my life, I've learned one thing: if you want to win, you have to strike first, stay in control, be strong."

That's how our world works. Only with Autumn, it's different. She would never hurt anyone on purpose. She's not part of this sensationalist, superficial world.

"That's no life," Autumn says now, reaching for my hand, unaware that this is far from everything.

"Sometimes they suspect something or just piece

together rumors." I hear the bitterness in my voice. "Some of them are even true, but officially they'll always remain baseless accusations."

"Which ones?" There's nothing but genuine curiosity in Autumn's expression, yet I hesitate to tell her this dirty truth as well.

But if this thing between us is going to have a chance, I have no other choice. I've been lying to her for days, while she's been giving me too much and holding nothing back.

I take a deep breath, salty sea air filling my lungs. "The speculations about how I made my career, for example."

What I was willing to give for my big dream. They've been circulating for years, flaring up again and again whenever there's no other sensation for the press to report. Autumn surely knows what I'm talking about, yet I take her with me into the memory I'm now sinking into.

The blonde's smile is honey-sweet. She's into the muscle-bound man in front of her. The one with the roguish grin, the chiseled jaw, the out-of-bed hairstyle. The one who radiates coolness down to the last strand of hair, the one bursting with confidence.

Everyone loves him. He's what everyone wants.

And I'm glad, because as long as they only want what they see, I'm safe.

Her lips curl. "Your last movie was amazing."

"Thanks." I lift the corners of my mouth out of habit.

She leans forward, showing off her cleavage. "My daughter's room is plastered with posters of you."

Just like the bedrooms of half of America's teenagers. They idolize me, think they know me.

They don't know shit. They only see what I show them, and I'm giving the blonde what she wants now. Not just because that's how the business works, but because the rest is none of her damn business.

I lean against the bar. "Would she like an autograph?"

"She already has one. But I want something." Her fingers trail across the counter. "You know, I have this idea for a movie, and you'd be perfect for it."

"Really?" I don't let on how desperately I need a new role, how badly I want to be in front of the camera, to be someone else.

"Yes, it's about a young woman who inherits a run-down bakery in Brooklyn and meets a grumpy neighbour there." Her eyes sparkle.

How original. I keep my sunny smile in place.

"The two of them renovate the bakery together, and there are all sorts of funny situations, and of course, there's some romantic tension," she chatters on cheerfully, without breaking eye contact.

Disappointment washes over me. This role isn't what I'm looking for. It won't give me what I so desperately need, and yet I know that doesn't matter. All that matters is that this woman is married to a well-known producer. She wants me, so I have to want her too. That's just how things work behind Hollywood's façades if you want to make it.

"That sounds fantastic." I nod appreciatively.

Her fingers drift further across the counter toward me. "You'd be perfect for the role." She lowers her eyelids, only to look at me intensely a moment later. "But I'm still not sure—maybe Scott Pears would be a better fit. My husband leaves the decision up to me, you know?" Her fingers inch closer to mine, her hand rests on top of mine, then trails up my forearm. "You'd have to give me a few good reasons if you really want the part."

I take in her hungry gaze, feel her fingernails gently scraping across my skin.

She's beautiful. Long blonde curls, blue eyes, high cheekbones, full lips. Silicone breasts, wasp waist.

"So that's how it is," I say, while weighing whether this offer is worth it. Of course, I already suspect how this will end. The way it always does. You scratch my back, I scratch yours. And if I ever want to land truly great roles, I'll need more than just this job—I'll need a network I can rely on.

She raises her eyebrows, her fingers tapping against my skin. "The offer is only valid today."

And to turn it down would be the dumbest thing I could possibly do.

Once again, I study her.

I could do worse. Much worse. Besides, it's just sex—nothing more, nothing less. A few pleasurable hours without any useless feelings to complicate things unnecessarily.

"Do you have the contract with you?" I ask, because I'm not about to let her take advantage of me. This is a deal between equals.

A pleased smile spreads across her face. "I like you." She quickly pulls a few stapled pages from her bag and hands them to me.

"In duplicate, even," I note as I take the pages from her. She's thought of everything.

I skim through the contract. Filming starts early next year, half a million in pay.

Half a million and the chance to further establish myself as an actor. For a few measly minutes with an exceptionally beautiful woman.

She pulls out a pen and hands it to me. I sign both copies and slide the contracts back to her across the counter.

Her expression is now content and full of anticipation as she signs the papers as well and hands me back a copy. Then she slides off her barstool and adjusts her miniskirt. "Shall we?"

I offer her my hand. "We shall."

That's me. That's Tay Lawson, the famous actor. That's what I did to survive.

"Wow, that's… intense." Deep concern shows on Autumn's face as a sea breeze blows a strand of hair across it.

"That's Hollywood. If you want to make it, you have to be willing to give everything." I shrug.

"Acting must mean an incredible amount to you." Absentmindedly, she smooths her hair.

I catch her gaze, the boat swaying gently back and forth. "It keeps me alive," I reply, thinking of the role of Dr. Cross, which I still haven't heard back about.

"What do you mean?" A small crease forms between her brows.

I tell her what acting does to me. How slipping into roles allows me to live out all the emotions I lock away in my real life. With every word, the crease on her forehead smooths a little more.

"I understand," she whispers afterward, and I'm sure she does. "Your job gives you so much, but in return you have to endure an incredible amount. How do you manage not to let it get to you?"

That's the advantage of a scarred heart—it's used to the fight. "Life gave me thick skin," I reply, and in her eyes I see that she understands what I mean.

"I'm sorry." She lowers her eyelids and reaches for her glass.

My thumb brushes over her fingers. "You don't have to be. My life made me strong; I learned how to protect myself."

I can't help but wonder if Autumn is built for what might come too easily to me. Whether she could endure it or if she'd break under the pressure of playing the media game.

On the other hand, they'd have no reason to go after Autumn excessively. She's a doctor from Halifax with a heart so big that everyone can't help but love her. Everything they'd find would be beautiful and true. They wouldn't be able to tarnish her purity, and would quickly lose interest in her.

A single tear rolls down her cheek. "So you're kind of like Superman. Invulnerable."

"Yes, to the world I am, and I have to be," I say, because that's something that will never change.

She lifts her eyelids, her expression infinitely sad. "But I'm not Lois Lane."

"No, you're not," I confirm. "You're my kryptonite." She's what makes me feel, what makes me vulnerable, what makes me human. "And I'm addicted to everything you make me feel."

Her shoulders sag lower, she takes a shaky breath, and I brace myself to ask her the all-important question. The question that could either end whatever this is between us—or truly begin it.

I look at her intently. "So tell me, Autumn, do you still think I'm the last thing you need in your life?"

Chapter Thirty-One

AUTUMN

I wish the answer to Tay's question were no, but deep down I know it's still yes.

His expression is full of longing, and mine probably looks the same. Slowly, I nod, watching as more pain fills his eyes with each passing second.

"I wish it were different," I say, and if there were anything I could do to change it, I'd do it in a heartbeat.

He opens his mouth, about to respond, but I raise my hands to stop him. My breathing quickens, my heart pounds like crazy. I look out at the sea, where the moonlight dances silver across the waves—I don't want to see his face the moment everything ends.

With shaky hands, I reach for my blouse and undo the top button. My chest heaves with every breath so violently that I can barely catch the next one.

"What…," he whispers soundlessly.

I look down, see my fingers undoing the next button, see the candlelight illuminating the edges of my scars.

The image blurs before my eyes, my lips tremble, my heart shatters into a thousand pieces.

Then I undo another button. And another. I keep working my way downward, tears streaming down my cheeks and mixing with the salty moisture of the wind on my lips.

Tay remains silent as I reveal more and more of the monster that I am.

Finally, I slip off the blouse, push my bangs aside with one hand, and lift my hair with the other.

Staring at the flickering candlelight, my chest trembling, I wait for Tay's reaction, but he says nothing.

I don't dare look at him. "When I was sixteen, I had a car accident with my dad," I begin to say. "He died, and I became… this." A sob escapes my lips, even though this is only the beginning.

His seat cushion rustles, the wooden deck of the boat creaks. Suddenly, he's beside me, on his knees, looking up at me. His hands rest on my thigh, his thumb gently gliding over my pants. He doesn't say a word, and I understand why.

Automatically, I think of all the men who weren't famous actors and still couldn't handle my scars. Of all those who were disgusted by me, of all those who felt ashamed to have me by their side.

His hand moves higher. I can barely stand it, want to push it away, but I'm frozen. He reaches the waistband of my pants, feels his way up to my stomach. To the place so scarred I can't feel anything anymore. I watch, see how he touches me, how he gently strokes the scars as if they weren't repulsive, but beautiful.

I lift my eyelids. There's no disgust, no shame. There's wistfulness, and there's pain.

Earlier, I would have rather seen David, but now I want Tay. Just as he is, that's how I want to see him. With all his outward beauty, which in the last few minutes has taken on a different meaning.

I reach for his cap, gently pull it off his head, and take off his glasses.

His fingers keep exploring, touching the edges of the scars that snake across my chest, reaching a spot where my nerves weren't destroyed.

A sharp tingling rushes through me. "I'm a monster," I whisper, preparing to show him the full extent of what I am.

"We both have our scars," he whispers into the silence between us. "You wear yours on your skin, I carry mine in my heart."

As crazy as it is, he's right. The way I got to know him—so distant, like he didn't even have a heart. But it's there, and it's deeply wounded. We both carry the scars of our past. We're both broken, just in completely different ways.

I turn more toward him, reach out, touch his fake beard, and pull it off. "Just because we're broken in different places doesn't mean we can be whole together."

"Maybe it means exactly that," he replies. "You've made a few of my scars disappear. Thanks to you, my heart can at least beat properly for a few moments again."

"My scars will stay." That's how it is, and it hurts like hell. No matter what he does, he can't heal me.

He shakes his head. "You're the most beautiful person I've ever met in my whole life. The scars don't change that," he says, and I want to believe him.

I want to believe that I'm beautiful and lovable, even now, sitting half-naked beside him. I want to be with him, just for a moment, and savor how it feels.

Slowly, I slide off my chair, sink to my knees beside him, and take his face in my hands.

Tay Lawson, the most attractive man in the world, looks at me with nothing but love in his eyes. Now he leans in, our noses touch.

A pleasant shiver runs down my spine, I feel his breath on my lips, his warmth on my skin, intoxicated by his closeness, by his words, by this moment in which we kneel before each other exactly as we are.

"Autumn?" His lips brush against mine.

"Mhm." Heat rises inside me.

"I don't want to be the last thing you need in your life." He looks at me intently.

For so many years, I was certain I would never hear words like that from a man. Hearing them now—of all people—from Tay Lawson shakes my world. Everything I ever believed in, everything I was supposed to be afraid of, all of it loses its meaning. There's only Tay and me and this glow in my heart that feels like miracles might be possible again.

I know I shouldn't do it. I know I should keep going, show him everything, explain why this between us could never work.

Instead, I tilt my head slightly to the side, close my eyes, and lean in until I feel the warmth of his lips on mine. One last shaky breath, then I let myself fall completely.

We kiss each other, as gently as if this moment were too fragile, as if we were both too fragile. With every passing second, I sink deeper into our kiss, forget the world around me, let this incredible feeling of happiness flood over me and take hold.

We kiss, hold each other, lose ourselves in the vastness of

the ocean, and when we part what feels like a thousand little eternities later, tears are shining in his eyes.

He blinks, a tear slips from the corner of his eye. I catch it, catch a part of Tay he's learned to hide from the world. A part that still lives inside him, and the fact that he lets me see it tells me more than a thousand words ever could.

I'm sinking into a whirlpool of emotions and only know one thing: no matter how broken we are, together we are truly whole.

Chapter Thirty-Two

TAY

The scent of Autumn's skin still lingers with me. Her words, the way she looked at me. How she held me, how she kissed me.

She's with me, even though we said goodbye half an hour ago.

Disguised as David, I walk toward the entrance of Halifax Harbor Hospital, keeping an eye out for journalists, but I don't see any. They've been looking for me for two days now; it won't be long before they find me.

How would they react if they knew about Autumn's scars? What would Autumn do if the thing she's fought so hard to hide from those around her suddenly became known to the whole world?

I saw it in her expression when she took off her blouse. The fear, the panic, the shame.

But I also know how strong she is. I've seen her stand up for others—just not for herself.

Thoughtfully, I slip through the entrance and take the elevator to the seventh floor. Even though Kayla is probably already asleep, I need to be with her now, to sort out my thoughts and feelings. Because whatever is going on between Autumn and me is too big and too beautiful not to fight for.

A little later, I quietly open the door to Kayla's room. The lamp on the nightstand bathes the room in a soft twilight, yet I immediately recognize the female figure sitting on a chair beside the bed.

"Chloe." I close the door behind me.

She looks up, her expression cold. "Nice to see you too."

Everything inside me tenses. "Why are you here?" I glance at Kayla's bed, wanting nothing more than to kiss my deeply sleeping daughter on the forehead, but I don't.

"The press already knows where you are, so I figured I might as well come."

"So far, they only had suspicions, they just knew I had been here, not that I still am." Chloe shouldn't have come, that was a mistake. "Now that you're here too, and without any disguise, you're giving them everything they need to know." How could she be so careless?

"If you hadn't refused to leave Halifax, I wouldn't be here. It's that simple. So if they find us, it's entirely your fault." She rubs her neck.

There's no way I'm letting her think her words affect me, so I stare her down. "No one invited you."

She nods toward the sleeping Kayla. She had just been cold toward me, but now warmth flickers in her eyes. "I wanted to see my daughter. My God, do you even know how hard it was for me not to be with her?"

"She's making good progre…"

"Kayla said you're having dinner with her doctor," she cuts me off. "She's supposed to be suuuper sweet."

Is she jealous? "We had a lot to discuss." It's harder than

usual to play the unfeeling block of ice, and I'm not even sure I'm pulling it off. Still, I do my best not to give Chloe any opening.

She looks tired now, maybe she's in pain. "On a romantic boat ride?"

My gaze shifts to Kayla. She knew what I was planning—of course she told her mom.

Whatever, I shouldn't react to that. I look at her firmly. "What do you want, Chloe?"

She gets up from her chair, takes a bottle of headache pills and some papers out of her briefcase—hopefully the divorce papers. With the documents in hand, she walks over to me.

Completely unfazed, she hands me the papers. "You got the part. Congratulations."

I got the part?

Oh, thank God!

A wave of relief washes over me. Soon I'll be back in front of the camera, doing what means the world to me. Soon everything will be back to normal.

I take the papers and skim the first page.

"Sign on pages three, seven, and fifteen. I've checked the contract, of course—it's all clean." Chloe unscrews the pill bottle and takes a tablet. "Come on, so I can leave. Apparently, I'm unnecessary anyway."

Once again, that intense jealousy creeps into her tone. Just a few days ago, I would have ignored it, but today I signal for her to follow me into the adjoining bathroom. Even though Kayla is asleep, we shouldn't be discussing this here.

"You wanted the divorce, Chloe. You wanted to end our marriage, remember?" I whisper, closing the door behind me.

Not that it hurt me. It was just unfortunate that it happened during one of the darkest moments of my career.

Her expression turns sad now. “That’s not what I wanted.”

Excuse me? I raise my eyebrows, bracing myself for the fight that’s sure to follow.

“I just wanted you to love me. To show me that our marriage meant something to you, that you’d fight for it, that you’d fight for me,” she continues, her voice choked with emotion.

“Why would I have done that?” I shake my head and lean against the tiled wall. “What we had had nothing to do with love.”

Not in the slightest, and even less than I realized until recently. What I feel for Autumn has to do with love. With emotions I’ve never had for a woman before. Chloe and I were nothing more than business partners.

“I married you after you got pregnant because you wanted to present a picture-perfect family to the press,” I say.

It was a tactical move, without any deeper meaning, and she knows that just as well as I do. Still, she now crosses her arms over her chest, trembling.

“All this time I hoped you might learn to love me.” She turns her back to me. “That you’d open up eventually.”

Could that be true? She was always just as focused on my career as I was—real feelings were never part of it, at least not between the two of us.

I look in the mirror and see the reflection of her sad face. Clinging to the sink like a bundle of misery, and I feel sorry for her.

I’m sorry that I don’t love her. That she apparently

hoped for something from me for years, even though I never gave her a single reason to.

Once again I realize that while my rules may not apply to Autumn, they still apply to the rest of the world. Letting others get close makes you vulnerable; if you love, you lose.

Chloe loved me—and she lost.

"I'm sorry," I say quietly. "I didn't want it to end like this."

With a surprised expression, she lifts her eyelids, our eyes meet in the mirror. "It doesn't have to end, Tay. We still can…"

I shake my head, which silences her. What we had isn't just over—it never existed. I don't want to hurt her, so I don't say it out loud, just apologize again without specifying what for, and feel like an asshole even though I never led her on.

She comes toward me, reaching for my arms. "I love you. Still."

"It's over, Chloe. You and me, we don't belong together." I shake her off, seeing in her face how much my words hurt her.

"I understand." With a sharp movement, she brushes her hair back. "Sign the contract," she asks me, clearly trying to keep her composure, and pulls a pen from the pocket of her blazer.

I take it from her and open the contract.

So many times in the past few weeks I've feared that my career might be over. Today, with the contract in front of me, I feel strong again for the first time.

Still, I hesitate. What if Autumn can't manage to stand by my side? What if I lose her by signing this contract?

"Pages three, seven, and fifteen." Chloe sounds impatient as I imagine what would happen if I didn't sign.

I would lose everything I've fought for my entire life. For a woman I've only known for a few days.

That would be completely insane.

"What are you waiting for?" she asks. Chloe steps up beside me with a stern expression. "I already agreed by email, your signature is just a formality."

Of course, she's done it like this many times before. And I want this role, I need it. So I sign the contract where indicated and hand it back to Chloe.

"From now on, I'll take care of Kayla." She gives a tired smile, clutching the papers to her chest as if they're holding her together. "It suits you just fine, doesn't it?"

Absolutely not! I'm not walking out that door like I don't care about my daughter.

"Don't worry." She bravely pulls the corners of her mouth up. "I'll be nice to your new flame."

Can she? After what she just revealed to me? As hurt as she is? Doubtfully, I follow her back into the hospital room, where she stows the contract in her briefcase and grabs her wallet.

"I'm getting coffee now. When I come back, you'll be gone." Her tone is so icy, I can hardly wait to not be near her anymore. Still, I can't let her leave—not like this.

"You're only leaving this room as Mary." There's no way she should still be walking around here as Chloe.

With a sigh, she pulls the blonde wig with the thick bangs, the wig cap, and the fake beauty mark from her bag and transforms from Chloe into Mary. Lastly, she wipes off the bright red lipstick that had become her trademark over the past years.

"Tomorrow morning we'll finally tell Kayla the truth, end the hiding from the journalists, release a press statement about our separation, and then you'll leave." The words leave her mouth like tiny poison darts.

I glance briefly at my sleeping daughter. Yes, we do need to tell Kayla at last, but that's the only thing we agree on. Leaving Kayla here in Halifax with Chloe is not an option. I want to be there for her, there's so much I've missed that needs to be made up for.

"I'm not going anywhere without my daughter," I reply.

A snort escapes her lips. "And suddenly you can love everyone—just not me," she says, shaking her head and stepping out into the hallway.

Chapter Thirty-Three

AUTUMN

Happiness and confusion, joy and longing—that's what I've been feeling since I said goodbye to Tay at the harbor last night. But now, as I'm setting up the easels for her exhibition at the community center with my mom, there's something else: worry.

I shouldn't have shown Tay just part of my scars—I should've shown him all of them. And then I should've told him what they mean. Instead, I gave in to my feelings, enjoyed the evening, and lost myself in a dream with him that we can't live.

"And the big one goes back there, next to the green plant." Mom's hair is sticking out wildly, her cheeks are flushed. She looks so happy you'd think she was healthy—but that stability is as fragile as glass, and I'm the one holding the hammer.

My God, I shouldn't have gone to that dinner at all!

Feeling agitated, I grab an easel. "On my way."

She follows me and helps position the wooden frame.

Then she taps her chin with her index finger. "I don't know, the light isn't good here. Let's try over there."

As I place the easel on the other side of the houseplant, I sink back into my thoughts.

Floating with Tay yesterday, imagining that this thing between us could become real, felt incredible. I just wanted to kiss and hug him, to feel boundless for a moment. To enjoy what I've longed for my whole life. To allow myself to dream of something that's out of reach.

"What do you think, sweetheart?"

Maybe there is a way after all. I'd have to manage to distract the press from what they must never find out. Just like Tay said yesterday. If it's only about giving the journalists a good story so they stop digging, then maybe we can pull it off.

"Hey." Mom nudges me gently. "What's going on with you today?"

I blink. "Hm?"

Mom points to an easel that wasn't there earlier. "What do you think of this spot?"

"Which painting do you want to display here?" I ask, trying to stop the carousel of thoughts that hasn't let go of me since last night, at least for a few minutes.

"Spring Garden." A wistful expression flashes across her face. It was the first painting she created after Dad's accident. It took her five years to pick up a brush again. Five years in which I held her up while losing all footing myself. "It starts things off, as a tribute to your dad."

I didn't know she had dedicated it to him. Does it hurt her to exhibit it now and relive the memory? "So, what happens next?" I ask, because this topic is too difficult for both of us.

Mom clears her throat. "Well, this is the start of the

exhibition. It begins in spring and continues into summer." Her hand traces an arc over the still-empty easels in front of the white walls of the community hall. "Over here will be the autumn section, with the cornflower paintings, the pumpkins, and the leaf studies."

"That's going to be great." I force myself to smile at her.

"What's wrong?" she asks, studying me closely. "You seem so… distracted today."

I wave it off automatically. "Everything's fine."

Now she smirks. "You're in love."

That's putting it mildly. But should I even talk to her about it? Won't it remind Mom that she once lost the love of her life? Could it trigger a relapse?

I search her face for answers to the question of whether she's stable enough to handle this news. All I see is openness and joy.

"You can go ahead and admit it," she says, stroking my arm. "It's obvious anyway."

"Maybe there's someone," I say. Worry hits me the second I finish the sentence, but it seems unfounded.

"That's wonderful." She pulls me into her arms. "I'm happy for you."

I exhale in relief. "It's complicated." Only if I manage to lie to the press as well as Tay does, is there a small spark of hope that we can actually be together.

"Love always finds a way." Though I listen closely, I don't detect any sadness in her words.

"Hopefully." I study her, confused.

I never would have thought she'd take it so positively. Her words remind me of Tay, of the fierce way he's protected himself for years. And of Kayla, who protects her parents far too much, which does her no good at all.

The little girl I have so much in common with.

Mom gently runs her hand along my arm, and there's nothing to indicate that she's actually ill. Could she be stronger than I imagine?

And if that's the case, wouldn't it be time for me to start thinking more about myself, to be there more for myself, to fight for my own happiness instead of only for others'?

There's only one way to find out. I should try to bring up at least one thing that until now would have been unthinkable.

"He's not from Halifax, Mom. It's possible that I…" Mid-sentence, my courage fails me. It feels far too selfish to leave her here alone in Canada.

She pushes me away, looks deep into my eyes. "For some of us, there's only one person in this world," she says in a choked voice, and I'm sure she's thinking of the one great love of her life. "If he's that man for you, nothing and no one should stop you. Hold on to him."

That's what I want. I want to hold on to him, to be with him, to be happy together. "I'd be several hours of flight away from you."

She brushes a strand of hair from my face. "Don't you think it's time you started living your own life?" Instead of mine, hangs unspoken between her words.

I never saw it that way before. Being there for Mom was always a given. Was I there for her too much? Did I protect her too much? More than was even necessary?

I don't know.

"I just want you to be okay." I want both of us to be okay—that's what I wish for.

"I am, sweetheart, don't worry," she replies lovingly. She's told me that so many times before, and I've always dismissed it as a well-meaning lie without thinking.

Today, for the first time since Dad's accident, I wonder

if it might actually be true. She just found out I might be leaving Halifax—and it didn't shake her.

Maybe she really is doing better than I thought. Or maybe it's just the upcoming exhibition giving her a temporary high.

"Okay, I'll think about it, thanks, Mom," I reply thoughtfully. "But now let's go get the paintings. I can't wait to see them on the easels."

Chapter Thirty-Four

TAY

I didn't get any sleep last night. As a result, my body feels heavy as I walk down the pediatric ward hallway.

Thanks to Autumn, my heart is beating in the right rhythm again—and now it breaks at the thought of what Chloe and I are about to do to Kayla in just a few minutes. It breaks at the thought that I hurt my wife so deeply. And it breaks when I imagine that Autumn might not be strong enough for a life by my side.

I'd love to run away from all of this, but it's time to at least make one of my mistakes right. It will hurt Kayla, but letting her live with this lie, in a home full of arguments and coldness, would hurt her just as much. So I enter the hospital room, where my daughter and the woman I could never love are sitting at the visitor table, drawing.

"There you are," Chloe says with a forced smile. She's wearing the wig, so she no longer walks around visibly as Tay Lawson's wife and agent. Let's just hope no one at the clinic recognized her last night or that the press already found out where we are through other means.

Who knows how close they already are. One small mistake and…

"Daddy!" Kayla's eyes light up in a way that makes it even harder for me to breathe. "We can finally get ice cream today. Autumn's definitely coming too, it's going to be great, just like I drew it. Only Nanny Mina's missing. Can she come too?"

I sit down next to her at the table, not knowing how to tell her that it's not going to happen. Especially not now, when we have to be even more cautious around the journalists than usual. My daughter studies me, and I wonder if she can see the pain inside me.

With arms crossed, Chloe steps beside me. "Listen, sweetheart, your daddy wants to tell you something."

I shoot her a reproachful look. "*We* want to tell you something," I correct her. "Your mom and I, together."

Frowning, Kayla looks back and forth between Chloe and me. "So I'm not getting an aquarium after all?"

My chest tightens, a faint buzzing takes hold of me. I can't do this, I can't tell my daughter that our family is falling apart. That the life she's known until now is over for good.

Chloe nudges me.

I gasp for air.

Kayla lowers her gaze and fiddles with her drawing. "It's okay, the aquarium was dumb anyway."

A heavy sigh escapes Chloe's mouth, the fringe of her fake bangs lifts. "You've probably noticed that Daddy and I haven't talked much lately, maybe you even heard us argue."

I glance briefly at Chloe; her expression is accusatory.

"Mhm," Kayla says without looking at us.

I take my little one's hand. "Fighting is dumb, we don't want to fight, but it just happens, and way too often."

"Your dad doesn't love your mom anymore," I suddenly hear Chloe say.

Up until that moment, I had felt guilty toward her, but now I despise her for her insensitive words.

She wanted the divorce first, for god's sake. And now she's making it look like I'm the only villain in this room.

"Mhm," comes again from Kayla, whose fingers are now curling into a fist.

I can practically see her little heart breaking into a thousand pieces, want to stop it, protect her from it, but I don't know how.

"Your dad doesn't want to be married to your mom anymore." Chloe's tone carries her deep hurt. "We're getting a divorce, Kayla."

Everything inside me is tense, the hospital room starts to spin. My pulse quickens, the buzzing in my head grows louder.

Panic rolls in like a ten-meter wave, and I know it won't be long before it swallows me whole.

"I figured as much," Kayla says tonelessly, her gaze fixed on the window.

"We're really sorry." I squeeze her hand. "This can't be easy for you, but both of us, Mom and I, will always be here for you."

"Yes, we will," my soon-to-be-ex-wife agrees, and I hear the lie in her words. She grabs her briefcase and turns to leave. "Then I'll take care of the divorce papers and prepare the press release."

What the hell is wrong with her? I get that she's hurt, but how can she not care about our daughter at all?

"Have fun cleaning up the pieces," she mutters as she passes me, then all I hear are her footsteps fading away.

The door slams shut.

I hardly dare to look at Kayla. "What do you think about all this?" I ask her.

Out of the corner of my eye, I see her shrug. "Will I still get my aquarium?"

I try to figure out if she really doesn't care or if she's just pretending. "Of course."

"Okay," she says, then sits up straighter in her chair. "I don't want you and Mom to keep fighting either."

So she did notice after all? "I'm so sorry," I say, letting her see all the love I carry for her inside me.

She lowers her eyelids again, I slide over to her and hold her tightly. For the first time in her life, I embrace her lovingly and protectively, and I never want to let her go again.

"That's silly, Daddy." Clearly, my daughter is trying to comfort me in the one way she thinks is right for me.

She's doing it for my sake – and that's wrong.

Is it the careless way I've treated her all her life that has shaped her into this little person who overthinks everything? I shift slightly away from her to look at her.

"It's great that you want to be there for me, but right now I'm here for you. Is there something you want to talk about?" I ask, and she shakes her head in response.

"No, it's okay," she replies compliantly.

I automatically think of Autumn, recognizing her in my daughter's behavior. She, too, should stand up more for herself, regardless of how much I wish we could just be together—she, Kayla, and I—and that nothing would stop us from being happy together.

That's what I want, and deep down I feel that I must not give up what's between us.

Autumn is stronger than she thinks. If she could learn to embrace her scars, then nothing and no one in the world could hurt her. If she could manage to fight for her own happiness, it would change her entire life—and mine along with it.

Chapter Thirty-Five

AUTUMN

I enter the Halifax Harbor Hospital and slip the textbook on hospital law back into my bag. It helped distract me on the bus ride here, but now my nerves are kicking in. I'm about to see Tay again—for the first time since I said goodbye to him at the harbor.

I adjust my hair. My shift starts in thirty minutes, but I need to talk to Tay first.

If he assures me that the press will believe the story I'm going to tell—that I suffer from a severe light allergy and therefore have to cover my skin even under artificial light—then we might have a chance.

Mom has been insisting for months that she's managing fine without me, and since I moved out, things have actually been going much better than I expected. Mom could handle it if I went to Los Angeles with Tay.

Only the press is a problem—if they don't believe my story and start digging. I know it's nothing more than a straw I'm desperately clinging to, but it's all I've got.

In front of the elevators, I run into Olive, who's once again living up to her nickname, Glamour Lady.

"Aha," she comments with a smirk, tossing back her perfectly blow-dried hair. "Where were you so late last night?"

I shrug, and in my mind I see Tay and me on the boat. The way he looked at me—without disgust, without fear. The way we kissed. "Out and about," I reply vaguely.

Her dark eyes widen. "Oh really, 'out and about' is what we're calling it these days?" She nudges me playfully. "Your patient's dad?"

With a sigh, I lean against the wall next to the elevator. Apparently, nothing stays secret in our apartment. "Possibly."

Olive steps closer without touching the wall. "Tell me everything."

I'd love to, but it's still too new and there are too many unanswered questions. "I think he might be the one. You know…"

A mix of astonishment and disbelief dominates Olive's expression. "That's great," she says eventually, and I can't shake the feeling that my happiness pains her.

"What about you? Nyla told me the other day that there's someone who…"

She hurriedly waves it off. "As much as I'd love to keep chatting, I have to go now, the patients are waiting."

Whatever is going on, it seems to make her uncomfortable, so I don't ask and instead wish her a good day before taking the elevator to the seventh floor.

With a fluttering in my stomach, I reach Kayla's room a short while later. Behind this door, Tay is waiting for me, and today will be different from all the other times I've entered this room.

Warmer.

More beautiful.

More hopeful.

I take a deep breath and step inside, but to my surprise, no one takes notice of me.

Tay, disguised as David, is sitting at his daughter's bedside, studying her with concern. "But you didn't eat anything bad, did you?"

Kayla shakes her head. "It hurts."

"Okay, I'll get Autumn right away. She'll make sure you…"

"I'm here," I say, walking over to the two of them. Kayla looks pale, as does Tay, whose hand briefly brushes my arm. "What's going on?"

Tay's gaze meets mine. "She has stomach pain. At first, she just felt a little unwell, but it seems to be getting worse."

With a hand gesture, I ask him to step aside. "Okay, Kayla, show me where it hurts." She points to her entire abdominal area, and I lift her shirt. "Would you say the pain feels more like a pinprick or like someone is pulling on your stomach?" I ask, trying to stay calm, especially as I notice how worried Tay is when he steps to the other side of the bed and fidgets with his cap. "Or does it feel like you have a knot in your stomach?"

"Don't know," the little one replies.

I ask more questions about the type and intensity of the pain and palpate her abdomen, but I can't detect anything unusual. "How long has it been hurting?"

"For about an hour."

"What did you have for lunch, tell me," I say as I begin to check her vital signs.

While she talks, I measure her pulse, blood pressure, and temperature.

Everything's within the normal range.

"And a yogurt," she finishes her report.

"Did anything taste strange?" I reach for my stethoscope to listen to her stomach sounds.

She shakes her head.

Tay looks at me pleadingly as I listen closely.

The sounds seem normal. Strange. Kayla's expression suggests moderate pain, but her body appears to be fine.

"And was there anything else today? Maybe before lunch?" I ask.

Suddenly, I see Kayla and her dad exchange glances.

"Kayla's mom was here," Tay says, while Kayla presses her lips together. "We… well, Kayla knows now…"

I signal to him that I understand, then turn to Kayla. "Everything's fine, it's just a little stomach upset," I say reassuringly. "I'll get you a hot water bottle for your belly and some tea, that should help you feel better soon."

Next to me, Tay exhales in relief, Kayla nods with a pained expression. Her glasses slip down her nose. I give her a smile, then stand up and signal Tay to follow me.

"We'll be right back," he assures his daughter and leaves the room with me. As soon as he closes the door behind him, he looks at me, filled with concern. "What's wrong with her?"

Lost in thought, I tap my chin with my index finger. "I'm not sure."

He reaches for my hand, intertwining his fingers with mine. Warmth floods the spots he touches, a gentle tingling spreads. "You suspect something and didn't want to tell Kayla?"

Unfortunately, he's right. "I haven't found a cause for Kayla's symptoms, the tests came back normal. The only thing that's different today compared to yesterday is that her parents are separating."

He furrows his brows. "You mean…?"

"It's just a thought, and I might be wrong." Kayla already suspected it, but it wouldn't be unusual if she reacted this way now.

"They don't say something hits you in the gut for nothing." There's a guilty tone in his voice. "You might be right. It started shortly after she found out."

"She might just need time to digest it," I confirm. Even if Kayla had already suspected something, suspecting something life-changing and being certain of it are two completely different things. "She needs a little time to adjust to the situation. The symptoms are mild and could disappear soon."

"I hope you're right." He moves closer to me, his fingers gently stroking mine.

As much as I'd love to enjoy his touch right now, Kayla is more important. "Go back to her and talk to her. Encourage her to tell you honestly how she's doing. I'll get the hot water bottle and the tea."

"Okay, thanks, Autumn, thanks for everything."

"My pleasure."

Every fiber of my body wants to kiss him, even if just for a moment. I can see in his eyes that he feels the same. Now he leans in and brushes a kiss on my cheek.

"Will I see you later?" he whispers in my ear.

We have to. "Yes," I whisper. "My shift ends at ten, then we can…"

"Definitely," he says before I can finish the sentence.

Definitely, the word echoes warmly inside me as he pulls away from me, and again as I watch him disappear into Kayla's room.

He's barely gone and I already miss him. Inevitably, I wonder how I would survive if I had to let him go. At the same time, I sense that my heart already knows the answer to that question.

Eight hours and many little patients later, I make my way to Kayla one last time for today.

In the hallway, I run into Dr. Parker. "How's our," she winks at me meaningfully, "very important patient?"

"She was doing better two hours ago, she even ate a little." Hopefully, her stomach pains have completely calmed down by now. "I was just about to check on her."

"Check on her or her father?" she asks with a smirk, but I don't respond, I just let my gaze tell her that her question is unnecessary. "Well then, don't let me stop you."

I say a quick goodbye. As I enter Kayla's room, I'm suddenly hit with a wave of nausea.

I've never seen the blonde woman at Tay's side before, but the way she's stroking Kayla's arm leaves only one conclusion: Chloe is here—the beautiful, elegant Chloe I've seen so many times on TV and in magazines—disguised as a blonde businesswoman.

Now she notices my presence, just like Kayla and David-Tay, who's leaning against the windowsill off to the side. Suddenly, all three of their eyes are fixed on me.

"Autumn's here," Kayla announces so cheerfully and brightly that under different circumstances I'd be happy about it.

But right now, the temperature in the room drops to freezing, thanks to the way Chloe is sizing me up.

"That is her?" A short snort escapes her mouth. She

tosses her fake mane, and the golden bracelet on her wrist jingles.

I can't help but stare at her. "Yeah... um... hi, I'm Autumn, the attending..."

"Yeah, yeah, it's fine, I know who you are," she cuts me off. "Kayla is fine."

I immediately look at Kayla, who nods in confirmation. "My tummy ache is completely gone."

"That's wonderful." I give her a warm smile. "If that changes again, you let me know right away, okay?"

"As always," the little one replies, pulling a funny face.

"Good, then that's settled." Chloe's voice slices through the budding cozy atmosphere like a samurai sword. "See you tomorrow morning."

Tay walks over to his daughter, whispers something in her ear, and kisses her cheek. While Chloe raises her eyebrows in disbelief, the sight fills me with warmth. Just over a week ago, I never would've thought I'd see the two of them together like this.

After letting go of his daughter, his gaze lands on me. Warm, longing, full of love.

I feel heat rising to my face and quickly turn away before Chloe notices. I hastily wish Kayla good night and leave the room with Tay. Only a faint light is on in the hallway, not a soul in sight.

"What did you whisper to her?" I ask.

Tay takes my hand. "Just that I'll be right back."

"I'm glad Kayla is doing better." I gently stroke his fingers.

"Hopefully it lasts." There's worry in Tay's voice. Worry and guilt.

"Did you talk to her about the separation?"

With a long breath, he leans against the wall beside me. “She assured me again that it’s okay.”

“Maybe it really had nothing to do with the separation,” I say, and his expression softens.

“Hopefully,” he says, leaning toward me.

I shouldn’t kiss him, not before he knows the whole truth, and yet our lips find each other, a pleasant shiver rushes through me.

I feel the warmth of his closeness, let myself fall, deeper and deeper, because it’s simply too beautiful not to.

“Hey,” he whispers hoarsely as we pull away from each other again.

“Hey,” I reply, so wonderfully dazed from his kiss that I wish he would kiss me for the rest of my life.

His fingers trail up my cheek to my temple, where they gently brush over the scar. “I missed you.”

We need to talk. That’s what I should say, but instead I kiss him again, with all the longing in my heart. We stand tightly entwined in the middle of the hallway, surrounded by the twilight of the night. We kiss for minutes, and nothing else matters. Just the two of us and what connects us.

“We shouldn’t stay here too long,” Tay murmurs tensely against my lips.

Something in his words alarms me. “Why not?”

He explains that his cover won’t hold much longer, partly because of Chloe’s appearance—maybe it’s already blown. Suddenly, everything I’m afraid of comes rushing back.

“If they see us together…”

He gently strokes my cheek. “No one’s here.”

No one’s here *yet.* “What do you suggest?” I automatically take a step back.

He pulls his cap lower over his face. "Inner Sambro Island, that's where our holiday house is."

Inner Sambro Island? "I thought the island was uninhabited."

"That's what most people think." He winks at me.

That sounds like the perfect place for the conversation we now need to have more urgently than ever. "Okay, you say goodbye to Kayla, I'll go change in the meantime. Let's meet at the boat."

I kiss him one last time, I can't help it, I need to taste him, feel him, have him with me. With a heavy heart, I finally release him from my embrace.

"See you soon." Warmth floods his gaze.

"See you soon," I reply, not taking my eyes off him.

He slowly lets go of my fingers, I savour our touch as long as it lasts, and when finally only our fingertips are brushing, I exhale shakily.

Chapter Thirty-Six

TAY

The night has settled over the sea like a velvet veil. Through the windows of the vacation house, the faint shimmer of moonlight filters in. The world outside feels quiet and infinite.

On the way here, Autumn was unusually serious. It wasn't until we reached the island and I took off my disguise that she could smile again. She's scared, I can feel it, but here she has nothing to be afraid of.

"We're safe here." I let the curtain fall back over the window, brush a kiss against her lips, and gesture to the sofa. "Make yourself comfortable."

While she sits down, I kneel in front of the fireplace, stack logs on top of each other, and light them. Soon the fire begins to crackle softly, casting flickering shadows on the walls and bathing Autumn's beautiful face in a warm, golden light.

"And you're sure no one can find us here? I mean, if…" Autumn trails off mid-sentence.

I sit down beside her, wrap my arm around her shoulders. She lets her head rest against my chest. "No one knows about this hideout." Only Chloe, Kayla, and I know about this house.

"Okay." A soft sigh escapes her lips. "I need to ask you something. Yesterday at dinner you said you can fool the press. Tell them a story and hide the truth that way."

I have a feeling I know what she's getting at. "I did say that, yes. But with your scars, it's too risky. It would only take a brief moment when your bangs aren't perfectly in place and they'd get suspicious…"

"And what if I had erythropoietic protoporphyria—a severe light allergy? I'd need to keep my skin covered all the time, always wear hats. There are rare forms of the disease where the skin even reacts to artificial light." She sits up, looks at me intently. "Would my secret be safe then?"

As much as I'd like to say yes, I can't. Even as I'm trying to figure out how best to tell her, I see in Autumn's face that she recognizes the thought in my eyes.

It's a moment of silence, only the soft sound of the sea and the crackling fire can be heard as the night wraps around us. Our legs gently touch.

"We can try, but there's no guarantee," I whisper tenderly. "I saw your scars too—the ones on your forehead—long before you showed me the others. You didn't even notice, did you?"

She presses her lips together, a deep sadness fills the green of her eyes. The shadows of the fireplace dance across her skin.

"You're worried that people will be disgusted by you, but does it really matter?" I ask gently, because showing her scars would be one way, even if she doesn't see it that way. "Isn't it their problem if they can't handle it?" And if she showed them to the whole world, wouldn't she even be an inspiration to all those who are ashamed of how they look?

She would be a shining example that you can overcome the blows of fate—that's something good, isn't it?

She turns her gaze away, staring silently into the fire for a while. "There's so much more behind these scars than what you've seen so far." In front of the crackling logs, her words are so quiet I can barely understand them.

I gently stroke her arm. "What do you mean?"

"Terrible truths that must never come to light." She exhales shakily, and I freeze inside.

What is this about?

As if she senses my tension, she nods knowingly, her gaze still fixed on the flickering flames in the fireplace. Is she thinking about the fire that gave her those scars?

"Even before the accident, Mom was battling depression, but Dad's death pulled the ground out from under her," she begins to explain. Bit by bit, she tells me that her mom saw no other way out than to take her own life—but fortunately, the attempt failed. How hard things were for her afterward, how much she got used to pushing her own needs aside to be there for her mom.

"You went through all of that alone?" I pull her into my arms, wanting to show her that I'm here for her. Because it seems like no one has done that for her in a very long time.

"It used to be just the two of us, Dad and me, we got through it together, helped each other." Now she looks at me sadly. "Right before the accident, he asked me to promise him something."

Her body begins to tremble, I kiss her forehead.

"He said: Promise me that nothing and no one will ever extinguish that light in you. Promise me that you'll always make the world a warmer place." Her voice breaks, the words linger between us, and slowly, things I hadn't understood before start to make sense.

The often overly warm-hearted way she treats everyone. How little she thinks of herself, how important it is to her to help others.

"And you've kept that promise to this day," I say, because I'm sure of it. Thanks to her, this world is a warmer place. "But what about your world? If you give all your warmth to others, what's left for you?"

She swallows hard. I'd love to know what's going on inside her, but her expression doesn't give me the slightest clue.

"Nothing," she finally whispers, barely audible.

Still, she's been doing nothing else for years, and I'm slowly beginning to understand why. "You're afraid the press will find out about your scars from the accident and, in turn, about your mom's illness." I entwine my fingers with hers, wanting to give her support, even though I suspect there's none to be had. "You're afraid it would make her illness worse if your story got splashed all over the media." And it will. Guaranteed.

She nods absentmindedly. "But that's not all."

I don't understand what's happening as Autumn suddenly pulls away from my embrace and gets up from the sofa. A queasy feeling spreads in my stomach as she positions herself a meter away in front of me. The firelight caresses her face and makes her hair softly glow.

"After the accident, my mom was devastated. I wasn't doing well either, but the last thing I wanted was to cause her more pain." She pulls off her sweater, revealing a spaghetti strap top underneath. She traces the scars on her chest with her fingers. "My boyfriend, my first love, dumped me because his princess had turned into a monster he didn't want to be seen with. Even at school, I wasn't Autumn anymore, just the monster. No one meant me harm, they were just scared, but it still hurt so incredibly much."

A burning pain shoots through my chest when I imagine what Autumn went through back then. What she endured, what it must have been like for her. How alone she must have felt. It must have broken her, and yet all she thought about was the others. About how they were afraid.

That was wrong. In that situation, her own needs should have come first.

"I wanted to be strong for Mom, but instead I was angry at Dad, because if it hadn't been for the accident, everything would have been different." Now she takes off her top, standing before me in just her bra and jeans. "I knew it was wrong to blame him, I didn't want to be selfish, I wasn't allowed to think about myself—after all, Mom was doing so badly."

I shake my head at her twisted logic, want to get up, go to her, hug her. But she signals me not to come any closer.

"My friends turned away from me, I hated my body, and I couldn't burden Mom with either of those things," she says, her voice filled with so much pain.

"That must have torn you apart inside." My God, it must have been hell. She was sixteen, and what she took on would have been far too much even for an adult.

Tears well up in her eyes as she unbuttons her jeans. "It broke me," she whispers and pulls down the zipper.

I can't stay on the couch any longer, I spring up, rush to her, but she shakes her head vehemently and directs me back to the sofa.

Why is she doing this? Why won't she let me be there for her?

"It broke me, but at the same time I knew I couldn't fall

apart. My mom needed me." She grabs the waistband of her pants and pushes them down.

I forget to breathe for a moment when I see what lies beneath. Countless elongated scars cover her thighs, some finer, some thicker.

One is fresh.

My heart breaks—for her, for her pain—and I couldn't care less whether she wants me near her or not, I have to hold her. I rush to her, embrace her, let her know she's not alone.

"Mom doesn't know about these scars on my thighs. If she did, she'd blame herself. She'd accuse herself of not seeing what was going on with me, of not helping me. Her world would collapse." Autumn's voice breaks.

A thousand thoughts race through my head like a roller coaster, and I don't know what to say or what to think.

With her head resting against my chest, she exhales shakily. "And that's not the only thing she doesn't know."

I pull her into my arms as tightly as I can, even though I suspect that holding her any longer might mean dragging her deeper into despair.

"That my dad would lose his job, that he was afraid of burdening her with it, that the only solution for him was to drown his worries in alcohol."

She sniffles and I sink deeper into the whirlpool of my emotions. "Your dad was…"

"Yes, he had been drinking, he had been drinking before the accident." A single tear slips from the corner of her eye.

"He drowned his sorrow in alcohol because he didn't want to burden my mom with it. He wanted to protect her too." Just like Autumn always wants to protect everyone at all costs—everyone except herself.

She can't do that, she matters too.

"If Mom finds out, she'll blame herself for that too. She'll blame herself for everything."

And that's even understandable, even though she's not responsible for her illness and certainly not to blame for what happened. My God, it's so paradoxical!

"I protected her from all these truths so she wouldn't completely fall apart." Her pleading gaze finds me. "If the press finds out about my scars, they'll find out about the accident. And from there, it's only a small step to uncovering what else happened back then." Autumn tries to be strong, but her voice trembles. "Some of my classmates know about the scars on my thighs."

Now I understand why she asked me a few minutes ago whether the press would believe her made-up story. Not because she's afraid of being ridiculed for her scars.

It's so much bigger than that.

When Autumn told me on the boat that I was the last thing she needed in her life, she was right. The spotlight my fame would shine on her life would destroy her mom.

She looks up at me intensely. "My mom has been through hell, and even though she's doing okay right now, that won't last if she finds out about all this. What kind of daughter would I be if I put my own happiness above hers?"

And what kind of man would I be if I placed my own happiness—the happiness of having her by my side—above Autumn's? The thought hurts too much to say it aloud.

I brush a strand of hair from her face, kiss her forehead, and try not to think about what all of this means for us.

"Before I met you, my world was cold, superficial, and empty." And the crazy thing is, I actually liked it that way. I felt safe there, where real emotions never played a role.

Where everything was smoke and mirrors and nothing was real. “You made it warm, deep, and meaningful.”

A wistful smile flickers across her beautiful face. She places her hands on my cheeks. “And it will stay that way, no matter what happens.”

How could she say that? The world is what it is, and to survive in it, I have to protect myself. Only with her is it different. “What if we keep our relationship a secret?”

Autumn’s thumbs move gently across my cheeks. There’s worry in her expression. “Could that work?”

“There’s no other option,” I whisper.

With a pained expression, she rises onto her tiptoes. “Can we really hide from the world? Would we be safe?”

The crackling fire, our quiet breaths, and the steady sound of the ocean fill the room. “Some of my colleagues have managed it for years.” Others have failed, but I can’t bring myself to tell her that. It won’t be easy, we’ll always be in danger, but I want to believe it’s possible.

Her eyes sparkle in the soft light, and I feel the familiar warmth that lingers between us.

“We have to try,” she says.

Yes, we do. Because if we really can't have this anymore, if this thing between us truly can't be—then I don't know how I'm supposed to go on.

Our lips meet gently, hesitant at first, then full of longing. It’s a slow, intense kiss, filled with passion. And even as I lose myself with her, I know it’s going to be hard. I know that years of sacrifice and limitations lie ahead of us. But I also know that I’ll protect what we have at all costs.

Chapter Thirty-Seven

AUTUMN

The night was a dream come true. I can still feel Tay's skin on mine, hear his ragged breathing, see his eyes filled with excitement and love, and let myself fall like never before in my life.

It was a dream—and we won't stop dreaming it.

Flooded with hope, I close my locker and make a mental note to stop by Kayla's room—and with that, see Tay—as soon as possible. As I step into the hallway, my pager buzzes.

Quickly, I pull the device from my pocket.

Code Red.

Oh no.

I rush off. What could have happened?

Brian—the boy with the heart defect. Has his condition become acute?

My steps grow faster and faster, only two more floors.

Mariah—has she had another epileptic seizure? Is she not getting enough oxygen? Did she fall?

Panting, I pass the entrance to the sixth floor.

Sarah—has her chronic kidney failure triggered organ failure?

I run to the nurses' station.

From a distance I see Sandra. "Where's the emergency? Where am I needed?"

"Teddy Bear Room," she shouts.

Oh God, no, this can't be happening.

An unending shiver runs down my spine, I quicken my pace and don't care that my hair is whipping around. Nothing else matters, only one thing counts: getting to Kayla as fast as possible.

Completely out of breath, I finally arrive. The door to the hospital room is barely open when I hear it: sobbing. Hasty breaths trying to suppress the tears, but failing.

A nurse is with Kayla.

"Show me exactly where it hurts," he asks her.

My stomach clenches, but I force myself to stay calm and march toward the bed.

Kayla is curled up in bed, her knees pulled tightly to her chest, and she's shaking her head vehemently. Her cheeks are wet, the pillow beneath her soaked through.

She has stomach pain—yesterday it was mild, but this looks like much more than that.

Her mother is sitting beside her—once again wearing the blonde wig—her hand desperately resting on her daughter's shoulder, but the touch seems to do little good.

"Hey, Kayla, don't worry, I'm here," I say gently, and the nurse steps aside.

"Severe, cramping abdominal pain, vomiting, nausea, fever. She doesn't want to be examined," he explains to me.

Looking at Kayla, I nod.

She looks at me, her eyes wide and full of fear. "It hurts

so much," she gasps, and I see her small body tense with every breath. She presses her hands against her belly.

I kneel down next to the bed so we're at eye level and glance briefly at David-Tay. Desperation is reflected in his eyes behind the horn-rimmed glasses.

"May I feel your belly?" I ask Kayla.

She opens her arms, and I gently place my hand on her stomach. Her skin is hot, almost feverish, and the whole area is tight. Her body flinches at my touch, and she starts crying again, this time louder.

"Here... here..." Her voice is barely more than a whisper.

It could be anything. Appendicitis. A bowel obstruction. I continue palpating carefully, but every inch seems to cause her agony.

"Don't worry, first we'll make sure you feel better, then we'll find out what's going on," I assure her while frantically searching for answers. Her abdomen doesn't feel rock-hard, but there's a clear guarding reflex. Not a good sign. "Ibuprofen two hundred milligrams, two milligrams of ondansetron. I also need blood tests," I say to the nurse, who immediately prepares a blood draw kit.

I turn my attention back to the girl. She's trembling, her breathing rapid. "We're going to give you something for the pain in just a moment, okay?"

While I wait for the nurse to bring the medication, I take her small hand, which disappears into mine. "I'm going to place an IV in the crook of your arm now, all right? We need it to draw blood for testing."

Kayla nods hesitantly. The fact that she trusts me so much touches me deeply, and I won't do anything to betray that trust, so I explain to her in detail what's happening as I insert the line and draw blood.

"You did wonderfully," I say at the end with an encouraging smile, handing the blood samples to the nurse, who has returned with the medication. "Basic blood panel, as soon as possible, please."

"What's wrong with her?" Chloe asks worriedly.

"We'll find out," I reply.

I look at Tay, whose face is gripped by panic. With my eyes, I let him know that I'm here and that everything will be okay, even if I can't explain Kayla's suddenly severe symptoms.

Kayla receives her medication. It will take a few minutes for it to take effect.

I take her hand and squeeze it tightly. "It'll get better soon, I promise."

Now that there's nothing more I can do, the air between Tay, Chloe, and me suddenly feels thick enough to cut through.

Without warning, Chloe jumps up from her chair next to Kayla's bed. "We need to talk," she says, addressing Tay. Just moments ago she was full of warmth and concern for Kayla; now, toward him, she's ice cold. "Outside."

Tay and I exchange a brief glance. I silently let him know that Kayla is safe with me, yet he hesitates. His wife doesn't seem to care; she hooks her arm through his and pulls him out into the hallway.

As the door closes behind the two of them, I can't help but wonder what they're discussing now.

Chapter Thirty-Eight

TAY

Only at the end of the hallway, where the sprawling green plants press against the glass front, does Chloe let go of me.

"This is a nightmare. Not only are we stuck here now," she says dejectedly. "Kayla, it's…"

I run my hand over the fake beard. What happened earlier hit me hard. On top of that, I saw in Autumn's expression that she has no explanation for Kayla's condition.

What if it really is psychological? What if Kayla just can't cope with the news of our divorce, even though she assured me several times yesterday that she could?

"Kayla doesn't have a sensitive stomach, she's always been healthy." Chloe tugs at her blouse, as if her fingers need something to do. "I don't understand this, what's wrong with her?"

Chaos reigns inside me, mixed with a kind of despair I've never known before. "Autumn will…"

"Don't start with that Autumn," she cuts me off. "This isn't about you, it's about our little daughter!"

Of course it's about Kayla, it's about nothing else. "Autumn is her doctor, she'll figure out what's going on and treat her. In a few days everything will probably be fine again," I reply calmly, wishing more than anything that it turns out to be true.

With her arms crossed, Chloe steps up to the window and looks out at the overcast day. "Something's not right."

I stand next to her. Automatically, my eyes scan Halifax Harbor for journalists, but thankfully, I don't see any. "We have to…"

"The stomach pains yesterday were already unexplainable." Chloe's desperate tone hits me deep in my heart. "Was it us, Tay? Did we cause this?" she whispers.

So she's been thinking about it too. "I don't know," I admit, because as much as I want to push the thought away, I can't. Since I can't bring myself to look at my wife, the mother of my daughter, my agent, the person I've shared so many years with, I lower my gaze to the floor.

I trace the marbling of the laminate floor as guilt and worry take hold of me.

"She needs us," Chloe breaks the silence between us. "Both of us."

"Maybe she's just sick." Autumn is treating her, and as soon as she's discharged, we can move on—Chloe and I will get divorced, Autumn and I will hide from the public.

Chloe shakes her head vehemently, the strands of her blonde wig swaying back and forth. "I know my daughter."

And I don't know her. That's what she thinks, and it's the truth. For years, I kept my distance. Honestly, I have no idea who she really is, what she's afraid of, what matters to her. I know nothing about her friends, about what she wants to be one day, and certainly not how well or badly she'll take the news of our separation.

My God, what am I doing to my little daughter right now?

"Good thing the press release hasn't gone out yet. Do you have any idea what would've happened then?" Her question echoes between us, just like the answer neither of us has to say aloud.

We both know it.

If Kayla's symptoms really don't have a physical cause —and Autumn already hinted at that yesterday. If she's already doing this badly because her parents are splitting up, then she'll never survive the media frenzy surrounding our divorce. The rumors flooding the press, the whispering it'll trigger in her personal life, the curious questions.

Kayla will go through something similar to what Autumn experienced after the accident. Will I be able to be there enough for her, or will it break her? I don't know, but I don't want to find out for anything in the world.

Chloe exhales slowly. "Look, I don't like this any more than you do, but I think Kayla needs stability right now."

A lot in her life has fallen apart in the past few weeks. Maybe too much. Maybe we're wrong. Maybe it's all completely different.

"Until we have a diagnosis, we shouldn't make any rash decisions," I say, thinking of Autumn. Of what it would mean for both of us if Chloe turned out to be right. Would we still see each other in secret? How long could that last if I'm lying not just to the whole world but also to my own daughter?

"Okay," I hear Chloe say. "But if we don't know what's going on by tomorrow, we have to at least try. For Kayla's sake. We'll claim we're not getting divorced, and if she gets better because of that, then we have to…"

I quickly raise my hand to stop her from saying anything

more. "We'll talk about that when the time comes. I'm going to check on Kayla—that's what matters most right now," I say and turn away.

Maybe I can talk to her again and find out something that helps me understand what's going on with her. Even if she doesn't say it outright, maybe there's something between her words that I've missed until now.

Chloe lingers at the end of the hallway, and as I make my way to Kayla's room, my heart clenches painfully. This heart, which I thought for years could no longer break, threatens to shatter under the weight.

Chapter Thirty-Nine

AUTUMN

The fire races toward me.

Closer and closer.

And even closer.

Instinctively, I grab the doorknob, shake it, but it won't open.

Tay is behind the window. With a desperate expression, he tries to free me.

I push against the door.

Nothing moves.

Tay looks like he's screaming, but I can't hear him. I only see his eyes, filled with pain and fear.

I press my forehead against the window, he does the same. We are so close to each other, yet we can't reach one another. Now the flames reach for me, heat rolls down my back as Tay and I look at each other.

Only the windowpane separates us. A piece of glass we should be able to shatter. Yet we look at each other and let the flames consume me.

A scream escapes my mouth, I open my eyes wide, and

find myself in the twilight of my shared apartment room. My sleep shirt clings to my body, Tay's face still dances before my mind's eye.

Tay.

Where there was fire just seconds ago, the same worries now rise in me that have been with me since yesterday. Kayla's symptoms have improved, but there's still much to suggest that her parents' separation is the cause of her stomach aches, even though she continues to insist that the divorce doesn't bother her. Since our conversation during physiotherapy, I know how much she wants to protect her parents. That she's now lying to do exactly that seems entirely possible.

The thought weighs heavily on my chest as I change out of my nightshirt and slip into my robe. Then I shuffle out of the room to make myself some tea. It's actually too early to get up, but going back to sleep and possibly reliving that nightmare is something I want even less.

To my surprise, a narrow strip of light falls through the ajar kitchen door into the hallway. Inside, I find June sitting at the kitchen table, her long blonde hair a wild mess, with deep shadows under her reddened eyes.

"Hey," she says as I enter, pushing her laptop aside. "Can't sleep either?"

I shake my head. "I'm making tea, want some?"

June runs both hands through her hair. "Do you have a kind that'll raise my IQ?" she asks, and I immediately have a feeling what this is about.

"Ashton?" I fill the kettle and switch it on. When we went shopping together at the farmers market the other day, she told me more about her patient with the mysterious illness and also what connects her to him.

"It's getting worse and worse. If I don't find a solution soon…" She trails off.

Thoughtfully, I lean against the kitchen counter while she confusedly runs through all the details of his illness and possible causes. By the time the water boils, I can no longer follow her and drift back into my own thoughts.

I don't know how to go on. How could I continue without Tay, the man who made me believe in miracles again?

A sigh escapes my lips. With June's rambling in my ears, I unwrap two tea bags, hang them in cups, and fill them with water.

June looks at me intently as I set the cups on the table. "I can do this. Nothing and no one can stop me, I will diagnose Ashton's illness."

"You will." Because she never gives up. She's always been that way, she fights for her happiness until she wins. She's incredibly strong, and not for the first time since I've known her, I wish I were a little more like her. But something is different today.

For the first time since I've known her, I feel that wishing alone isn't enough.

I wrap both hands around my teacup. "I've got a mysterious case too," I tell her, even though she hasn't asked what kept me up tonight. She hasn't offered to help, but I need her. "Would you go through it with me?"

To my surprise, she nods. "Sure."

"Only if you have time," I add after all, not wanting to burden her further. Her patient's well-being is important to her, and pushing myself to the front feels selfish.

Frustrated, she rolls her eyes toward the ceiling. "I'm already stuck in a dead end again. Other thoughts might help me see Ashton's symptoms more clearly." June pulls her teacup toward herself. "Alright then, go ahead and tell me."

Full of gratitude, I tell her about Kayla's abdominal pain, the progression of her symptoms, the blood test I ordered, and also that it didn't yield any results indicating an illness.

"Hm," she says, tapping her chin with her index finger. "Maybe an intolerance? Has she received any new medication because of her leg?"

Shaking my head, I take a sip of my tea. "But something else happened," I reply, because it makes no sense to deny the most likely cause. "She's had the abdominal pain since she found out her parents are getting divorced."

"So you think it's psychosomatic?" June's fingers tap on the kitchen table. "It's possible, but as a diagnostician, I can't be satisfied with that. There are still countless other possible causes."

I gesture for her to continue. She must have an idea that I haven't thought of yet.

"Diabetic ketoacidosis, for example." June's cheeks begin to glow. "A previously undiagnosed case of diabetes in your patient, now causing abdominal pain and nausea."

"Then she'd also have excessive thirst, which she doesn't. And her blood sugar level would be elevated," I reply, since I've already considered that. Still, I reach for my phone to take notes. "I'll order a daily blood glucose profile and a ketone test. Better safe than sorry."

"Then there are also bacterial causes that don't show up on a standard blood test: yersiniosis, for example. Or it could be a parasite like giardiasis," June continues.

Giardiasis? That's impossible. "She's been in the hospital for almost two weeks—how could she have come into contact with contaminated water?"

My roommate chews on her lower lip. "Okay, that's actually unlikely, and there's no other way to contract the parasite."

I slide forward in my chair. "Let's think this through again," I say, listing everything that makes even the slightest bit of sense. "Each of these illnesses would show some indication in the ordered blood work, but there's nothing." Desperation colors my words. "Elevated white blood cell counts in infections and inflammatory bowel diseases, low hemoglobin in sickle cell disease or autoimmune disorders…" My God, now I sound just like June did earlier.

"Maybe someone mixed up the prescribed medication and gave her too much?" June now suggests. "It would be something that fits the symptoms but wouldn't necessarily show up in a standard blood test."

"That would've been noticed—the medication is checked multiple times," I reply, frustrated. Besides, I don't believe it. Even though Sandra spends most of her time gossiping and betting instead of working, something like that wouldn't happen to her, I'm sure of it.

June shrugs. "I'm just saying, the little one is probably getting painkillers for her leg, right? Some of them can cause those symptoms if dosed incorrectly."

That may be, but it still can't be right. "Kayla has only been getting painkillers for physical therapy for days now, and the dosage is definitely always correct." After all, I accompany her to therapy and see how much paracetamol she takes. I slump in my chair, forced to admit I'm going in circles.

Again.

June looks at me, tired. "Then maybe it really is psychosomatic," she says, frustrated, and with that, the last spark of hope for another explanation fades within me.

Chapter Forty

TAY

I sat by Kayla's bed all night while Chloe got some rest. I held her hand, brushed her hair from her forehead, soothed her when she was in pain.

The whole time, I kept thinking about Autumn, missing her warmth, her smile, the way her voice makes everything inside me vibrate.

When she finished her shift yesterday, she didn't have any new information. She looked at me with such longing that I had to pull her into my arms. I had to hold her.

It won't stop, I won't be able to stay away from her. I'll keep wishing, every single moment, to have her in my life.

Lost in thought, I watch my daughter, who's finally getting a little sleep. Her breathing is shallow, her mouth slightly open, beads of sweat glistening on her forehead even though she doesn't have a fever.

A scraping noise draws my attention to the door. Chloe walks in, the blonde Mary wig on her head.

"Is she doing better?" She kisses Kayla's forehead.

"A little," I reply.

Suddenly, I feel Chloe's hand on my arm. "We have to try."

She's right, we do—but I'm scared. Scared of what it means if Kayla's symptoms disappear after she finds out her parents aren't getting divorced after all. Scared of the life that's waiting for me. I can lie to the world, but Kayla? And every free minute I spend with Autumn would be one I'm not with Kayla.

My little one lets out a grunt. "Daddy," she murmurs sleepily.

"I'm here," I say quickly. "How are you feeling? Are you thirsty?"

"Mhm," she responds, looking at both of us with her big blue eyes.

I hand her the water bottle. She sips through the straw, and I try to tell if she's feeling any better.

"Sweetheart, Daddy and I have good news for you." Chloe moves her chair closer and strokes Kayla's healthy leg.

I glance at her—my wife, the person to whom I so thoughtlessly promised to stand by in good times and bad.

Kayla sinks back into her pillow. "What is it?"

My wife smiles gently, and if she hadn't made it clear that she wants this just as little as I do, I'd think she didn't mind. "Your dad and I have decided that we don't want to fight anymore."

"I know that." Kayla looks back and forth between us, confused. "That's why you're getting divorced."

Chloe shakes her head. "We remembered how much we love each other, and we don't want to separate anymore, sweetheart. We're staying a family."

A family.

Chloe, Kayla, and me.

I think painfully of Autumn, who will have no place in this family.

Kayla shrugs. "Okay."

Frowning, I study her. If it had been weighing on her so heavily, shouldn't she be happier now? Then again, she's always claimed that our separation didn't bother her. Are her stomachaches really psychosomatic? I still can't believe it, but the next few hours will probably tell.

I force a smile onto my face. "Besides, I'll be home more from now on so we can spend time together," I say, because that's the only thing I'm looking forward to in this future. I want to be there for her, want to finally be the dad she deserves.

"Yay!" Kayla shouts despite her stomachache. Has it already gone away? "We'll feed the fish together and play Barbie and go pony riding."

"Can I talk to you for a second?" Chloe turns her head so Kayla can't see her face and gives me a venomous look. "In the bathroom."

Why? I look at her questioningly; she nods toward the bathroom door. "We'll be right back, Kayla," I say to my daughter and follow my wife into the bathroom.

"You can't promise her things like that. Filming for your movie starts soon—you won't have time for her," she hisses quietly as soon as the door closes behind her.

"We'll find a way." Kayla is important, I can't lose her too. "I want to spend more time with Kayla—on weekends, on holidays, after filming." I used to party constantly with the crew; I didn't want to be at home. But that's changing now.

Just a moment ago Chloe agreed that Kayla needs stability. Why is she looking at me now like I'm suggesting something impossible? "Well, tough luck. Your contract states that filming goes on without a break—seven days a week."

Excuse me? "For heaven's sake, why didn't you fix that clause?"

"Because you should damn well be grateful to even get this chance after your last film flopped so badly." Her expression turns angry now. "Do you really think I had any room to negotiate?"

"Fuck," I mutter, prompting a scornful snort from Chloe.

"Thanks, Chloe, for taking such good care of me and my career while I screw my way through strangers' beds. *That* would be the right reaction," she replies, her voice cracking. "And now, if you'll excuse me, I'd like to take care of our daughter."

With those words, she leaves me in the bathroom. I lift my gaze to the mirror, see David and how he's falling apart piece by piece because he's suddenly letting so much more get to him than ever before.

Be a man, my father warns me in my thoughts, and maybe he's right.

Eight hours later, I'm standing across from Autumn. We're on the roof of the Halifax Harbor Hospital, one of the few places where we're safe, the place where Autumn caught me after my panic attack. The smell of salt and seaweed hangs in the stormy air, and the roar of the surf can be heard even up here.

I only have to look at her to feel that I can't breathe without her. But I also know that too much stands between us.

Kayla's symptoms actually improved after this morning's conversation, and just now Autumn also told me that the additional tests ordered didn't yield any results either.

"I don't want to believe that, it can't be," I say tonelessly.

Her red hair flutters in the wind. "Still, it's probably the truth." Despair clouds her face. "Even my roommate—a brilliant diagnostician—with whom I discussed the case, came to the conclusion that…"

"But you treated her and now she's doing better—much better, even. That could also be an explanation." The medication helped, albeit slowly overnight, but then increasingly throughout the day. So she was sick—physically sick.

"Unfortunately, it's not that simple." She steps up to the railing and leans on it. "Physical symptoms triggered by psychological stress are real. In such cases, belief in the effectiveness of a treatment can actually lead to improvement, even if there's no direct organic cause that was cured."

Unable to grasp what that means, I shake my head. "How can she be healthy? She must have something, a virus or some other infection? Food poisoning, an intolerance?"

Fighting back tears, Autumn presses her lips together. I can see how hard this is for her. "All the tests so far show that Kayla is healthy."

I'm slowly beginning to sense what's going on inside my daughter, apparently deep in her subconscious: If she's sick, she stays here at Halifax Harbor Hospital. If she's sick, we can't go home—to a life where separated parents await Kayla.

What am I doing to my little girl?

"Can't you run more tests?" The moment the question leaves my lips, I feel like an asshole. Kayla should be the only thing that matters right now, yet my heart breaks at the thought that there might be no future for the woman standing just a meter away from me and me.

Her eyes turn sad now, infinitely sad. "Of course we can, and we will. But we shouldn't get our hopes up too much. The chance of a different result is..."

Our eyes meet. For a while, we just look at each other, neither of us wanting to say the unthinkable, neither of us ready to let go.

Just as I reach out to her, Autumn's phone vibrates loudly in her lab coat pocket. She ignores the buzzing, steps closer, wraps her arms around me, and exhales shakily.

"Tay, I can't do this. If Kayla's hurting because her family is falling apart, I can't be with you in secret...," she whispers desperately.

Neither can I, but the words won't come out. Yes, Chloe wanted the divorce—that's how it all started. But she's willing to try again, only I'm not, and Kayla will feel it if my heart is always somewhere else.

Autumn's phone buzzes again. She flinches in my arms, and I gently stroke her back.

Another buzz fills the silence between us. Whoever's trying to reach Autumn, it must be urgent.

"You should..." Before I can finish the sentence, Autumn pulls away from my embrace.

"Maybe Mom needs something," she says in a hoarse voice and reaches into her lab coat pocket.

Chapter Forty-One

AUTUMN

Hopefully nothing happened.

Without taking my eyes off Tay, I pull my phone from the lab coat. Relief washes over me when I see that the messages aren't from Mom, but just from Olive.

"Busted," I read in one of the message previews. "Why didn't you…" in another. "Ooh la la" in the next.

"What's going on?" Tay's voice sounds far away.

Shaking my head, I tap on one of the messages. "No ide…"

Wait a second.

That's… that's me…

No!

A feeling like the world is starting to tremble beneath me, above me, and all around me takes hold as I stare at the screenshots Olive sent me.

Tay and me.

Tay—not David—Tay!

In front of the vacation house on Inner Sambro Island.

Along with the headline: Affair – Tay Lawson cheats on his wife with red-haired femme fatale.

That's what the journalists conclude from this photo, even though Tay and I aren't even touching in it? There's nothing to suggest we're having an affair!

"Oh God…" I gasp as horrifying scenarios start brewing in my head. That was the night I showed Tay all my scars.

Was I standing at the window? Near the window? Was the curtain drawn? How bright was the firelight?

Panic creeps up inside me, and I can barely manage to go through the photos and reports Olive sent me one by one.

All about the mysterious woman at Tay Lawson's side.

Tay steps behind me and inhales sharply when he sees what I'm seeing. "Fuck."

The blood freezes in my veins as I skim through the article. They know my name, they've found out that I'm a doctor at Halifax Harbor Hospital, and they know that Kayla is being treated there.

"My God, how did they find all this out so quickly?" I stammer, unable to form a coherent thought. How did they track this down so fast? The night those photos were taken was just two days ago!

Tay tries to pull me into his arms again. "They know you're Kayla's doctor, so we can easily explain your visit to my vacation house. The pictures don't show anything incriminating, the rumors will fade away quickly."

Maybe— but only if we're not seen together again. Right? I don't know, I can't think straight anymore. Holding my breath, I open the next message, in which Olive has sent me a link to a forum.

My fingers are trembling—no, my whole body is

shaking—even though Tay is holding me so tightly from behind that it shouldn't even be possible.

"I'm sorry," he whispers in my ear, as if he senses what I'm about to read.

A wave of speculation crashes over me. People are wondering how this unremarkable woman managed to snag the superstar Tay Lawson, whether it's an affair or something serious, and what's going to happen next.

Nowhere do I find rumors about me personally. No one is wondering who I am as a person or where I come from—instead, they get lost in their own versions of how far Tay and I have gone and what will happen when his wife finds out about me.

That's good. I think. As long as my scars are safe from them, Mom is safe too. Still, it doesn't feel that way. Just one photo taken in an unguarded moment could trigger an avalanche that might drag Mom down with it.

Tay kisses my cheek, my temple, my forehead. I want to melt into his embrace, shut out the world, just be with him. Still, my eyes stay glued to the screen.

"How selfish can someone be, to destroy a family? Has she even thought about the poor child?" writes one user. "That woman has no decency whatsoever. It's disgusting!"

"They hate me. Deeply." They don't know me, know nothing about me, yet they despise me—and from the outside, it's even understandable. I'm a disruption in Tay's life, I'm destroying his supposedly happy family.

Tay seems to be searching for words in vain, and I no longer know what to say either.

Kayla's symptoms, for which there's only one logical explanation. The way things between Tay and me appear to the outside world. Mom.

Everything in me resists a reality I didn't want to see

until now. But there is only one truth, and I can't ignore it any longer:

Sometimes you meet someone who pieces together the broken parts of you, only to lose them again. Sometimes miracles glow in our hearts, only to eventually surrender to the darkness. What remains is the realization that it was never a miracle, just a fleeting moment we desperately mistook for one.

Until this morning, I still wanted to hope that there could be a future for Tay and me, but now there is no hope left.

I turn to him, see in his eyes that he's understood it too. A mix of despair, longing, and pain reflects on his face. He cups my face in his hands, and I do the same to him. We hold on to each other, even though we both know we've just lost one another.

"I'm so sorry," he repeats soundlessly. The wind carries his words away. Far out over the sea.

How could this have happened?

How is it possible that the only man in this world who makes me feel whole, the man who loves me despite everything that isn't perfect about me, the man who made me believe in miracles again—how is it possible that this man is slipping away from me?

His thumbs gently stroke my cheeks. "Kayla is getting older," he says. "One day she'll be old enough to handle the divorce. And your mom will keep recovering too. In a few years, we might get another chance."

Years? That's hundreds of weeks during which we won't be close to each other even once. Thousands of days when I'll have to fall asleep and wake up without him.

"You'd be willing to wait that long?" I look deeply into his eyes.

His expression turns serious. "I would wait for you for all eternity."

"So would I." My lips curl into a wistful smile. My heart doesn't know whether to break from sadness or explode from love. This moment is bittersweet, and yet it is and remains a goodbye.

"Kiss me," he pleads longingly. "Kiss me one last time."

I do. I kiss him one last time with all the love I carry for him in my heart, and he returns my kiss so tenderly that no further words are needed.

Since my accident, I thought fate couldn't be defeated. That it strikes, eats into our lives, breaks us beyond repair, hollows us out until nothing is left. But now, in this moment, I want to hope again for the first time.

What connects Tay and me must be stronger than any fate. It will endure for decades if it has to, and one day we'll stand before each other again. We'll kiss, the miracle of our love will glow within us, and just like now, tears will stream down our cheeks.

Tears of joy.

I hope for that with all my heart as we don't stop kissing. I soak in every second, every touch, every breath.

We're going to make it—have to make it—yet the moment we end our kiss, it feels like a goodbye forever.

A goodbye that hurts more than every single scar on my body. A goodbye that leaves a fresh wound that will never fade.

"We'll stay in touch, text, call," he suggests now, his lips still so close to mine that I can feel his breath on my skin.

"We could do that. But then it would feel like this every time." Every goodbye would be torment, our days filled with longing. We'd be close, but never close enough.

Seeing something you need so desperately and knowing

it's out of reach is far worse than allowing life to take on a new order for a while. I know that—I've experienced something similar with Henry and Lucy. Seeing them every day tore me apart, and this—this with Tay and me—is so much bigger than anything Henry and I ever had.

I force a smile. "When we see each other again, it'll be forever."

With a wistful look, he brushes my hair back. "You made my heart beat again."

And with that heart, he gave me, for a moment—for a brief instant—so much more than just his love. "Promise me it'll keep beating." Because only then does what happened make sense, even if it hurts.

For a brief moment, fear flickers across his face. "I promise," he says, pulling me into his arms.

I wrap my arms around his back, hold him and am held by him, savor his closeness, breathe in his scent. And as inevitably as the sun dips toward the horizon over the ocean, our final moments together slip away.

A single ray of sunlight breaks through the clouds. I close my eyes. Orange-red light flickers behind my lids, and I imprint this moment deep in my heart as we hold each other until darkness surrounds us.

Chapter Forty-Two

TAY

Outside the window, the surf roars while I let my fingers glide over the cold leather of my boxing gloves.

Whoever strikes first has the advantage, whoever hits harder wins. Whoever lets others get close becomes vulnerable, whoever loves, loses.

Those were the rules I lived by for years. The rules that lost their meaning because of Autumn.

But what about the rest of the world? Regardless of what happened between Autumn and me, Hollywood is still the same. Superficial, scheming, artificial. As much as I love my job and as eager as I am to play the role of Dr. Cross, I'm not looking forward to the life that awaits me in Los Angeles.

The thought weighs heavily on my chest. I set the boxing gloves aside and lift my gaze to the window.

I'm going to miss this. The vastness of the ocean, the freedom, the ease. But even more, I'm going to miss Autumn. Her warmth, her gentleness, the way she understands me without saying a word.

Like a film, our all-too-brief time together plays before my mind's eye. There's the tender way she looked at me from the very beginning. The green of her eyes, so deep, so full of love. How she protected Kayla and me, understood us, and trusted us unconditionally.

If the world could see this film, wouldn't people's hearts open just a little? If they understood what I've come to realize over the past few days, wouldn't they see those they meet in a different light?

Would they stop hurting each other thoughtlessly?

Just a few weeks ago, I would have answered that question with a clear no, and today that hasn't changed. But deep down, I suspect that meeting a cold world with coldness may only make it colder still.

I, too, have contributed to that over the past years—that's something I no longer want to do, yet at the same time, I have absolutely no idea how to survive in Hollywood any other way.

I take a deep breath, sling the bag over my shoulder, and set off. Autumn comes with me, in my heart, where she will always be and make sure it beats the right way.

A little later, for the first time in a long while, I steer the boat across the sea toward Halifax not disguised as David and check the messages on my phone. Yesterday it was announced that I'll be playing the role of Dr. Cross.

"Tay Lawson is back—better than ever," headlines a gossip magazine. In the article, they sing my praises to the skies. There's no more mention of me being a bad actor. That's how it goes with the press—their opinion shifts with the winds of time, and that's not likely to change.

"All clear—Tay Lawson's daughter healthy again, family happily reunited," reads the next headline.

Happily reunited…

The skyline of Halifax appears on the horizon. I head toward the harbor, behind which the Halifax Harbor Hospital rises into the sky. That's where Autumn will be overseeing Kayla's discharge today. We agreed that Chloe should handle it. That it would be easier if we didn't see each other anymore.

But knowing that I'm so close to Autumn at this very moment, as I sail into the harbour, and yet can't reach her, is anything but easy.

As expected, a horde of reporters is waiting at the dock. I brace myself, fully aware that I can no longer do what I've perfected my whole life. Undoubtedly, I have to stay in control, but I don't have to appease them with a fake smile, and I'm also no longer going to be the first to strike—those days are over.

No sooner have I docked than they pounce on me. Flashes go off, voice recorders are thrust in my direction, there's even a cameraman present.

"Mr. Tay, are you picking up your daughter now?"

I shake my head. "Chloe is with her." They don't need to know more—not even that I'll be flying ahead to Los Angeles without the two of them.

"How is Kayla doing?"

The stomach pains are completely gone, and she'll continue her physiotherapy in Los Angeles. "Excellent, thank you for asking," I reply—anything else they'd twist around anyway—and politely ask them to let me through.

They follow me all the way to the taxi. "What about that doctor? Did you have an affair? What does your wife say? Has she forgiven you?" a woman's voice calls out.

Inwardly, I flinch. "Dr. Hall treated my daughter, as well as the rest of the Halifax Harbor Hospital team, excellently, and I'm very grateful to her for that."

"Why was she at your holiday home?" the journalist presses.

With my hand on the taxi door handle, I study her, see the hunger for sensation in her eyes, the shallowness, the ruthlessness, and I'm on the verge of asking her whether she can even look at herself in the mirror anymore. But a split second later, I feel something I haven't felt in a long time: regret. Doing this job is anything but easy.

"We coordinated Kayla's treatment," I reply, and my heart grows heavy when I think about what we actually did.

What we won't be doing for a very long time. How much I'll miss her, with every breath, with every beat of my heart.

The journalist briefly furrows her brow. She opens her mouth, but closes it again without asking another question. Did she see the pity in my eyes? Is that why she's silent? Maybe.

"As much as I'd love to keep talking, my plane is waiting," I say quickly before she can finish her question, and give her a warm smile. Then I slip into the taxi to the airport, from where I'll be leaving Halifax for a damn long time.

Chapter Forty-Three

AUTUMN

Thanks to you, my heart can beat properly again.

Tay's voice is everywhere inside me as I step up to the window at the end of the hallway. Here on the seventh floor, I can see over the rooftops to the harbour. I didn't want to come here, shouldn't be standing here looking out, but I couldn't help myself.

I had to see him, even if only from a distance. Just a few minutes ago, he left the boat. He's gone, but I still can't grasp it.

As I turn away to focus on my work, I wonder how I'm supposed to return to the life I had before Tay. Whether I can endure the loneliness I had long since come to terms with all over again. How I can fall asleep without knowing how he's doing.

The only bright spot of the day is that Mom handled seeing her own daughter in the news along with those nasty rumors surprisingly well. Still, I walk down the corridor with heavy shoulders.

"Oh dear."

I look up and spot Dr. Parker standing at the nurses' station with Sandra.

"I warned you...," says my supervisor.

Yes, she did. "I need Faith Scott's file," I say, addressing Sandra, because this is the last topic I want to discuss right now.

Sandra hands it to me, and I don't miss the way she studies me as she does. "Everything okay with you?"

"Perfect," I reply. After all, I swore to Dr. Parker just a few days ago that my feelings for Tay would in no way affect my professionalism.

As I turn around, I hear the two of them whispering.

"Well, I guess you owe me twenty dollars," says Dr. Parker.

She doesn't, because Sandra won that stupid bet among the colleagues – Tay is the love of my life.

I still hear Sandra sigh, but I no longer catch what she says afterward.

I throw myself into work, but even that can neither cheer me up nor distract me, and when I head to Kayla's room a few hours later, I feel anything but ready for another goodbye. And even less ready to face Chloe, yet it's precisely that woman—in all her unmasked beauty, with dark hair and bright red lips—that I find in Kayla's room.

The woman who has what I long for: the man my heart beats for.

"Autumn, very good. Do you have the discharge papers for Kayla?" She quickly opens the travel bag on the bed and pulls open the nightstand drawer.

I wish she were less warm, less likable, a woman nobody likes. "Yes," I reply, nodding toward the documents in my hand. "Where's Kayla?"

Her gaze finds mine. "At physical therapy. I thought it

would be good for her to get one more session in before we fly."

"An excellent idea." I smile at her. "Then I'll say goodbye to her later."

"That won't be possible." She pulls Kayla's coloring books from the drawer and packs them into the suitcase. "Right after therapy we have to leave immediately, the plane is waiting, and unfortunately the timing is extremely tight. But I'd be happy to pass something on to her from you."

"We can surely manage a quick hug," I reply, because as much as the thought of saying goodbye to the little one hurts, I don't want to let her go without a farewell.

Chloe picks up the loose colored pencils one by one until the drawer is empty. "Do I have to sign the discharge papers?"

"No." I hand her the folder, trying to read her face to understand why she's changing the subject. "The documents also include all the information about the treatment and the follow-up therapy," I say absentmindedly.

She takes the folder and opens it.

"If your doctor in Los Angeles has any questions, he's welcome to contact me. My phone number…"

"That won't be necessary." When she looks up, she seems friendly, yet I get the impression she wants to get rid of me. "Thank you for taking such good care of my daughter. Goodbye."

Am I imagining it, or did she emphasize the word *my*? "You're very welcome."

Chloe quickly closes the folder and unzips her briefcase to put it away. As she slips the documents into one of the compartments, I spot a large white container inside the bag.

A pill bottle—it's so huge that I get curious. Who needs such an enormous supply of tablets?

Chloe, now heading to the closet to pack Kayla's clothes, doesn't notice me stepping closer and peeking into the bag.

Maybe they're antacids or vitamins. That would at least explain the size of the container. I tilt my head to read the label. Paracetamol—nothing unusual, but why does she need a jumbo pack? Is she sick?

"What is this?" Suddenly Chloe is standing next to me, a stack of Kayla's hoodies in her hands. "What are you doing?"

I look at her thoughtfully. The makeup is so thick that I wouldn't be able to tell if her skin underneath were pale or if she had dark circles under her eyes. "That's quite a lot of paracetamol."

"That's none of your business," she replies, grabs her bag, and zips it shut. Her movements suddenly seem frantic.

"Are you all right?" I ask directly, studying her body. She's noticeably slim, bordering on underweight.

She smiles magnanimously. "Of course, I just get the occasional headache, that's all."

You don't need a bulk pack of painkillers for the occasional headache. My gaze drifts over her hair. It looks healthy, but it could just as easily be another wig. I lock eyes with her; she looks away.

"Thank you for your help, I can manage the rest on my own." The way she clutches her bag, as if she wants to protect it from me. The tense jaw. The fact that she clearly wants to get rid of me, that she doesn't want me to say goodbye to Kayla.

Something isn't right here. But what?

While Chloe packs Kayla's socks and underwear, I rack my brain, trying to figure out where this feeling is coming from.

"Goodbye," Chloe says again, much more forcefully than before. It almost sounds like a warning.

"One more question." I step toward her. "Why don't you want me to say goodbye to Kayla?" I ask, hoping for a clue.

She stuffs the socks into the travel bag. "That's nonsense, we just don't have enough time."

Shaking my head, I fix my gaze on her. That's ridiculous—Kayla and I are in the same building, it wouldn't take a minute to say goodbye.

"You want to keep me away from her, you're afraid I might find out something I'm not supposed to know." I have no idea where the thought suddenly comes from, but it feels right. "What is it that I'm not supposed to see?" My tone becomes more intense. "What are you hiding from me? Has Kayla's stomach pain returned?"

"Kayla is perfectly fine," she replies indignantly. "If she wasn't, you would know it as her doctor."

That's true—the attending physicians are the first to be informed of any issues with their patients, provided they're on duty, and I've been on duty for hours. But if it's not about Kayla's health, then what is it about?

"You don't want her to talk to me." Heat rises in me. "What is it she's not supposed to tell me?"

Her movements grow increasingly frantic as she packs Kayla's belongings. "Listen, I get that your little heart is broken, but that's no reason to start imagining things that have nothing to do with reality."

I try in vain to fit the puzzle pieces into place in my mind. If Chloe is healthy, it must be about Kayla. The girl had long known that her parents didn't, or no longer, love each other. During physical therapy, she seemed like the constant fighting between them was the worst part for her.

When she began having those unexplained stomach pains, I was sure the girl was unaware of many things.

But what if that's not true? What if she really doesn't have a problem with the divorce? But she apparently didn't have a disease either.

So why the stomach pains?

Wait a minute.

Didn't the pain start shortly after Chloe showed up at the clinic?

"Did you put the idea of stomach pain into your daughter's head?" I ask Chloe. Children are very impressionable, especially by their parents, and it would be something that could explain everything.

Is she that kind of person? Could she do that? And if so, why? To drive a wedge between Tay and me?

No, that can't be it—after all, she was the one who wanted the divorce. Or was she?

"This is getting more and more outrageous," she snaps at me. "If you don't want to get sued, you'd better withdraw these baseless accusations immediately."

My head is spinning. Are these baseless accusations? Am I being unfair to her? Is my broken heart just grasping at straws that couldn't save it either way?

She zips up the travel bag and slings it over her shoulder. "Get out of my way." Her gaze turns ice-cold as she reaches for her briefcase.

A faint rattling sound can be heard as she lifts it up.

The pills.

Paracetamol.

"Some painkillers can cause the mentioned symptoms if taken in the wrong dosage," I hear June say in my mind, and out of nowhere, the loose threads come together.

Suddenly, there's another possible answer to all the

questions. An answer that pulls the ground out from under my feet.

"You poisoned Kayla." The words leave my mouth without a sound.

Chloe freezes.

So it's true?

"You gave her paracetamol, and more than was good for her." My God, what kind of person is this woman? "Because you knew Tay would stay with you if that was best for Kayla." But why did she want that?

Chloe's reaction is a hysterical snort. "I'm leaving now. Expect a defamation lawsuit, because that's a given." She spins on her heel and heads for the door.

I sprint after her. "Don't you realize this can be detected in Kayla's blood? The standard blood panel showed nothing abnormal, but as soon as we take a closer look at her liver values, there will be no more doubt." I barely catch up to her before I pass her to block the door. "The samples still exist, we keep them in case they need to be analyzed again."

Suddenly, she turns chalk white.

That's the proof.

I can't believe it. I can't believe she actually did that.

"Why?" I ask, horrified.

"I love Tay. Without him…" Tears shimmer in her eyes, and the tension drains from her body.

Suddenly, I feel sorry for her. Even though I can't comprehend how she could go that far, I understand her pain, her helplessness. And as crazy as it sounds, part of me wants to protect her from the truth she so clearly denies.

What's wrong with me?

Am I really hesitating to confront a woman who risked her child's health for her own benefit with facts that simply can't be changed?

Yes, it hurts—of course it will break her heart—but isn't living a lie by any means possible even worse than that? Doesn't the truth give her a chance to start over? To find someone who loves her back, with whom she can experience real happiness?

"But Tay doesn't love you," I say, and in that very moment, I know it was right to say it out loud.

Tears stream down her cheeks, smudging her makeup. "He will. As soon as he forgets you, he'll learn to love me."

I shake my head sadly. I don't know much about this marriage, but I know a lot about Tay. "He's not the man he used to be anymore."

Her expression is full of wistfulness. "Exactly."

What? Chloe knew? She always knew about Tay's scarred heart? That's why she wanted the divorce. But then, when she saw him again here at Halifax Harbor Hospital, she noticed the change in him. She felt that he could open his heart to others. That he had become the man she had wished for all those years.

She loves him, now more than ever. So much that she's willing to cross any line for him.

I don't know how to deal with this. What to think or feel. I only know one thing: that she—love or not—went too far.

Far too far.

"You risked Kayla's health." This is insane. Chloe is insane!

"Kayla was never in any danger," she replies, her voice hoarse. How can she act as if it's completely normal—even understandable—to poison her daughter to save a marriage? "The dosage was precisely measured."

"You're not a doctor, how…"

Her expression turns almost pitying now. "You clearly have no idea how vast my network is."

Is that supposed to mean a doctor friend advised her? Who does something like that?

I gasp. "If Tay finds out, he'll…"

"If I were you, I'd think twice about that," she cuts me off. Her eyes narrow menacingly. "After all, there are a few things about you that no one's supposed to know, right?"

I immediately step back. Is she bluffing, or does she really know something about me?

"The accident, your father's blood alcohol level." A triumphant grin spreads across her face as a cold shiver runs down my spine. "Your mother's suicide attempt."

I gasp, but no air comes. How did she get this information?

"When you know where to look, you can find everything—and your dear school friends gave me a few more interesting details too." Her gaze drifts to my thighs. "Poor Autumn… so alone… so torn…"

The hospital room around me starts to spin, faster and faster. Chloe's flawless face blurs before my eyes. She researched me or hired a private investigator. It only took her a few days to uncover every detail.

"You wouldn't want your mom to find out about all this from the newspapers, would you? Who knows what might happen then, right?" I barely notice her brushing the bangs from my forehead. "Or is that a risk you're willing to take—for Tay?"

A familiar fear sinks its claws into me.

Even though I've increasingly suspected lately that I've protected Mom too much over the past few years. Even though she keeps insisting she's doing fine. And even though, through Tay, I've come to understand that there's no clear answer to the question of whether it's better to protect yourself or others, as I always thought.

Could I do that? Could I take that risk?

Oh God, I don't know.

"I knew it." A smug smile flashes across her face. She strokes my hair, and when she reaches the ends, she tugs on them. "Tay belongs to me. Forever," she says, then lets go of my hair and pushes me aside.

Still unable to comprehend what just happened, I watch her disappear from the room.

Nothing in this world is fair. With those words, Tay gave me a glimpse into his life a little over a week ago on the roof of the Halifax Harbor Hospital.

I didn't want to believe it, thought that as long as there were people who brought enough light into this world, it wouldn't sink into darkness.

But now I suspect that there are battles you can't win with that. That there are people who will always strike out for their own happiness and don't care who they hurt in the process.

Chloe is one of those people.

She plays dirty, poisons this world and everyone in it—and gets away with it because no one is willing to go further than she does. That's probably exactly how she handled the doctor who helped her dose the paracetamol.

She'll keep poisoning Tay and Kayla too—in the name of love—and she won't need a single pill to do it.

I don't know much right now, in this moment, as I lean tiredly against the wall and slide down. But I do know that she can't be allowed to get away with it.

I know I have to act—for Kayla's health, for Tay, and also for myself.

And I already know how.

Chapter Forty-Four

TAY

With my hands buried in my pockets, I look out the window, where the lights of Los Angeles spread out beneath me. More and more stars begin to awaken in the sky.

I'm still alone in the villa, in this world whose superficial safety I once sought refuge in, but which now feels like it's no longer mine.

Everything here is cold. The furniture is simple and expensive—a cream-colored sofa, a massive coffee table, an artfully arranged bookshelf.

More than anything, I want to call Autumn or at least text her. To find out how she's doing, to hear her voice, to feel close to her for just a few minutes.

Since I landed in Los Angeles, I haven't wanted to do anything else. I barely paid attention during the meeting with the producers of my next film.

Lost in thought, I lower my gaze to the mirror-smooth marble floor. How can I be here in Los Angeles with a woman I don't love? How can I breathe here while on the other side of the continent, a woman is waiting for me who owns my heart?

It will take years before Autumn and I get a second chance—if we ever do.

"Daaaddy!" I hear Kayla call out loudly, cutting through my thoughts.

I smile automatically. "I'm in the living room."

Leaning on her crutches, she hobbles in. Her cheeks are flushed pink, her eyes widen as they land on the aquarium she had wanted so badly. I rush over to her and hug her tightly.

"Isn't it amazing?" I gently stroke her hair, so glad to have her back. She's my ray of hope, my reason to keep going.

"Wow!" she breathes in awe, staring at the colorful fish with her mouth open. "You're Nemo and you're Dory and you…"

Her excited murmuring fades into the background as Chloe appears in the living room and gives me a tired smile. "Hey, how was your meeting?"

I remind myself that the situation we're in doesn't make her happy either, and that we both still have to hold it together—for Kayla. "They want me to attend a promo event tomorrow night. Did you have a good trip?"

"Better not ask." She rolls her eyes, slips off her high heels, and pads into the open kitchen to pour herself some wine.

Kayla calls out to me. "Can we make a video for Autumn?"

Chloe shoots me a venomous look. "Autumn doesn't care," she replies as coldly as I've rarely seen her speak to Kayla. "She has other patients to take care of now. She's already forgotten you."

"She definitely hasn't," I correct my damn wife and place a hand on Kayla's shoulder. "Autumn will be happy about the video."

My daughter cheers. "Can I have your phone?"

"There's no time for that now." Chloe's eyes narrow to slits. "Off to the bathroom with you, the bed is calling."

"But it'll only take a minute," Kayla protests.

"No backtalk." Chloe downs her glass in one gulp, marches toward us, and grabs Kayla's arm.

I quickly hold her back. "I'll take care of it tonight," I say with a firm expression.

Her forced smile sends a shiver down my spine. "Fine."

On the way to the bathroom, Kayla is unusually quiet, and I'm also lost in my own thoughts. I wonder whether Chloe will continue to punish Kayla for everything she dislikes about me. Even if Kayla's nanny resumes part of the childcare starting tomorrow, we won't be able to avoid spending time together as a trio.

I find no answers, not even when I kiss my sleeping daughter on the forehead an hour later, put the fairy tale book aside, and stroll back to the living area of our villa.

On the way there, my phone buzzes. A message from Autumn appears, and my heart skips a beat.

She misses me too, can't stand being without me, wants to hear me, see me, feel me.

I lean against the wall and open the message, but as soon as I skim the first words—where she asks me not to tell anyone what she's about to write—I start to feel uneasy. Moments later, the hallway begins to spin around me.

No psychosomatic symptoms, paracetamol, poisoned, blood samples, evidence, Chloe.

The words dance before my eyes, I can't grasp what they mean, can't believe Chloe went this far.

My God, what is wrong with this woman?

How could she possibly…

My hand trembles with rage, heat builds inside me, fury that needs to come out—but must not.

There it is: Chloe knows everything about Autumn and threatened to make it public if she told me the real reason for Kayla's stomach pains. And now it's dawning on me who made sure Autumn ended up in the tabloids. Chloe must have tipped off the reporters. She wanted to drive a wedge between us—and she succeeded.

My fist slams against the wall behind me, a sharp pain shoots through my forearm, but it doesn't hurt nearly as much as Autumn's words.

I love you, Tay, and I love Kayla. That's why I broke our agreement not to have contact this one time. Whatever you do now, if Chloe finds out I told you, she'll destroy me.

Chloe must not get away with this—and she won't. I thank Autumn and assure her that she doesn't need to worry. I would never do anything to hurt her.

Never.

On the way to Chloe, I take a deep breath and prepare myself for the most important role I've ever played in my life: the clueless husband who has to expose his wife without confronting her with the truth he already knows.

No one wrote me a script for this, there are no stage directions I can follow. All I have are my own feelings, and I'm going to trust them.

Chloe is sitting with another glass of wine on a designer stool at the kitchen counter. The bottle next to her is empty.

"What was that earlier?" I ask her, sliding onto the stool next to her.

She runs her fingers along the stem of the wine glass. "What do you mean?"

As if she didn't know that. "This." I point first at her, then at myself. "We're doing this for Kayla. So she's happy, so she's okay."

A quiet snort escapes her lips. Her gaze drifts to the window, behind which the nighttime sprawl of Los Angeles stretches out before us.

"What's the point of the whole charade if you then deny her such a small wish, like making a video for Autumn?" That makes no sense, and she must realize that too.

"Autumn…" She takes a sip of her white wine, then looks at me sadly. "She's not part of this family. Kayla should forget her as soon as possible." And so should you, hangs unspoken between us.

"This family. As if it still existed," I hear myself say bitterly.

Suddenly, Chloe places her hand on my arm. "Give us a chance, I'm trying too." She starts to gently stroke me. "We're trapped in this life, so we should make the best of it, don't you think?"

And what is that supposed to be, the best? I shake off her hand, grab her wine glass, and take a big gulp. "And what, in your opinion, would be the best?"

She moves closer to me than I'd like. Her expression softens, she lowers her eyelids. "I loved you, and maybe I can love you again. If I can manage to forget what you did to me, maybe I could love you again."

What the hell is this now? "What I did to you? What are you talking about?" I didn't do anything to her. "You wanted the divorce, remember? That's how it all started—it's the only reason I was even in Halifax."

"I never wanted to leave you," she replies quietly, without looking at me. "I thought you wanted the divorce and just beat you to it."

"Bullshit, Chloe. If you're going to lie, at least stick to the same version." I slap my palm on the counter, letting my anger out, showing her how furious she makes me. "The other day you claimed you wanted the divorce so I would fight for you." My God, does she really think I'm buying this charade?

She flinches, but only for a moment. "I've always loved you."

Another lie—I can see it clearly. In all our years together, I never tried to read her. Her feelings didn't matter to me; I wasn't interested. But now that Autumn has made my heart beat again, I see Chloe in a different light.

Shaking my head, I study her. "No, you didn't," I say with feeling. "Why did you even marry me back then?"

For a while, she silently stares at her wine glass. "Out of love."

"Stop lying to me already!" I yell at her. She poisoned her own daughter—she can't love, she's not capable of it. "We got married because you were pregnant."

She chews on her lower lip.

"You pushed for this marriage, thought it was a smart tactical move." Yeah, that's what it was—that's how she framed it back then.

Did she manipulate me? Not for a second did I open up to her—I never let her see what was going on inside me, always kept my wall up.

My God, I thought I was safe. I thought we had a shared goal. Was I really just Chloe's puppet?

She didn't hurt me—I made sure of that—but she manipulated me, and that's just as bad.

"I loved you, I loved you from the very first day," she whispers, her voice choked.

Lies, all lies. But if she's hoping I'll change the subject and leave the room, like I've done our entire life together in situations like this, then she's wrong. Today, I'm diving to the bottom, to where the painful truth is buried.

"If you loved me, you would've negotiated breaks in my contract for the doctor role so we could see each other." I raise my eyebrows pointedly, sure she sees the heated spark in my eyes.

"I had no choice, there was no room to negotiate." Shaking her head, she lowers her eyelids. "I knew how important this role is to you, so I agreed—because I love you."

I'm slowly starting to wonder why she never became an actress herself. She undoubtedly has the talent for it.

"But I don't love you, you know that, I've never claimed otherwise." I force her to look at me. She has to stop shaping the truth to suit her. "And I never will love you." How could I? As cold and false as she is. That woman has no heart. Maybe that's why, in a twisted way, she was right for me when mine was still half-dead.

She empties her glass, takes a new bottle of wine from the fridge, and pours herself another. "Because you love the little doctor, right? Can't you see she's only after your money and your success?"

The contemptuous tone with which she speaks about Autumn drives me mad. I cross the living area, needing to put distance between us before I do something I'll regret. "My money and success are the last things Autumn wants from me," I say, looking out at the sea of lights below me in Los Angeles.

"That little whore's really messed with your head, hasn't she?" I hear Chloe grumble behind me.

I spin around instantly. Her eyes gleam devilishly; she

enjoys hurting me. "No, you're the little whore who messed with my head." Even as I say the words, I realize how true they are.

There's so much more than her insane attempt to "save" our marriage by poisoning Kayla. She lied to me from the very beginning, always twisted the facts to suit her needs, and I, the idiot, believed her. I believed her when she said I'd have to sleep my way to the top if I ever wanted to become someone. I believed her when she said we made a great team.

What else did she lie to me about?

Was her pregnancy really unplanned, or was it just her way of tying me to her?

Far too many thoughts are racing through my head like a roller coaster, flipping over, losing their grip, plunging into the depths.

"You're calling me a whore?" Chloe presses her hands to her chest in mock shock. "Me, the woman who was always there for you, who picked you up off the street and made you a star?"

It's true, a lot of what I've achieved in life, I owe to her. But she didn't do it out of love, I'm sure of that. And besides, she's wrong about one thing.

"Aren't you forgetting something?" I ask her sharply. "When my career was in danger, were you there for me then?" No, she wasn't. She wanted to let me fall, just not go down with me.

That's it.

That's why she wanted the divorce!

"It's not Autumn who's after my fame and success." My God, why am I only seeing this now? "It's you, and it's always been you."

There was no love.

There was only her addiction to fame. To money. To admiration.

She wanted to be in the spotlight, to be successful and wealthy, and thanks to me, she made it.

Suddenly her expression changes, becomes hard and calculating. "Your success is entirely my doing. Do you really think I'd give up everything I worked so hard for because of some random little slut?"

A cold shiver runs down my spine, and I make sure she sees it in my expression. "You were ready to give it up when you thought my career was over, for fuck's sake!"

She punished me because I wasn't who she wanted me to be, just like my father used to. And she manipulated me, just like my brother did. She made me believe I needed her, that I was nothing without her, a failure, worthless.

And I didn't see those obvious parallels. Because I had locked my childhood away so deep.

Chloe curls her lips into a disgusted sneer. "You think you're so important, Tay."

At last, she drops the mask.

This is her. The real Chloe. The one who would walk over corpses. The one who doesn't care who she hurts, the one for whom everything revolves around herself.

She is how I used to be before I met Autumn.

"How could I not see for so long who you really are?" My words carry all the disappointment—about her, this marriage, and myself—that I've been holding inside.

"Oh dear, are you about to cry?" Chloe gets up from her chair and steps toward me. "Shit, yeah, you are, aren't you?" Her index finger finds my chest. "I always knew it: You're not a man, Tay Lawson, you're a wimp pretending to be one, and you're doing a shitty job at it."

I back away, a buzzing starts in my head, my chest tightens, my field of vision narrows.

For a moment, I feel like the boy from the ranch again, bullied by his brother and looked at with shame by his father. For a moment, I'm once more the little good-for-nothing who knows he has to be a man—strong, tough, and emotionless—who has to strike before others do, and who will be laughed at if he misses.

As if by instinct, Autumn appears before my mind's eye. With her light, she broke a spell inside me that not even my daughter had been able to break until then.

What I suspected this morning becomes a certainty in this moment: Meeting a cold world with coldness only makes it colder.

I won't allow Chloe or anyone else to drag me into their darkness. Under no circumstances will I let the woman who now stands before me with such contempt destroy what has awakened in me over the past few days—something so beautiful, so warm, so pure.

"That hurt," I admit openly, and I mean so much more than Chloe's accusation that I'm not a man, but a wimp.

My wife stares at me with her mouth open.

"What happened in your life to make you this kind of person?" A wistful expression flickers across my face. It must have been terrible, maybe even worse than what happened to me.

"What's that supposed to mean now?" she asks, nervously reaching for her wine glass.

"I'm sorry, Chloe." I take the glass from her and set it back on the counter. Then I place my hand on her cheek.

"What are you sorry for?" she asks.

"That you fought so hard and still lost," I reply. From

the confused look on her face, I can tell she has no idea what's going on. "I want a divorce."

"And what about Kayla?" she asks accusingly. "Are you willing to risk her health just to run off with that doctor?"

As if our daughter ever meant anything to her. She was just a means to an end. I lift my gaze and look out the window into the night. I'd love to confront her with everything, but for Autumn's sake, I stay silent.

"The other day we completely blindsided her with our separation, she wasn't prepared." And the words Chloe—presumably on purpose—chose were more than inappropriate. "We'll proceed carefully, involve a child psychologist, give her time."

Chloe looks at me in shock. Damn, the woman is the greatest actress of all time. "You're willing to risk that? You'll ruin her."

On the contrary, I'm saving her. Frantically, I search for something to say in response. Something that will take the wind out of her sails and at the same time never let her suspect that I know about her despicable act.

What would make her want to divorce me? If she no longer gets from me what she so desperately needs.

Yes, that's it!

I know what I have to say to get rid of her without betraying Autumn.

"Besides, I'm ending my career." The words leave my mouth with full conviction, even though the thought alone causes me immense pain. But that pain is worth it, because I'm sure Chloe understands what the consequences would be: there would be no spotlight left for her to bask in. It's the only thing that truly matters to her, and now she has no choice but to admit it.

"That way, I can be there for Kayla during the difficult

time of our separation, and the press won't be a problem," I add.

"Well, tough luck," hisses my soon-to-be ex-wife, pointing her index finger at me. "The contract explicitly rules out resignation. The only reasons not to shoot the film would be your death or a serious accident that disfigures or mentally impairs you."

Just a few days ago, I would have believed her without question—today, I'm certain that's another one of her lies. I demonstratively cross my arms over my chest. "Good thing I know Phil, the producer, so well. I'll talk to him—he'll understand and can sort it out for me."

It's the perfect trap—and I can see in Chloe's face that it just snapped shut.

Thank God. I probably couldn't have kept up the charade any longer.

A mocking laugh escapes her mouth. "Fine, if you want the whole world to think you're a loser who'd rather give up than fight for the Oscar you swore you'd win in every interview, then..."

"...then so be it," I finish Chloe's sentence.

In my mind's eye, I suddenly see Mike and the man who once called himself my father standing next to my soon-to-be ex-wife.

All three stare at me with wide eyes, no one says a word.

They can't hurt me, none of them, but not because I'm protecting myself with all my might.

The opposite is true—my heart is wide open and full of compassion. They're trapped in their lives, with their small-mindedness, their emotional coldness, their ruthlessness. Their inability to feel and act out of love.

"You were a complete waste of time," Chloe hisses.

I smile gently. "Pack your stuff and get out."

Chapter Forty-Five

AUTUMN

Restlessly, I pace back and forth in my shared apartment room. It's been dark outside for hours, stars cover the sky, and moonlight falls on the painting Mom made for me that hangs on the wall.

Since I texted Tay, I haven't let go of my phone for a single second. I've imagined a thousand different scenarios, seen Chloe's furious face and Tay's disappointment in my mind. I pictured them arguing, getting more and more worked up. Or maybe it's going completely differently—maybe Tay is still thinking about how to expose Chloe. He promised not to say anything, and I know he won't. But what if Chloe finds out anyway?

My God, I hope this doesn't go wrong.

I check my phone again.

Nothing.

He probably won't get in touch anyway—we agreed not to have contact, and what good would it do?

I tap my phone, the screen lights up.

Nothing.

What's happening in Los Angeles right now? What is Tay doing, how is Chloe reacting?

Finally. A message from Tay!

My heart skips a beat as I open it.

"Chloe is gone," he writes.

I should leave it at that, but I still ask what happened and sink onto the bed while I wait for his reply.

In a few words, Tay tells me about an argument. About how he gradually realized what a cruel game Chloe had been playing with him all these years. About how unscrupulously she behaved in their marriage. Not because she loved him, as she had claimed to me.

"She only ever wanted my fame," he writes.

Yes, that fits the woman I met at the clinic today. I wait briefly to see if he'll say more, but nothing else comes.

"I'm so sorry," I type, tears in my eyes, knowing I should say goodbye now. "Chloe won't just leave it at that, will she?" I ask anyway, because it's just too important. That woman knows no boundaries, no compassion, no scruples. Kayla is out of danger. But Tay and I are not.

For a while, nothing happens.

Then his reply comes: "As long as we're not seen together, we're safe."

Yes, there's some truth to that.

Resigned, I set the phone aside, fully aware that this conversation is now over. Tay's last sentence echoes inside me.

As long as we're not seen together, we're safe.

Chloe will find out if we meet in secret; she might even be waiting for it. The only things standing between Tay and me are my scars and the worry about my mom.

You don't want your mom to find out about all this from

the newspapers, do you? Who knows what might happen, right?

Chloe's words from this afternoon are pounding in my head. A sense of unease spreads through me, and I start pacing in my room.

What would actually happen?

Back and forth.

Thirteen years have passed since the accident, and not once have Mom and I talked about what happened. I've protected her all this time—maybe too much.

Back and forth.

Maybe she's stronger than I thought. Hasn't she been saying for years that she's fine?

Back and forth.

What if those weren't lies?

Back and forth.

And what if they were?

I stop, my gaze falls on the painting Mom made for my apartment room.

Thoughtfully, I step closer, reach out my hand, let my index finger glide over the frame. She painted it because she's doing well. She's been painting again for years.

Could she possibly handle the truth?

"Is that a risk you'd be willing to take for Tay?" Chloe asks me again in my thoughts.

In the painting, a woman stands with her back turned to the viewer in a field of cornflowers. Her red hair flutters in the wind.

What if my fears are unfounded and I'm making the biggest mistake of my life by continuing to protect Mom from something she doesn't even need to be protected from?

My fingers leave the frame, brush over the textured paint on the canvas. On my fingertips, it feels like my scars.

Completely sacrificing yourself for others is just as wrong as ruthlessly putting your own happiness above that of others. Somewhere between these two extremes lies a point where we can find balance. A point where we yield and accept, hold on and let go, win and lose.

My fingers reach the red-haired woman.

And deep inside, I finally allow myself to acknowledge the thought that has been with me for days: to take that one path I've so far refused to walk.

As I get off the bus at dawn and tuck the textbook—whose pages I've only stared at absentmindedly rather than read—into my bag, a queasy feeling settles in my stomach. As I step onto the driveway, cold sweat runs down my back. In my mind, memories flash by—long buried, yet today they feel as if they happened just yesterday.

Mom in her bed.

Motionless.

An empty pack of sleeping pills on the nightstand.

I breathe against the memories, try to push them away—I don't want them, not now, not when I'm supposed to be full of hope and courage. The door I'm approaching is closed, and just like back then, all those years ago, I have no idea what's waiting for me on the other side. Only that it scares me—that much I know.

But what scares me even more is the thought of what will happen if I don't even try.

I have to talk to her, yet I stand frozen in front of her door, only able to think about what happened the last time fate shook her life.

Aunt Lanie, who just picked me up from the hospital, pulls into our driveway. "Are you excited to be home?"

My fingers tremble as I undo the seatbelt. "Definitely," I say, because I don't know what the real answer is.

Her question lingers inside me as I get out of the car and step onto the paved path leading to the front door.

Am I excited to be home? The place where Dad is no longer, but Mom is in bad shape. Every time she visited me in the past few days, she seemed numb. The medication keeps her calm, helps her get through the days. She seems almost normal, maybe a little dulled, emotionless, but I know it's because of the pills.

"She'll get through this," I hear Aunt Lanie say gently.

I look at her resolutely. "We'll get through it together." As soon as I've settled in at home, my aunt will return to her own family. I'll be there for Mom, make sure she takes her pills, keeps her therapy appointments, and gets out regularly.

A little later I'm standing in front of the closed door, behind which my new life is waiting. The one I don't know how to live.

I push it open, look into the dark hallway, see Dad's jacket hanging on the coat rack, his work shoes on the tiles as if he just took them off. There are even a few wood shavings next to them. It feels like he could call out to me at any moment, come around the corner, hug me.

But no one calls out to me, no one comes around the corner, no one hugs me. There's only Aunt Lanie, who steps behind me and exhales tightly.

"Come on, there's cake." She places her hand on my back.

I stare at the threshold, take a deep breath—and step inside for her sake.

A few minutes later, the house was full of paramedics. Even today, I still hear them shouting, see the blue lights flickering across the walls, feel Aunt Lanie's arms around my trembling body, smell her perfume.

Thirteen years have passed. One hundred and fifty-six

months in which I haven't left Mom's side. Nearly five thousand days in which my entire life has revolved around hers.

Time plays out before my inner eye like a movie. I see a teenager who dealt with everything on her own. Who only gave and never took, not even when her own fate broke her. I see a young woman who lives for others, just to have something—anything—she might be loved for. I see a doctor who sees the world through the eyes of others, who always tries to find compromises. I see a woman who never doubted that this was the right way, and I know she was wrong.

Suddenly, the door swings open. Mom's radiant face appears behind it. Her cheeks are rosy, her eyes lively, her movements full of energy.

"Autumn, what a lovely surprise." She hugs me. "What are you doing here?"

Talk to you. About everything we never talked about.

Oh God, what if she's not ready yet?

Mom pulls away from me, her hands brushing my arms, a worried crease forming on her forehead. "Is something wrong, sweetheart?"

I swallow down my panic, then nod silently. Since the accident, I haven't even managed that. Letting them know something was wrong. Because I didn't want to be selfish, because my problems were never allowed to be more important than hers.

"Come on, let's have a cup of tea together," she says and pulls me into the house with her.

While she fills a pot with water, I watch her movements, wondering if she's tense, if she feels weak, if she's worried.

"Tell me." She turns on the stove and places the pot on the burner. "Does it have something to do with the man we talked about the other day?"

Searching for enough courage, I take a deep breath. "I need to tell you something," I finally force out.

"You're going to leave Halifax." Mom smiles gently. "That's okay, really, believe me."

I shake my head. "It's about…" Oh God, why is this so hard? "…about the accident."

For a split second, she flinches, then looks at me with a mix of wistfulness and concern. I meet her gaze, show her my fear.

"So you're finally ready to talk about it," she says softly and sets out two teacups.

"I didn't want to burden you with it because…" My voice fails me.

Lost in thought, she lets her fingers glide over the handle of a cup. "I know, and I'm sorry."

There's nothing she needs to be sorry for. I get up and walk over to her to give her a hug. "There's nothing you need to apologize for."

She starts trembling in my arms. "On the contrary, I need to apologize for everything."

Something about her words makes me pause. I don't know what it is, only that they sound like she knows more than I do. "For what exactly?" I ask hesitantly.

The water in the pot is boiling, Mom pulls away from my arms and fills the cups. "I should've told you a long time ago, but you never wanted to talk about the accident, so I kept it to myself."

What is she talking about? "What?"

"That your dad was drunk wasn't the cause of the accident."

Excuse me? "You knew he'd been drinking?" How long has she known?

She shrugs. “Of course, the police test for that, I was informed.”

“And I thought…” I was so sure that my silence would protect her from something. How distorted is the reality I’ve been living in for so long?

“It wasn’t the alcohol, it was the car. I had promised to take it to the shop, but I didn’t manage to.” Her fingers tremble as she fishes out two tea bags from the supply. With lowered eyelids, she pulls on the strings. “I thought it wasn’t that bad, that it could wait a few weeks, until I was feeling better.”

“What was wrong with the car?” I take the tea bags from her and hang them in the cups.

“There was a rattling noise when I drove over bumps.” Her expression turns desperate now. “I didn’t know that parts of the steering were loose and that it would be so bad…” She claps a hand over her mouth.

Immediately, I’m by her side and hold her tightly. “It wasn’t your fault,” I tell her. “It was a chain of unfortunate circumstances. Fate.”

“You sound like my therapist.” There’s a surprising gentleness in her voice. “She also said I have to forgive myself.”

There’s nothing to forgive. “You have an illness, Mom.”

She shakes her head vehemently. “But I have it under control,” she corrects me. “I’ve been doing well for years, I’ve overcome the past.”

I release her from my arms to study her face. She’s sad, clearly, she’s not well. Talking about all this hurts her. “But you…”

Mom places her hand on my cheek. “Just because not every day is good doesn’t mean I’m sick,” she says earnestly.

I never stopped worrying about her. Wondering if she

was okay or if she was on the verge of falling back into the abyss. Every tiny sign was a warning to me.

Even those that everyone shows from time to time, even when they're healthy.

I was blind, so endlessly blind. "When did this happen?" I ask my mom, shaken.

"In your first year as a resident. You were gone a lot, even at night. I felt it was time to stand on my own two feet and forgive myself." She picks up the teacups and hands me one. "Yes, the accident was my fault, and that will never change. I live with it, day by day, and I make the best of it."

She does, I can see it. For the first time, I see her as she truly is today, not as I always wanted to see her. She's no longer the mom she used to be—she's a strong woman forging her own path.

How could I not have seen that for so long?

Maybe I didn't want to.

Maybe it was easier for me to worry about her than to worry about myself. Maybe it was easier to protect her than to stand up for myself.

My God…

Was my mom the perfect excuse for me to hide? And were all the others, too?

The ones I didn't want to burden with the monster were, in truth, the ones I was ashamed to show my scars to.

The ones I wanted to protect, the ones I wanted to see happy at any cost, were in truth the ones I wanted to be loved by for my big heart, because I was convinced it was the only thing about me that could be loved.

One by one, these thoughts rise up inside me. And suddenly I realize something that knocks the ground out from under my feet: I never wanted to be selfish, but in truth, that's exactly what I was. Because it was never about the others—it was always only about me.

About my scars.

About my pain.

About my shame.

"I have to confess something to you," I say to my mom. "Something I should have talked to you about a long time ago."

She gestures for me to sit. Holding our teacups, we settle into the chairs at the kitchen table, and then I tell her everything.

How I felt back then, how terrible it was for me to lose Henry, that taking care of her was the only thing that still made me feel like I had any worth.

How lonely I was, that I felt like a monster, and how it destroyed me to keep all of it bottled up inside.

"I promised Dad I'd make the world a warmer place," I finally tell her. "And I was sure that meant being there for you first and foremost."

Mom wraps her hands around her cup. "I noticed that you weren't doing well."

She brought it up, I remember, often even. But I didn't want her to see how weak and broken and torn I was, I was ashamed.

"I hated my body, and secretly I blamed Dad for my situation," I admit, fully aware that I was the one who truly turned myself into this monster.

Not Dad, who left me alone with Mom.

Not Mom, who gave everything in the fight against her own demons.

It was me. I'm the one responsible for the scars on my thighs. They were my outlet, my way to release the anger I considered selfish and therefore forbade myself to feel. And they're also signs that I didn't value myself enough to ask for help during that difficult time.

Mom's expression is understanding. "Why did you never tell me?"

"I thought I was protecting you," I reply tonelessly. "From everything that was wrong with me—and there was so much."

"Wrong with you?" Mom tilts her head to the side, still seeming composed.

I know she can handle the truth. Searching for the right words, I take a sip of tea.

"Mom?" I reach for her hand, my fingers trembling. "There's something I still need to tell you."

She nods at me encouragingly.

Thinking of Tay and the future we might have gives me courage. Still, my heart pounds in my throat as I open my mouth. "I used to hurt myself, back in the time after the accident, and I was so ashamed that I couldn't tell anyone."

Tears well up in her eyes. "You did what?"

It hurts her—I can see it—and it hurts me to know that I'm the reason.

"It's over," I say, gently stroking her hand. "But there are marks on my skin. Marks that soon the whole world will know about," I say, and then I tell her about Tay.

About how we met. How we grew closer. How he reacted to my scars and healed a part of me I thought was broken forever.

"Tay Lawson?" Mom clasps her hands over her mouth.

Yes. Tay Lawson. "I know it's totally crazy." My cheeks start to burn. "If we want to be together, the press will find out about my story. About our story, about Dad, about the accident, about all the scars." I look at Mom searchingly, looking for any sign that she can't handle this news, and indeed there's worry on her face. "Do you think you can..."

"This isn't about me, sweetheart," she interrupts before I can ask whether she can handle it. "For years, you were too ashamed to tell me the truth. Do you really think you can tell the whole world now?"

I press my lips together, because that's exactly the crucial question. That's what everything has revolved around since I found out that David is actually Tay Lawson. That's what I didn't want to admit to myself, what I made excuses for, the same ones I used back then. That I have to protect Mom—from something that, in truth, only I was afraid of.

Do you think you can tell the whole world? Mom's words echo inside me.

"Maybe it's time I do exactly that," I reply.

Tay and I could grace the covers of glossy magazines as Beauty and the Beast. They might judge me for what I did to myself. Call me out, criticize me, laugh at me.

But if I have to choose between a life in the spotlight with the man who makes me feel whole, and a life of loneliness where I don't allow myself to stand up for who I am, then I know the answer.

"Maybe it's time I live my life." Even as I speak the words, I can feel how much strength they give me.

That's what Mom said to me a few days ago at the community center. What she's known for so much longer than I have. What she's tried so many times to make me understand. What I never wanted to hear, because I was afraid of what it meant.

Mom smirks. "I think so too," she says. "So, what are you going to do now?"

Something that will change my life forever. "What Dad

actually asked of me that day." He didn't want me to warm the world of others alone, that was just what I understood. My world matters too, it deserves warmth as well. "And for that, I have to fly to Los Angeles."

A wide smile spreads across Mom's face. "Sounds like a plan."

I pull my phone out of my pocket. My fingers tremble as I unlock the screen, and while I search for a suitable flight, I feel my heartbeat quicken even more.

Chapter Forty-Six

TAY

The sound technician clips a microphone to my shirt while I let my gaze wander across the still-empty television studio.

In a few minutes, the reporter will ask me questions on that red sofa—questions I don't yet know. Until now, Chloe had always handled these things with the media in advance, but there wasn't enough time to find a new agent, and I had more important things to do in the last few hours than worry about this interview. Because this morning, I talked to Kayla about the fact that Chloe and I are now officially separating. She responded with an "Okay," and by now I'm sure she really is okay with it. She confessed how long she's felt that we're not a real family.

To sort out the details of Kayla's care, I'll probably need a lawyer, since Chloe hasn't responded to any of my messages about it.

Mentally, I add the search for a lawyer to the overflowing list of things that still need to be done because of our separation. The only good thing about it is that the chaos might at least distract me a little from how much I miss Autumn.

I let out a heavy sigh at the thought of her.

The TV journalist enters the studio with her hair flowing behind her, and the sound technician wires her up. An assistant asks me to take a seat on the sofa, which is brightly lit by spotlights in the center of the studio.

As I shake the host's hand, I see the dangerously aggressive sparkle in her eyes, even though she gives me a deliberately warm smile.

"You're not getting away from me today," her look tells me, and she gestures for me to sit down.

This is the moment when I used to remind myself of my own rules and put my walls back up. Today, I think of Autumn and her mission to bring more warmth into this world.

"We're live in three…" calls a voice from the darkness backstage.

Since I said goodbye to Autumn on the roof of Halifax Harbor Hospital, I've asked myself so many times why our paths crossed when there's no future for us. Why fate brought us together only to tear us apart again.

"…two…"

It doesn't make sense, but maybe I just haven't seen it yet.

"…one…"

With her warm openness, Autumn accomplished something I had thought impossible until then: she healed me, at least a little. And I want to believe that even the superficial, artificial world of Hollywood can be healed a little too.

The upbeat theme song of the show plays. "Welcome to Five to Five, the celebrity magazine with the hottest news," the host chirps into the camera, then turns to me. "Today's guest: Tay Lawson, welcome!"

"Great to be here." I give her a warm smile and lean back on the sofa while the host scoots forward in her armchair.

"How is your daughter?" Feigned interest laces her words.

"Excellent, thank you for asking," is what I would have said just a few weeks ago. "Her accident was a shock, and I'm immensely relieved that she's now on the road to recovery," I say today.

She tilts her head to the side. "Rumor has it there's a doctor who supposedly helped you get over the shock," she replies with a devious grin.

I suppress the wistful smile that wants to creep onto my lips. I've spent years perfecting the art of deceiving and manipulating this world, and to protect Autumn, I'll have to keep relying on it.

"She did, by taking such good care of my daughter." This time, I need the slick smile I've trained for so long, so no one sees how painfully my heart tightens at the thought of my time with Autumn. Fortunately, nothing about my divorce has leaked yet, so she has no reason to dig deeper. "And I'd like to take this opportunity to thank all the doctors and nurses at Halifax Harbor Hospital for their work. They've done an outstand—"

"Yes, yes, of course," she cuts me off. I knew this would happen, and I also knew that would be the end of that topic. "Let's talk about your new role. Your last film was a complete failure. Are you afraid of another flop now that you're returning to the screen as Dr. Cross?"

The host's manicured fingernails drum against the cards with the interview questions in her hand.

"Not in the slightest." That's how I would have responded before. "In front of the camera, I play a role that I immerse myself in and deeply connect with. When I'm filming, I become the person I'm portraying," I now explain to the host.

"Um..." Clearly confused, she furrows her brow.

No one has ever heard such honest words from me about my work, so I meet her with an understanding look. "There's only one situation where I'm afraid in front of the camera: when the character I'm playing is afraid."

She's silent for a moment, then sets the cards aside. "And when you're not in front of the camera? Does the role scare you then?" For the first time, there's genuine interest in her voice, however faint.

Without taking my eyes off her, I nod. "Sometimes," I reply, because it's the truth. "But that doesn't stop me from doing what I love."

Playing roles was a vital outlet for me for a long time. The only way to show emotions—and even though that's changed, slipping into characters, transforming into someone else, feeling life in all its breadth—is what makes me happy. And that's exactly what I let the host and all the viewers at home see.

"Wow," my counterpart murmurs. Backstage, someone holds up a sign with a big three to remind her that the show is almost over. "Thank you for those surprisingly candid words, Tay."

"It was my pleasure," I reply, imagining Autumn watching this interview. I see the soft glow in her cheeks, a mix of disbelief, pride, and longing in the green of her eyes. But I also see a tear slide down her face and feel my heart grow heavy along with hers.

With practiced ease, the host turns her dazzling smile to

the camera. "If you want to see more of Tay Lawson, come to the Beverly Hilton Hotel. In two hours, he'll be walking the red carpet at an event there, and who knows, maybe you'll even snag a selfie with him." Music begins to play in the background. "We'll see you again tomorrow at five to five, the celebrity magazine with the hottest news."

Until we get the signal that the show is over, I keep smiling at the camera, then I rise from the sofa. My schedule is extremely tight, so I say a quick goodbye and immediately head home, where both my tuxedo and the stylist are already waiting for me.

The fact that the interview went so well gives me hope. It'll take time to find a new balance between self-protection and openness, but I can feel that I'm on the right path.

Smiling, I leave the studio, but as I sink into the back seat of the waiting car and check my phone, the smile vanishes from my face in an instant.

Chapter Forty-Seven

AUTUMN

My pulse is racing, my chest heaves with every breath beneath the tight evening gown I bought at the airport and put on immediately.

Now I regret the decision. The dress is way too revealing, but I can't change it anymore—it's too late for that.

Again I glance at the time display above the center console. In twenty minutes, the event Tay is attending today will begin. When I researched this news on the plane, I knew it was the perfect opportunity.

I haven't written to him; he has no idea how close we already are. If he knew what I was planning, he might try to stop me. He'd be afraid I couldn't handle the glare of his fame, that the press would tear me apart—and Chloe too.

But they can't. Not if I beat them to it.

I have to make it in time, or I'll miss him on the red carpet. It's going to be close—at least if the GPS showing our route is to be believed.

"Would you please drive a little faster?" I beg the taxi

driver taking me to the Beverly Hilton Hotel, reaching for my mascara.

Nothing can go wrong.

She raises her eyebrows, our eyes meeting in the rearview mirror. "That'll cost extra."

"No problem." I signal her to step on it and dig the hairbrush out of my bag. "How much longer until we get there?"

She shrugs. "Ten minutes, maybe."

Then it's ten to seven. Tay's event starts at seven.

The lights of Los Angeles blur past me—red, blue, white, and yellow blending together. My thoughts are with Tay as I pin up my hair.

The sudden flash of blue lights in front of the windshield pulls me out of my thoughts, sirens wailing. The car slows down, and as it dawns on me that there's probably been an accident, it comes to a stop.

This can't be happening.

I stretch to see, but all I can make out are the other cars that have already formed a line ahead of us.

My God, they're not moving an inch!

Is this a full roadblock?

"I'll be right back." I quickly wrap my jacket around my shoulders, get out of the taxi, and walk in high heels along the line of cars toward the flashing lights.

With every step, my heart pounds faster, my breathing grows heavier. When I reach the accident site, where a wounded man is being loaded into the ambulance, I realize we won't be getting through here anytime soon.

The crashed car is blocking the entire road.

We have to take a different route, so I rush back to the taxi. It has to work, even if I might not arrive at the venue before Tay, at least I can still get there at the same time.

As soon as the taxi comes into view, I realize that this is exactly what's going to happen.

I'm not going to make it.

Never.

By now, the taxi is stuck. A long line has formed behind the car, turning around is out of the question.

The taxi driver gets out of the car and lights a cigarette.

My heart skips a beat, just like my breath. The surroundings blur.

I have to run, so I grab my handbag from the car and pay the fare.

"Where do I need to go?" I ask the taxi driver.

With the cigarette, she points me in the direction. "Take a right at the third intersection, then go straight until you see the red carpet."

"Thanks." I slip off the strappy high heels and gather up my dress with one hand.

"Good luck, sweetheart."

I barely hear the woman's words anymore—I'm already running.

Chapter Forty-Eight

TAY

"Five more minutes," my driver informs me, stopping the car at a red light. Then he turns to face me. "Is it true, what they're saying online?"

It happened shortly after the interview—Chloe informed the press about our breakup, and she did a thorough job of stirring up the rumor mill. Gossip about our divorce is dominating the headlines, and the public's reactions are dominating me.

I bet it has something to do with that red-haired Canadian.

Poor Chloe, he cheated on her.

He acted so warm and loving on Five to Five, but in truth, he dumped his wife without a second thought.

Sentences like these—and others just as bad—circle in my head while my driver watches me with curiosity.

"We've grown apart." A sigh slips from my lips. It's not the whole truth, but it's more than he would have gotten from me three weeks ago.

The driver shrugs. "It's probably not easy, being in the public eye like that."

I lower my gaze to my hands. "Like in any life, there's light and shadow," I reply, eyes fixed on my bare ring finger, thinking of Autumn and the way she looked at that ring before she found out it meant so much less than she thought.

Just under two hours ago, I took it off and made myself a promise: if I ever wear a ring on that finger again, it will be different. It will stand for the fact that Autumn and I made it. That our love outlasted the time her mom's wounds needed to heal.

If I ever wear a ring on that finger again, it will mean the world to me.

"Yeah, I guess that's how it is," the driver murmurs.

I crack the window open. The mild night air flows in. The car turns the corner, headlights flare a few hundred meters ahead. My driver slows down and merges into the line of limousines.

"Three minutes," he informs me.

On the red carpet, my colleagues bask in the flash of cameras. We draw closer; I see them striking poses, sucking in their stomachs, faking smiles.

The murmur of voices outside the car grows louder. The reporters are lying in wait, and they definitely have way more questions than the host on Five to Five.

They'll want to know if Autumn is the reason for my divorce—and I'll lie, because I have no other choice if she's to remain safe.

The driver stops the car. "Here we are."

I adjust my tie knot, wait for him to open the door for me, and get out.

Dozens of reporters rush toward me, shove microphones in my face, fire off questions, jostle each other aside, acting as if there's nothing more important in the world than uncovering the dirty secrets behind Tay Lawson's divorce.

"Are the rumors true, Tay?"

"Why are you getting divorced?"

"It has something to do with that doctor, doesn't it?"

"Is Chloe still your agent?"

All the questions rain down on me, and I brace myself to answer them as best I can.

I smile at them openly. "Well, it's…"

Something flickers past in my peripheral vision, making me pause mid-sentence.

What was that over there in the audience?

I turn my head, look more closely.

There it is again.

"What's going on, Tay, why are you keeping us in suspense like this?" a journalist calls out.

Red hair, pinned up. A side-swept fringe revealing a scar.

Autumn?

The red hair vanishes into the crowd, and a split second later I'm no longer sure it was ever really there.

"Sorry." I shake my head, clearly already so mad with longing for Autumn that I imagined seeing her for a moment. "What was the question?"

With those words, I turn back to the journalists, but they're no longer focused on me—instead, they're staring at something slightly behind me.

Their eyes widen, the cameras pan to the side.

Silence spreads.

"Is that…," someone whispers.

"I think so," a woman's voice breathes.

A split second later, I feel a hand on my shoulder.

A delicate scent of strawberries reaches my nose.

Warmth floods my chest.

My heart beats stronger.

Am I imagining this? Or is it really happening?

"Yes, it has something to do with that doctor." That was Autumn, who had just answered the journalist's question.

She is here.

My God, she is here!

I whirl around and see her—see the woman who owns my heart—standing right in front of me. Only the barricade separates us. There she is, cheeks flushed and breath coming in gasps, her hair pinned up. Tears glisten in her eyes.

There stands Autumn in a storm of camera flashes—trembling, yet with a determined expression. Her chest rises and falls rapidly. She knows the images of a staff member now moving the barricade aside to clear her path onto the red carpet toward me will be seen around the world tomorrow. And still, she is here—the woman I love—in an evening gown that reveals the scars on her décolletage.

But that's not all.

Because as she takes a step toward me, she shifts the high slit of her dress with her leg, letting the whole world catch a glimpse of her bare thigh for a moment.

Completely overwhelmed, I look at her. I see her fear, the courage it's taken to do this—but also that none of it can stop her. Because there is hope, too, and love—so much love.

Now she wraps her arms around my neck and looks at me intently.

"Yes, it has something to do with that doctor," she

repeats, her voice thick with emotion, echoing the words she said earlier.

Slowly, I begin to understand what's happening. And now, tears rise in my eyes as well.

Chapter Forty-Nine

AUTUMN

In front of all the cameras, I pull Tay close, close my eyes, and press my lips to his. Flashes flicker behind my closed eyelids, a thousand questions hammer at my eardrums, mixed with cheers and boos—some euphoric, others disapproving. I feel eyes all over my bare skin and know that the images of my scars will circle the globe by tomorrow.

But none of that—absolutely none of it—matters. That Tay and I are kissing, that we can be whole together, that we will be free—that is the only thing that matters.

I let myself go, kiss him more deeply, savor his closeness, knowing I no longer have to hope for a miracle.

It's here.

I feel it everywhere, like tiny fireworks in my chest. A thousand sparks. So much light and warmth.

Miracle glow.

"You're crazy," Tay murmurs hoarsely against my lips a few minutes later.

"Crazy about you," I reply, and kiss him again.

"So she's the reason for the divorce?" a journalist shouts. "Can you confirm that, Tay?"

"What does your daughter say about it?"

"What's the story behind those scars?"

These and a thousand other questions are fired by the reporters, and they sound like they're on the hunt, like they're tearing every word we say apart in midair, ready to sink their claws into our bodies and rip us to pieces. But in Tay's arms, I feel safe.

"Come on, Tay, you have to give us something," a man urges.

I end our kiss, look around, and see countless pairs of eyes, all fixed on us.

"Hi, I'm Autumn," I say, and although there's a queasy feeling in my stomach, I also know that this is right. "I'm the doctor who treated Kayla. The woman who…"

Tay places his hand on my arm to stop me. "The woman who completely changed my life." He smiles warmly, and that doesn't change as he turns to the journalists.

He doesn't shut down.

There's no wall, no aloofness, no dishonesty. Just Tay, exactly as he is.

"In what way?"

"What do you mean, Tay?"

"How changed?"

The journalists' calls grow louder, more sensational. They smell a good story for their front pages. High click rates, sold-out editions.

"She didn't know me, didn't know where I came from, what had happened to me. What I had done, what kind of person I am." He takes a deep breath. "And yet she saw something in me that I had forgotten how to see myself."

With my arm around Tay, I watch as the journalists lower their microphones and cameras. It's as if they can sense that this is more than just a sensational story. That it's about something deeper than they've ever seen on the surface.

That Tay isn't the person they always thought he was.

"Thanks to her, my heart can beat properly again." His gaze shifts to me, full of love and warmth.

The fact that the two of us are now standing side by side in the public eye is a miracle in itself. But that such an incredibly attractive man would ever make a declaration of love like this to me—the monster—on a red carpet in front of rolling cameras? I never would've believed it.

A wistful sigh drifts over to me. It must have come from one of the female journalists. Out of the corner of my eye, I see another pulling tissues from her pocket, a reporter smiling dreamily.

All of them, standing around us like this, seem enchanted by Tay's words. They can hardly believe it—but I do all the more: Tay, the man who seemed so unreachable when we first met, has just given the world a glimpse into his soul.

And I feel that this was only the beginning.

"Shall we?" Tay points to the red carpet leading to the entrance of the Beverly Hilton Hotel.

Still moved, I nod.

Suddenly, the journalists snap out of the little miracle that had just surrounded them. "What did you mean earlier when you said she didn't know what had happened to you?" someone asks, far less sensationally than before.

"We'll talk about that another time," he replies, intertwining his fingers with mine before we walk side by side through the flashing lights and the enthusiastic cheers of his fans.

Chapter Fifty

TAY

One week later

With a cup of herbal tea in hand, I step to the bedroom window, where Autumn is watching the first rays of sunlight touch the horizon beyond Inner Sambro Island. Mist hovers above the sea, slowly dissolving, fishing boats head out, and seagulls glide through a sky streaked with soft pink clouds.

Today it will happen.

"Thank you." Autumn takes the cup, and I step behind her and gently wrap my arms around her. "Is everything okay with Kayla?"

"Mina is with her, she's watching her for now," I reply. "But I had to promise that we'd go get ice cream afterward."

Autumn laughs. "As much as she wants."

Together we look out over the water, her back close against my chest, the scent of her hair in my nose. Having her with me, falling asleep beside her, waking up with her, taking care of Kayla together—it all feels more right than anything ever has in my life, despite the endless rumors about us. We still have a lot to sort out before Autumn moves to Los Angeles with me, but she already has a new job lined up. Soon, she'll continue her amazing work at the LA Children's Hospital.

Hopefully, she'll be able to do her work there without being bothered by journalists. But what she plans to do today will certainly help with that.

I kiss her temple. "Are you sure?" I ask her, as I have so many times since she told me about her idea.

With both hands, she brings the cup to her lips and blows the rising steam from the surface. "We all have our scars—everyone in this world carries something around that hurts them."

Everyone makes mistakes.

Everyone regrets something.

Everyone sometimes wishes they could turn back time and do things differently.

Autumn is right, but that doesn't automatically mean everyone thinks the way she does. "Not all people are beautiful despite their scars," I remind her, even though it hurts.

She rests her head on my shoulder and nods absentmindedly. "That may be true, but that doesn't mean every one of them is lost forever."

In my mind, I see myself as I was just a few months ago. I was one of those people Autumn is talking about. My scars had made me ugly.

Now she sets the tea aside, turns to face me, and looks at me intently. "If they listen, they'll understand why you love me despite my scars—and maybe they'll do the same."

Shaking my head, I brush her bangs from her forehead and kiss the small scar at her temple. "It's not despite your scars that I love you," I whisper, my lips close to her skin, and trail kisses across her cheeks toward her lips. When I reach them, I stop just a few millimeters away.

Our eyes meet.

I feel her breath on my lips, the warmth of her skin, feel my heart beating—strong and free.

"It's not despite your scars that I love you," I repeat, letting my gaze tell her that what I'm about to say is nothing but the truth. "It's with them."

Her eyes begin to glow in a wondrous way. Fascinated by the sparkle, I kiss her without closing my eyes.

We kiss—tenderly, gently—and keep our eyes on each other. I feel her glow take hold of me, feel the incredible miracle it stirs inside me, feel how some of the scars on my heart begin to fade.

I know they'll never disappear completely, but they don't have to. They're no longer a sign that someone once broke me. They're a sign that I survived my fate.

The green of Autumn's eyes blurs, I lower my eyelids, kiss her more deeply, taste the salt, and don't realize at first that it's not only Autumn's tears brushing my lips.

We kiss for minutes, outside the sea laps at the shore, seagulls screech. I'd love to stay here with her, but the soft thudding rising from the living room reminds me that we still have something to do.

With a heavy heart, I put some distance between us. Autumn intertwines her fingers with mine. "Shall we?"

Earlier I asked her if she was sure. If she really wanted to do this, and the thought of what was about to happen scared me. But now there's so much determination in her expression, and I want to believe with her that today we can make another small miracle come true.

Hand in hand, we walk down the stairs, the thudding

from the living room grows louder, a jumble of voices drifts toward us. Now a bright light flares up.

"Test, test," someone says.

We step up to the doorframe, look inside. The journalist is sitting on the sofa, adjusting his shirt.

I squeeze Autumn's hand. "Ready?"

She returns the squeeze. "Ready."

Epilogue

AUTUMN

Two and a half years later

The air in the Dolby Theatre is electric; around me, dresses sparkle in gold, silver, and ruby red like a sea of shimmering fabrics and jewels.

Joshua Friedberg, who just accepted the Oscar for Best Original Score, leaves the stage to thunderous applause.

I glance at Tay, who's sitting next to me. His black tuxedo is impeccable, the bow tie perfectly tied. His right hand rests loosely on his knee, but his fingers tap out a silent, irregular rhythm.

We both know what's coming next on the program.

I can practically feel Tay's heart stop beating as the host turns toward the microphone.

"Now we come to one of the highlights of the evening: the award for Best Actor," she announces with a radiant smile.

Carefully, I intertwine my fingers with his. Winning this

Oscar and receiving the recognition for his work that means the world to him has always been his dream, and there's nothing I want more than for that dream to come true tonight.

I automatically remember how I gave that interview two and a half years ago in the little holiday house on Inner Sambro Island. How openly I spoke about everything, taking the wind out of the gossip magazines' sails. With Tay by my side, I let them see my vulnerability, my mistakes, and every one of my scars. But also my dreams, my deep desire to help children avoid falling into the vicious cycle I once did.

The reactions were overwhelming. My story went around the world. Complete strangers wrote to me to say that what I had experienced changed the way they saw themselves and others.

June, Nyla, Sonora, and even Olive—who until then had been the most perfect person I had ever known—told me about their fears, weaknesses, and mistakes.

And then another small miracle happened: someone asked where to send donations for the clinic I want to open one day, and by now, so much has come together that my goal is within reach.

Since that evening when I stepped onto the red carpet with Tay, so many dreams have come true for me, and I know that the same is possible for Tay.

We both know that.

The host reaches for the envelope.

This is the moment everyone in the room has longed for and feared. I unconsciously hold my breath as the host unfolds the paper.

"Five outstanding artists are competing for the title, with five performances that made us laugh, cry, and marvel."

The host's words bring a wistful smile to Tay's lips. He's probably thinking about how much emotion he poured into that role. I was on set, I saw him, and he was so incredible it took my breath away. Experiencing his passion for his work up close even made up for the fact that we barely saw each other during filming.

"The nominees in this category are…" She reads the names one by one, including Scott Pears, who once snatched an Oscar away from Tay.

When Tay's name is called, a camera flash flares up in front of us. It's still unfamiliar for me to be so in the spotlight. Unfamiliar, but not uncomfortable. Not even in my low-cut evening gown do I feel uneasy. On the contrary, it fills me with pride to show my scars.

Because they are so much more than just letters, words, and lines of a story that life burned deep into my skin without asking for permission. They also tell of how we can overcome what fate imposes on us. That we can go on and that we can find our way back to a happy life.

I wave at the camera, thinking of Kayla, Mom, June, Olive, Sonora, and Nyla, and all the people now sitting at home in front of their TVs.

"And the Oscar goes to…"

The host opens the envelope, and the audience collectively holds its breath. The camera stays on us, just as four other cameras are doing with the other nominees at this exact moment, to capture the announcement.

Tay and I exchange a conspiratorial look.

No matter what happens, I silently let him know.

He nods.

"…an actor who has surpassed himself. He showed us what it means to fully dedicate oneself to a role and, in doing so, revealed life's truths to us."

No matter what happens, Tay will make his dreams come true.

"Ladies and gentlemen, the Oscar goes to…"

No matter what happens. Tay and I will be happy.

"… Tay Lawson. Congratulations!"

He did it?

My God, he really did!

The crowd erupts and suddenly all the cameras are pointed at us. Without letting go of my hand, Tay rises from his seat, and he doesn't even think about releasing me as he makes his way to the stage.

We hadn't discussed me going with him, but everything is happening so fast that I can barely react.

Spotlights follow us as we walk, along with numerous cameramen who only back off once we step onto the stage.

The lights, the faces, the roaring crowd—all of it blurs before my eyes. All I see is Tay, taking the golden statue that means so much to him.

It's an incredible moment for an incredible achievement. His whole soul went into this role; he gave everything of himself, felt every moment.

Now he steps up to the microphone, the applause fades, and he lets his gaze wander.

"Ever since I was eighteen, I wanted to win this Oscar. I had to have it; it's considered the highest honour an actor can receive." The host smiles, Tay wraps his arm around me. "But today, it's not just a reward for my hard work, it also represents the greatest thing I've ever achieved in life."

To be a person again, someone who feels and loves with an open heart. To no longer need a valve for his emotions and therefore be an even more sensitive, more complete actor. That's what he means, even if the audience, now erupting into another round of applause, doesn't have the faintest idea.

"That I stand here today with an Oscar in my hand, I owe to this woman," he continues in a gentle tone. "Because she made me realize who I am when I'm not playing a role."

With infinite tenderness, he brushes a strand of hair from my face in front of the cheering, whistling crowd, and when he turns back to the audience, his eyes are glazed with tears.

"She is the person who brought me back into balance, and without that balance I wouldn't have been able to play the role of Dr. Cross the way I did," he says with conviction.

Tears well up in my eyes. Seeing him like this, so pure and so true in the way he meets the world, moves me deeply.

Tay turns his gaze to me. "You're my kryptonite. You're what makes me feel, what makes me vulnerable, what makes me human."

He's used those words before, and just like then, they strike me straight in the heart. Unable to say anything nearly as beautiful or meaningful, I blow him a kiss as tears stream down my cheeks.

But I don't seem to be the only one feeling this way. The audience rises to its feet in applause. The artificial smiles so typical of Hollywood fade from the faces around us, replaced by emotion, wistfulness, and longing. The host places her hand on her chest with a sigh, even Scott Pears in the front row blinks discreetly.

Now Tay comes closer, our eyes lock, our noses touch. In front of the crowd's cheers, we melt into a kiss, and in that moment I know one thing for sure:

Sometimes you meet someone who puts the broken pieces back together until you recognize yourself again. Sometimes miracles glow in our hearts to remind us that they never truly went out. What remains is the realization that it was never a miracle we needed, but rather the courage to believe in ourselves.

Afterword

This book was not an easy journey.

Some stories flow effortlessly; this one fought back. Autumn, Tay, and I had a tough time. It took us a long while to get to know each other and to create this story together. The two of them pushed me to my limits, made me question everything that defines me as a writer. More than once, I wondered if this book wouldn't be better off disappearing forever into my digital drawer.

Still, I didn't want to give up, because the message of this book was just too important to me.

Today, I'm incredibly glad I stuck with it. Because what ultimately came out of all that uncertainty is something I truly love. Not just because of the message, which I hope touched your heart too. But also because this book showed me that hard times do pass.

That it's worth holding on.

That in the end, everything can turn out okay, as long as we don't stop fighting for that happiness.

This story has everything I love so much about Halifax

Harbor Hospital. The deep emotions, the love that shows up in the most unlikely moments—and the people who save each other even when they're barely holding on themselves.

By now, Halifax Harbor Hospital feels like a second home to me, and every story set there draws me in even deeper.

I hope you felt the same way while reading. I hope you empathized, hoped, and suffered along with them.

But now it's time to say thank you. Without the people who have stood steadfastly by my side for years, none of this would mean anything. A thousand thanks to my family, to the tireless book professionals, test readers, bloggers, and release helpers—there are now so many of you that I can't even name everyone anymore. I'm at a loss for words to express how grateful I am.

But most of all, I want to thank you—for buying this book, for reading it, and maybe even for loving it.

More by Belinda Benna

vinci-books.com/thedreams

I was hired to care for his daughter... not his heart.

Single dad and world-famous pianist Josh Friedberg is focused, distant, and impossible to resist. Spending time with his daughter Sophia brings us closer, and the slow-burning spark between us is undeniable—but risking love could cost me my heart all over again.

Turn the page for a free preview…

The Dreams We Share: Chapter One

MAYA

A heart-wrenching whimper reaches my ears. Though barely audible amid the lively sounds of the kindergarten group, I am immediately alarmed.

It's Frida.

I look up from the cardboard butterflies I'm cutting out for the summer festival, blowing a strand of my long black hair away from my face. The bright June sunlight streams through the windows, casting a colorful glow over the whimsically decorated room. The glass beads of the mobile above the entrance sparkle with a rainbow of colors, and the vibrant red of the play kitchen glows even more intensely.

My gaze continues to wander until I find the crying girl, who shows up at the kindergarten day after day, only wearing tights and a T-shirt. Over in the corner with the building blocks, she buries her head between her tightly drawn-up knees.

"There she goes again." My boss, Nadine, shakes her head with an exasperated snort and reaches for the hot glue gun. "Can't this child go a single day without creating drama?"

I look into her icy-blue eyes. "Why did you become a preschool teacher, anyway?"

Of course, she's the boss, and if I've learned one thing during my internship here, direct criticism is unwelcome. Nevertheless, I can't help but ask her the question.

"That's none of your business." Nadine shrugs indifferently and crumples the red tissue paper in her hand into something that was supposed to be a lovingly shaped flower for the wall decoration.

If it were just about me, I wouldn't say a word. But her cold demeanor is directed at the little innocent beings we have the privilege of caring for.

"Not mine, but it is the children's business." I reply so quietly that she probably can't hear it, pushing the tiny wooden chair behind me as I stand.

I walk past the dollhouse, the construction workshop, and the painting corner. I almost stumble over a miniature train that one of the wild rascals left in the middle of the room.

A few seconds later, I sink onto the soft carpeted floor of the building corner and pull three-year-old Frida into my arms. Her red curls reek of cold cigarette smoke.

"What happened?" I ask the little one, stroking her back reassuringly.

She doesn't answer. I only notice how she plays with my oversized earrings, sparkling in all colors. Frida sure loves that.

"Together, we can solve any problem, you know," I whisper while gently rocking her back and forth. "You remember, don't you? We're both..."

"Superheroes." Frida's voice is so faint that I can hardly hear it.

I smile. Because suddenly, I feel strong too. "Exactly. And what do superheroes do?"

She pushes herself away from me slightly and looks up at me with her green eyes. "They can do anything." A conspiratorial grin appears on her freckle-covered face.

"So if a superhero can handle anything, nothing can happen to them that they can't fix, right?" I lovingly wipe the tears from her cheeks. In the corner of my eye, I see Nadine throwing her arms up in the air. Due to her sour expression, she looks completely out of place in the group room, which appears so cheerful with its yellow curtains and children's drawings on the wall.

"Do I have to do everything alone?" She rants in a volume she knows I can hear. Then she turns with a grim expression to the rainbow-colored stack of construction paper sheets on the craft table.

"Nadine is mad at you." Frida wrinkles her button nose.

Though I flinch inwardly, I mimic the little one's grimace. "So what?" I whisper back. Then I turn my face away so Nadine can't see it and contort my features until the little one giggles.

Experiencing her laughter is worth any sacrifice. No matter how difficult it can be having Nadine as my boss, time with the children makes up for it. With them, I am in a different world. A place where there's no pressure. They don't pretend; they don't lie. And they see the world just the way I love it. Like through a magical kaleidoscope that casts a rainbow hue over everything.

I nod encouragingly to Frida. "Do you want to tell me now why you were crying?"

She lowers her eyelids in shame. I can barely understand

what she murmurs, but as I also let my gaze fall, I don't need to understand anymore. She tries to hide the dark stain on her beige tights with her hands, but I can still see it clearly.

"Please, don't tell on me," she whispers with a voice choked with tears.

Instantly, I empathize with her. I feel her shame and guilt as if they were my own. Still, I smile at her reassuringly.

"You can rely on me. And you know what? Coincidentally, I brought a magic cloak with me today." I pretend to pull a cloth from my bright blue flowing skirt. "Anything this covers becomes invisible."

The girl's eyes widen. "Really?"

"Yeah, of course. What do you think?" I hold the nonexistent piece of fabric in front of her face. "My goodness, Frida, where's your head?"

She leans to the side as if peering out from behind a curtain. "I'm here!"

"Thank goodness. I thought..." I pretend to be relieved, wiping away imaginary sweat from my forehead. The numerous plastic bangles around my wrist make a dull clacking sound while I wrap Frida in the imaginary cloak. One last time, I hug her tightly. "Now you can follow me unnoticed to the restroom. On the count of three, okay?"

"Okay," she whispers almost inaudibly. She nods against my shoulder.

Hand in hand, we make our way through the group room. Fortunately, none of the other children take notice. Melinda and her best friend David are drawing ships, and the preschoolers are having a tea party with the dolls.

Only Nadine notices that we're sneaking outside. She scrutinizes me, the color of her eyes resembling an iceberg.

Without reacting to her, I turn toward the exit. Only Frida matters now.

After tending to the girl, I reluctantly take a seat next to Nadine at the craft table. I can feel her eyes on me as I reach for the scissors. Immediately, I'm filled with tension, which threatens to overwhelm me.

"Did she wet herself again?" Her thin eyebrows rise. The hot glue gun in her hand oozes, and the adhesive smell fills my nostrils.

I shouldn't lie to her; that has gone wrong several times already, leading to reprimands. "No, she just wanted to show me something," I say anyway. For Frida's sake. After all, I made her a promise. Hastily, I take the pine-green cardboard and place the leaf-shaped stencil on it. My brightly painted fingernails add a cheerful mood to the plain surface.

"Don't get too attached to the little ones, Maya. You supervise them, teach them something, and when they're old enough, you release them into their future lives." She lazily sticks a tissue paper flower onto the wire stem. "That's it. They're not your children."

Is it supposed to be that simple? Even though my intuition tells me otherwise? "I understand that, but..."

She raises her hand. "I don't want to hear it."

"Something may be wrong at Frida's home." I shouldn't speak that thought out loud, but I can't help it. "Her shoes are too small, and her clothes are frayed and rarely washed. Shouldn't we do something?"

Heat rises within me as I think about what could be happening in her life.

"Enough of that," Nadine warns me emphatically. "Maybe her parents don't have much money, but they're doing their best. And it's not uncommon for a three-year-old to forget to use the toilet while playing. I can recognize children with problems, and Frida isn't one of them."

Surprised, I let the paper and scissors drop. So she has been observing the little girl too. Has she been to her home or talked to her parents? Perhaps Frida's family isn't as bad as I imagined?

It's possible, yet I search Nadine's face for signs that she might be lying to me.

"You're just an intern." She suddenly sounds as if she pities me. She puts her hand on my forearm. "Why do you think that after a few weeks, you can assess a situation better than a seasoned educator?"

Ashamed, I lower my gaze. Because the facts can't be denied. She's the professional, and I'm the intern.

For now.

This internship is the foundation for my special education studies. Only if I accumulate the required practical hours, submit a written assignment, and pass the four partial exams for study eligibility will I be allowed to attend university. If I had completed school until graduation, it wouldn't be necessary. But that's just not how it turned out. At twenty-six years old, I haven't accomplished much in general.

That's about to change.

I want to help children with problems. Children like Frida. This dream has accompanied me my whole life, and a few months ago, I finally found the courage to pursue it.

I'd love to tell Nadine about it. But I don't dare. She wouldn't believe that I could follow through anyway.

Her strained cough doesn't bode well. "And one more thing: I would strongly advise you to dress like an adult. Just a tip." With a disdainful sniff, she scans my rainbow-colored T-shirt.

The children love my cheerful style. And so do I. "A little color brightens up anyone's life," I reply defiantly, but I can't even look her in the eye while saying it.

With a loud creak, Nadine pushes her chair back. "Did I ask you a question?"

No.

"Exactly." She stands up and tugs at her mouse-gray T-shirt as if trying to conceal her rounded hips beneath the fabric. Then she tilts her chin up and calls the children to the gymnasium at a deafening volume.

After all the children have been picked up in the late afternoon, I enter the group room. Completely alone, Nadine sits at the craft table, struggling to handle the decorations for the summer festival. She cuts the leaves so carelessly that I almost want to take the scissors out of her hand. I straighten my back and cross the room, which feels eerily quiet without the children.

"Where should I continue?" I ask as cheerfully as possible, taking a seat on one of the small wooden chairs next to my boss.

She doesn't respond.

Better to start working right away. But as I reach for the box with the pre-cut tissue paper flowers to assemble them on the wires, Nadine stops me.

"We need to talk," she says wearily.

I follow her into her office, which is more of a storage closet than an actual workspace. There, she gestures for me to sit on the chair in front of her desk, piled high with folders and books. I feel uneasy. She maneuvers past the table and rests her head on her hands.

Heaven, when she looks at me like that, I feel like I'm four years old again.

"Maya," she begins, letting out a heavy sigh. "This is an educational institution for children aged three to six."

Yes, I'm aware of that. I might be scrunching my face because I have no idea where she's going with this.

"For two months, you've been working here, and I've done my best to make this fact clear to you," she continues, leaning back in her chair. The squeaking of the backrest pains my ears. "I don't like to admit a mistake, but if you have made one, you have to own up to it."

What? Nadine wants to admit a mistake? Something stirs within me. A spark of hope that perhaps my future holds more for me than financial worries and temporary jobs that no one could endure for long.

Positive thoughts are the beginning of all good things, I hear my father's voice echoing within me. For years, I've carried his voice inside me, and whenever he whispers something in his warm bass, I feel a little stronger than before. Even today.

What if behind Nadine's rough exterior, there's a soft core? What if she's been testing me all this time? And what if I've passed the test?

With anticipation, I gaze at Nadine, barely able to contain myself and eager to finally hear what she has to say. She grabs a piece of paper on her desk with the blank side up.

This could be my evaluation.

My legs refuse to stay still any longer. With a fantastic internship certificate, the first step toward admission to university is taken. In just three days, I'll take the second step by completing the required biology exam. A warm tingling sensation runs through my arms, while my palms become damp and simultaneously colder.

Everything seems to be happening in slow motion. Nadine turns the paper over and places it directly in front of me. Curiously, I lean forward.

Termination.

Does it say termination?

No, that's impossible. I read the word again, but *termination* stubbornly refuses to turn into *evaluation letter*.

"Dammit, what's going on here?" Did I say that out loud?

"Your behavior has been unacceptable in this institution from the beginning. Today, you lied to me again. Frida did wet herself," Nadine says.

Dammit. How did she know...?

"The replacement tights had a different color." Nadine raises her eyebrows. "Did you really think I wouldn't notice?"

Dammit. She must have noticed during the changing for the gym class. I shouldn't have lied to her. But abusing the trust of the little ones would have been just as wrong. "I wanted to—"

"Enough," she interrupts me. Suddenly, she looks exhausted. "I've never witnessed such unprofessional behavior. Denying it only makes it worse."

But that wasn't my intention. "Let me explain," I stammer.

Nadine shakes her head. "That's not all. You can't handle criticism and consistently execute my instructions incorrectly." She looks at me, full of disappointment. "You know we've discussed this before. You're not suited to be an educator. In fact, you should be thankful that I'm telling you this early."

"But..." Nadine's words circle in my head, but I can hardly comprehend them.

None of our little charges has ever complained. I'm there for them, so it can't be wrong. Or can it?

What if my dream is bigger than I am? What if I'm not meant to help children?

Disappointed in myself, I lower my gaze. "I—"

Once again, she doesn't let me finish. "My decision is final. Today was your last day of work."

What? I can't even stay until the end of the kindergarten year?

What will happen to the summer festival? I had planned game stations and rehearsed songs with the children. And what about Frida? Who will remind her she's a superhero when I'm no longer around?

"How can I make it right?" The pleading in my voice is unmistakable. I slide forward on the chair, almost landing on my knees. "Give me another chance."

Nadine's body tenses up. "You've had too many already."

"I've learned my lesson, honestly. This internship means everything to me. Don't take it away from me." I look at her desperately. She has to understand that my entire future is at stake.

Nadine bites her lip. "Don't make it harder on yourself. Just sign it." She nods toward the termination paper.

Defiantly, I cross my arms in front of my body. "And if I don't?"

"You see, that's part of the problem. You're behaving like a child. Grow up already."

Grow up? Why should I? So that I can become as cold-hearted as she is? I shrink on the chair, feeling hardly taller than a Lego figure.

She stands in front of me and thrusts the pen into my hand. "Just sign it." Her index finger impatiently taps on the paper. "Working with children is not for you. You need a job that suits you."

I swallow hard. Even if my heart refuses to understand, at least my head has to. My goal is unattainable. It always has been; I was just foolish enough to hope it would be different.

"Go ahead." Nadine's tone leaves no room for argument. So I do it. Resignedly, I let the pen glide across the paper. My jagged signature seals in blue on white the end of my dreams.

It's over. I have failed. Once again.

The Dreams We Share: Chapter Two

JOSH

Warm air builds up under my jacket, and the headlights blind me. I turn my head so that I can still see the host of the television show. Maybe it would have been better not to because looking at her is anything but calming.

Her forced smile and the hair tightly tied up in a bun make her appear like a wax figure. Only one thing seems alive, and that's her eyes. They are alert like those of a tiger, and my gut feeling tells me that this predator in the little black dress will soon bare her teeth.

"We are live in three, two, one..." a voice calls out from the darkness behind the four cameras, all focused on the two of us. The lively murmur of the audience in the hall fades away.

This is the moment to check my posture once again. I run my hands through my short-cropped hair and straighten my shirt collar while the host greets the viewers at home and in the studio with her melodic voice.

"Tonight, I have the pleasure of introducing a special

guest to you." She pauses, presumably to build suspense. "As a composer and pianist, this thirty-year-old fills even the largest concert halls, and many female fans have already tried to win his heart." Another insincere smile, but this time, I see her teeth. "Good evening and welcome Joshua Friedberg."

The camera pans to me, and the audience applauds.

"Thank you for the invitation. I'm delighted to be here." I smile back. Not for her, but for the people who have come to see me.

She nods politely, then turns her attention to the cards in her hand. "Joshua, your rise in the past years could certainly be described as meteoric. What makes your success?"

Answering this question is routine, yet it always takes my breath away to utter these words. Because they are as important to me as nothing else in the world. "Playing the piano is my great passion. I owe being able to live it solely to my fans. Without the fantastic people who allow themselves to be touched by my music, I wouldn't be sitting here today."

The host's eyes suddenly glisten with tears. She quickly clears her throat. "Critics say your music cannot be categorized. It is neither classical nor modern. They call it nothing more than the naive background melody of an intermediate world that shouldn't exist. What do you say to these accusations?"

I hold her intense gaze. "My compositions are new and unlike anything that has come before. They don't require extravagant stage shows, nor do they belong in dusty opera houses. They belong solely to my listeners, whom I want to carry away from their everyday lives for a few minutes. If I can achieve that, I'm happy."

Unimpressed, she scrutinizes me. "As a child from an affluent background, it was easy for you to establish yourself with your new concept, wasn't it?"

Of course. Because talent and hard work can be easily bought. Actually, my wealthy dad just invested a few million, and that's how I became a successful pianist. Even if my father had ever believed in me, his money alone wouldn't have been able to do anything.

I suppress the rising memories of the dark sides of my childhood and smile at the host as composedly as possible. "My parents have always supported me, and I'm very grateful to them for that."

Although I have delivered an answer, the camera remains focused on me. I feel the pressure to keep speaking, but I stand my ground. These seconds of silence are a popular way to get the interview guest to reveal more than they want to. The woman sitting across from me also searches for a vulnerable spot. She needs an opening through which she can intrude and delve deep into my soul, in pursuit of scandal or sensational news. Anything that boosts ratings is welcome.

I endure the silence because I am just as professional as she is.

Now she wrinkles her nose. It's clear to her that she won't get as close to me as she would like. Internally, I relax. Interviews are always challenging. Words get twisted too quickly, opinions are formed, and wrong conclusions are drawn.

Her mouth curves into a triumphant grin. "Rumor has it that your first piano teacher was certain that you lacked talent," she says, raising her eyebrows and fixing her gaze on me, causing a murmur to ripple through the audience.

Dammit, where did she get this information?

I didn't see this blow coming. I have to respond. And appropriately. "I had my first piano teacher when I was four years old. You'll understand that I can't remember everything he said."

That was meager. We both know it. Now it's entirely up to her. Will she pounce on me once and for all? Or can she hold back? Beads of sweat form on my forehead. It's difficult for me to maintain a casual smile.

She straightens up in her cream-colored leather chair and leans slightly toward me. "Are you implying that false information has been fed to us?"

Actually, I mean to convey that there's nothing I desire more than to end this conversation immediately. She must not poke around in this wound, as it has yet to heal.

Feeling somewhat helpless, I raise my shoulders, my gaze flickering to the wristwatch. The interview will be over soon; I just have to preserve a bit more composure. "Do you have every detail of what you did or experienced as a child at the forefront of your mind?"

A crease forms between her eyebrows. "One never forgets impactful experiences," she says with a dangerous undertone.

I must refrain from nervously tapping my fingers on my thighs. In any case, I cannot show any reaction. I regulate my breathing, endure the silence once again, and focus.

Twenty-one, twenty-two, twenty-three.

Disappointed, she leans back in her chair, and the audience begins to buzz with excitement.

Twenty-four, twenty-five, twenty-six.

"Your divorce last year must have been an equally impactful experience for you," she continues mercilessly. "How did it come to this?"

Not that I enjoy discussing it, but at least my manager prepared me for this topic. "We grew apart, and I'm glad we were able to separate amicably, remaining the best of friends."

"For Sophia?"

"For everyone involved." I smile again, although I've had more than enough of it by now. When will this charade finally be over?

"Of course, our female viewers are particularly interested in your love life. An attractive, successful man like you..." Her gaze sweeps over my body as if I were every woman's dream even though I'm just an ordinary human.

The press has tried so many times in the past months to uncover something about my love life. But the truth is, it doesn't exist.

"My love belongs to music, and it will always stay that way," I respond.

A resigned sigh escapes her lips. "If that's the case, of course we want to hear you play now." She gestures toward the concert grand piano located on the side stage next to us. Its half-open lid glistens under the spotlight, the stool covered in blue velvet, and the keys magnetically drawing my fingers.

This is what I've been waiting for. Interviews are not my favorite pastime, but everything else becomes unimportant when I sit at the piano.

Relieved, I rise and approach the piano. I let my fingers rest on the pleasantly cool keys for a moment, close my eyes, and release all the tension from the interview through my breath.

Let's begin.

I cautiously play the first notes. My fingers dance across

the keys, finding their place and creating a melody that carries me away.

Every movement is perfect—no mistakes and not even the slightest hesitation. The sequence of tones becomes more and more intense, and everything within me begins to resonate.

I smile, no, I radiate, as I pour all my passion and emotions into this one piece. As I approach the grand finale, even my heart beats faster. The music permeates me, and I become one with it, forgetting the world around me. This is happiness in its purest form.

Another triplet.

The crescendo.

Then the final chord.

With my eyes still closed, I wait until the last notes have faded away in the room. This moment belongs to me and my listeners. We are all connected, experiencing the power of music and letting it affect us.

Only when absolute silence sets in does the audience begin to applaud. I hear enthusiastic cheers and open my eyelids. The lights in the hall turn on, allowing me to see the people in the audience. There's a little girl with thick glasses clapping devotedly. And an old lady, sticking her fingers in her mouth like a teenager and whistling so loudly that I can hear it from here.

I know I'm beaming. My eyes are moist, and my cheeks are glowing. Because at this moment, above all else, I am grateful.

After so many years of rigorous practice, of striving to be seen and never giving up despite countless setbacks, I am finally able to live my dream of playing the piano.

Shortly after, I leave the studio through the back exit, get into the car, and drive to the nearest shopping center. Once I arrive, I put on the dark baseball cap for safety and slip into the subtle gray sports jacket. That, along with my inconspicuous jeans, should be enough to stroll through the center unnoticed.

Walking along the wide corridor with glossy tiles, I focus on my mission today. My daughter, Sophia, will be spending the summer with me. I want to give her a warm welcome and provide her with everything she needs. That's why I make a stop at a toy store. My gaze searches the display. The horses and the horse stable might appeal to Sophia. Every little girl likes that sort of thing, right? Or does she prefer one of those wooden train sets?

Feeling more uncertain than I'd like, I enter the shop. The dusty smell of the carpet hits me, and a faint children's laughter can be heard amid soft background music.

"Please, Daddy, the pirate ship is so beautiful," says the little boy by the side shelf, unable to keep his legs still.

A man who is undoubtedly his father lovingly strokes his blond hair. Then he crouches down in front of his son. "We can build it together and go on an adventure. What do you think?"

"Oh, yes!" The little one's face lights up, and with a cry of joy, he throws himself into his father's arms. "You're the best dad in the whole world."

Hearing those words pierces my heart.

Because as much as I look forward to having Sophia with me soon, I mainly feel fear. Her mother always took care of everything, freeing me up to focus on my career. My daughter and I hardly know each other. Moreover, since the divorce, she has oscillated between two extreme emotional states: silent and quick-tempered.

Will she look at me the way the little boy looks at his father? Will she ever reach for my hand and hop alongside me like that little guy who now disappears with the man toward the cash register?

Longing and doubt simultaneously creep up within me. The fear of not being a good father threatens to overwhelm me.

To stop that, I hastily look around for a salesperson. The man at the cash register, who looks exactly like I imagined Santa Claus as a child, is busy. The lady with the knitted vest and oversized glasses is already assisting a customer.

In the back, I spot a young woman with long black hair, her top sparkling as conspicuously as the doll she holds in her hand. Indecisively, she looks back and forth between the doll and the shelf. The miniature Christmas tree ornaments on her extra-long earrings sway in rhythm. She appears nervous, almost desperate.

Helplessly, she looks around and places the doll on a shelf. It immediately falls out.

"No, no, no," I hear the woman murmuring in the distance, her voice growing increasingly panicked. She nervously brushes her hands against her expansive blue skirt.

She appears anything but competent. I doubt she can help me find the right welcome gift for Sophia. As I skeptically observe her, one of my pieces plays through the speakers. "Freedom."

The delicate notes begin to sound. Soon, the orchestra will join in. The music will swell, and the intensity will increase.

But it's not there yet. Only the piano can be heard, and although the melody is soft, the stressed woman's face suddenly relaxes. With the doll in her hand, she closes her eyes and sways to the rhythm.

A smile spreads across her lips. The clearer it becomes, the more the cute dimples flash on her cheeks.

Spellbound, I watch her. I see the peace that suddenly dominates her expression. And I realize how her chest rises before she exhales with a deep sigh.

Then she starts to dance. Right in the midst of the bustling shopping mall. Holding the doll tightly against her chest, she twirls around. She stumbles over her skirt, regains her balance, and laughs for a moment.

All of a sudden, I'm overwhelmed with emotion. Because I know it's my music giving this woman a carefree moment. It makes her radiate with such warmth that it reaches me despite our distance.

Her facial expression carries a special kind of bliss that I have never seen before. I feel connected to her.

Perhaps I shouldn't stare at her, but I can't look away. Not even as the last notes of the piece slowly fade away. And certainly not when she opens her eyelids and looks directly at me with a dreamy gaze.

Without any effort on my part, my mouth corners lift.

A fraction of a second later, her expression changes. It's as if she just woke up and realizes where she is. With a startled look on her face, she turns her back to me and tries once again to place the doll on the shelf. Her hands tremble, and her upper body shudders.

Strange.

Something like this has never happened to me before. Has she mistaken me for someone she fears?

Confused, I return my attention to the toy shelf where I still stand.

"How can I assist you?" a female voice asks from behind me.

It's the saleswoman with the cardigan, looking at me kindly.

"Um..." Why was I here again? Ah yes, Sophia. "I need a gift for a five-year-old girl."

"Well, let's see if we can find something." She claps her hands enthusiastically. "Mr. Friedberg, right?" she adds with a conspiratorial undertone. "I'm a big fan, you know."

The day has been long, and the interview drained my energy. But I'm happy to be there for the people who have contributed to my success. So I reveal my identity, give her an autograph card, and smile for a selfie in her phone camera.

Unfortunately, our interaction doesn't go unnoticed. Within a short time, more and more people surround me.

"When is your next album coming out?" an attractive woman with small dark curls asks, pressing her cheek close to mine for a photo.

Slightly dazed by her sweet perfume, I place a finger on my lips. "That's still a secret. But I can reveal that there will be news soon." My manager, Tamika, would expect me to convince the woman to subscribe to my newsletter or follow my social media accounts.

But that's not my style. Despite my success, it still feels like I'm imposing myself. So I discreetly pull out the pen again and turn to the other fans.

Only when everyone is satisfied do I bid farewell and quickly make my way to the car. Accompanied by the city lights, I traverse the evening streets of Vienna until I reach the driveway of the villa I've been living in since last autumn.

My house lies before me, deserted. The exterior lighting

enhances the intricate decorative elements and the bright whiteness of the facade, giving it an exquisite look. I've always liked Art Nouveau, and today, I have the privilege of living in such a magnificent estate.

I open the dark green wooden door and step into the entrance area, tiled in a checkered pattern. The key lands with a clink in the tray on the antique cabinet. The bright sound reverberates through the vast space, in stark contrast to my footsteps, barely audible despite the silence.

Like a ghost, I wander through the kitchen, the living room, and the dining room in semi-darkness.

In just a few days, the house will be filled with life. I look forward to it. Yet I can't help but wonder how I will manage to establish a connection with Sophia. My God, I should have figured it out by now. After all, she's my daughter!

The worries drive me farther into the music room. Once a library, this room still houses books, sheet music, and scores, reaching up to the high ceiling of the old building. I've removed the furniture, leaving only the piano and a leather seating group in the style of the thirties within the grand expanse of the room.

I lift the lid of the grand piano, sit down, and begin to play.

But before I can fully immerse myself in the most beautiful of my worlds, the doorbell rings.

It must be Tamika. No one else would pay me a visit at this hour.

As expected, my manager stands at the front door. She wears a mysterious grin on her bright red lips.

"Do we have an appointment?" I ask, confused as she bustles past me in her midnight-blue jumpsuit, making her way into the house.

She brushes back her perfectly smoothed platinum blond hair. "No."

"Please, come in," I say, even though she's already in the hallway. "Would you like something to drink?"

"Champagne, please." She'll be turning forty next year, but she looks like a mischievous little girl right now. "Come on, don't just stand there. Where are the glasses?"

"Kitchen," I say as I watch her practically float through the foyer. I follow her, and when I arrive, I see her standing in front of the open refrigerator. The light from inside makes her diamond-studded necklace shimmer.

"Perfect," she says, taking out a magnum bottle of champagne. "You could at least help me."

Even though I don't know why, I walk over to the glass cabinet and take two champagne flutes. "Will you tell me what's going on?"

Skillfully, Tamika pops the cork and fills the glasses. She hands one to me, and I can see that she's practically bursting with excitement.

I raise my glass. "What are we toasting to?" I scrutinize her.

"To you," she returns. "And..."

Raising my eyebrows in question, I urge her, "Enough now. Spit it out."

"And to your nomination for the International Music Award!" With an elegant gesture, she pulls a piece of paper out of the pocket of her jumpsuit and waves it in front of my face. Her cheeks are glowing. "You did it!"

I stare at her in disbelief. Did she really just say that, or am I dreaming? "You mean..."

She nods, her head bobbing wildly up and down and back again. Deep laugh lines form around her eyes. It's real.

The radiance, the joy, the triumphant clenched fist. Everything is real.

The nomination. It's real!

In a trance-like state, I lower my glass and take the letter. Indeed. In the upper right corner, the logo of the International Music Awards proudly shines. And in the subject line are the words I've been reading in my dreams every night.

"Congratulations! You are one of the ten nominees for this year's Best Newcomer category."

I don't need to read further, and it's not necessary. I know the process and rules of the most important music industry awards by heart. I know a shortlist of three contenders will be selected by mid-July. And that ultimately, in early September, during a magnificent show, the audience will decide who receives the award.

This prize means the world to me.

One day, I will be the greatest pianist of them all. Count on it. I made that promise to my father, but he just laughed at me.

He was convinced I would never be good enough.

But I am. If I win. Even he won't be able to ignore that proof. It's my chance to make him understand that choosing the piano was the right decision. And ultimately, to prove it to myself.

I barely notice Tamika jumping into my arms with a shout of joy. My thoughts are scattered, and emotions are overflowing. But gradually, a clear image forms in my mind.

"We should plan a tour," I say. Besides the musical concept, the jury values sales figures the most. But the fans, who will ultimately decide, can only be convinced by my music. I have to be better than I've ever been. I have to surpass myself; only then do I have a chance at this prize.

"Don't worry, preparations are already underway. Ralf and I are developing a new show. We need fresh compositions from you, preferably with a romantic touch, nothing too extravagant." Tamika's eyes light up. "We're planning an open-air tour, performing in all the capital cities and musical centers of Europe. Additionally, we'll ensure plenty of positive press coverage."

"Yes, yes, and yes." I can already vividly imagine myself sitting at the piano on the stage in the Arena di Verona, pouring my soul out. I hear the accompanying orchestra, see the fireworks rising behind the ancient arches of the amphitheater, and feel the energy of the moment. "That sounds amazing."

"The fans will love you. And they undoubtedly have to," Tamika grins mischievously.

I nod excitedly, but behind all my enthusiasm, a heavy thought suddenly emerges. "What about Sophia?"

Tamika shrugs. "She'll come with us, of course. She'll find this journey exciting, and in the fall, she can brag to her kindergarten friends about it."

Even though Tamika takes it lightly, my thoughts darken further. "But she's only five. Who will take care of her on tour?"

"We'll hire a nanny. I'll take care of that. Between rehearsals, performances, and press events, you can do something nice with Sophia," she says, casually uttering the words as if it's not a problem at all. As if there would be any time for anything during a tour.

I sink onto one of the kitchen stools, resting my head in my hands. How could I neglect Sophia like this when I finally have the chance to be a good father to her? This is wrong.

Suddenly, Tamika's forearm is heavy on my shoulders.

"Don't even start thinking that way," she says, as if she knows exactly what's going on inside me.

I look up at her. Her expression is serious.

"You've worked too hard to let up now. If there ever was a right time to give it your all, it's the coming months." She looks into my eyes intensely, her hand tightening around my shoulder.

"That's true..."

"Besides, you have many more summers ahead with your daughter. Next year, you can even take a whole month off and spend exclusive time with her. But you can only win the award this year, and maybe never again." It's fascinating how Tamika sees the world so pragmatically. But she's my manager for a reason. She knows what's best for my career.

However, no matter how right she may be in this matter, I can't give in to her urging without a fight. "Isn't there another possibility? A smaller tour, more concert breaks? Or we could skip the press events?" I look at her hopefully, but I can already read the answers to the questions on her face.

She hands me my glass again, somberly. "Your competitors will fight with all means necessary. If you don't go along, negative headlines will rain down on you. Your fans will turn away, and then you can forget about the music award."

Right. I have to deliver. This nomination is an honor, and if I don't do everything to win the prize, my father will be proven right once and for all. I would be forced to admit that I'm actually not good enough. And that I never truly was.

That must not happen!

I have to find a way to reconcile my most important career goal with the desire to be a good father. There's no other way.

"Well, it's settled then," I say, my voice firm as if I'm trying to convince myself that I can achieve both. I nod emphatically, then I place the champagne glass on the kitchen counter without taking a single sip.

Grab your copy…
vinci-books.com/thedreams

About the Author

Belinda Benna is an award-winning author whose moving romance novels are filled with emotion, allowing you to lose yourself between the lines and find yourself at the same time.

Experience stories that will make you cry, laugh, and fall in love—each with a message that will stay with you for a long time.

www.ingramcontent.com/pod-product-compliance
Lightning Source LLC
LaVergne TN
LVHW030916080826
845145LV00013B/2914

* 9 7 8 1 0 3 6 7 2 7 4 0 6 *